# THE
# MISTRESS
## OF
# *Pemberley*

## Delaney Jane

### In Collaboration with Chera Zade

# DEDICATION

To Theodore

For the inspiration.

# ACKNOWLEDGMENTS

I have to give thanks to my dear friend, Allison Teller,
for lighting the fire under my backside to finish this novel.
Thank you to Whitney, not only for reading all my books,
but for loving Mr. Darcy *almost* as much as me.
Yes, I said almost. Don't fight me.

And of course, thank you to the Jane Austen Centre in
Bath, England.
I wear my Darcy pin with pride.

# CHAPTER ONE

## *The Wedding Guest*

———◆———

*It is a truth universally acknowledged, that a woman on the day of her wedding, must be in want of a stiff drink.*

And the soon to be Mrs. Darcy could vouch for that, and never more wholly than when Mrs. Bennet announced the arrival of a Mr. and Mrs. Wickham.

"Goodness, what must Lydia be thinking?" Jane asked, fighting to pin her long, golden curls up behind her ears.

She'd been fighting with the same curl for an hour now.

Elizabeth shook her head. "She isn't thinking, darling sister. That's how she got herself in the predicament she's currently in."

Jane covered her mouth with a gloved hand, trying to stifle her laugh. The laugh soon faded as Jane returned her attention to the mirror and grew ever more flustered with the unruly curl.

"Here, let me do it," Elizabeth said, moving to stand at Jane's shoulder.

The two of them were tucked away in the parlor of one of the guest suites in Pemberley House. Though Mr. Fitzwilliam Darcy and Mr. Charles Bingley were to be found somewhere on the ground, Elizabeth was fighting to remove him from mind. She didn't want her sister to see her

1

blushing, yet again.

"There you go again," she'd say, laughing at Elizabeth's expense.

She couldn't help it. Whenever she thought of Fitzwilliam – of his nearness and his professed and proven love – her mind drifted to the events expected of her later that very evening.

She would be a wife.

No longer a maiden.

And all before bed.

The fact Jane wasn't blushing was far worthier of note, she thought.

"What was your sister thinking? Is the girl trying to kill me?"

The two sisters turned to find Mrs. Bennet standing in the doorway, leaning against the doorjamb as though it alone held her on her feet.

Ever the dramatic.

"Come, Missus. Let the brides prepare in calm repose." Mr. Bennet said, shooting a wink to his daughters before offering an arm to his wife.

"Calm?! How can any of us be calm, right now? Good grief, Lydia is going to ruin this wedding! I swear, Mr. Darcy will be calling the whole thing off when he lays eyes -"

Her voice faded down the long hall as father led her back to the drawing room. He'd been doing his best to wrangle his wife all morning.

She wasn't easy to wrangle.

Elizabeth set the last pin in Jane's hair, releasing her sister to inspect herself in the mirror. After a moment of stern looks, Jane was satisfied.

Elizabeth did her best not to sigh in relief.

"Can you imagine, sister – this is how our fates would unfold. Married on the same day?"

Jane was gushing again, as she was often wont to do when it came to the subject of her dear Charles.

Elizabeth gave a half smirk. "I don't imagine anyone

2

imagined this."

Jane turned in her seat, grabbing up Elizabeth's hands. "I'm so glad for it. I can't imagine a more perfect way to spend my wedding than side by side with you. My dearest sister."

Jane was in rare form.

Elizabeth smiled. She could forgive her sister for the added flair of drama, today. She did come by it, honestly.

"Don't forget who among us was married first," a voice said from the door.

Jane rolled her eyes, but Elizabeth turned and opened her arms to Lydia.

"It is good to see you," she said, and it was the truth. However much scandal Lydia brought – or nearly brought to the family, she was by far the most fun of the Bennet sisters.

Erratic, certainly, but fun.

"Jane, you dear Charles has summoned you to the drawing room."

"Oh!" Jane said, a yelping sound similar to a surprised pup, and without pause, she was darting out into the hallway, her lace wedding gown flitting through the doorway behind her.

"I thought she'd never leave," Lydia said, giving a raised eyebrow to Elizabeth.

Lizzy couldn't help but laugh. "Come now, don't be cruel."

"Ah, I know. She's giddier than usual, I see."

Elizabeth took a deep breath, taking in her own reflection in the mirror. "Can you blame her?"

Lydia moved up behind Lizzy to stand at her shoulder. The two sisters gazed at their reflections for a long moment as Lizzy turned from side to side. Her dress was like Jane's, but the fabric under the lace overlay was a light sky blue. Jane's was as pure white as it could be.

"You look better than I did, you dreadful girl."

Elizabeth laughed. "Well, you did get married on a whim,

3

love."

"That I did," she said, and the tone almost saddened Lizzy. The thought of her baby sister being married so young, and to a man with a reputation like Wickham's – it wasn't what she'd wished for her, certainly, but it wasn't far from what she'd expected.

Lydia was a woman of her own mind.

"Oh, I've brought you gifts! I wanted to give them to you when Jane was out of the room."

"Really?" Elizabeth said, turning with sudden curious excitement. She turned to find Lydia bent over a nearby chair, looking into a lovely satin satchel. Lydia pulled a small bundle tied with navy blue ribbon from inside, cradling it in her gloved hands as she held it out to Lizzy.

"Keep these somewhere private, but here you are."

Elizabeth held out her hands to take the two small books. She shot a surprised glance at her sister. This was not an expected gift from Lydia. Mary or Jane perhaps, but not Lydia. She smiled. "Why private? When did we start hiding our literary interests?"

She gave her sister a sarcastic look, but Lydia's expression did not change.

"You won't want your houseguests discovering you reading these titles. I've a few more that are being shipped up from London. I will bring them to you once they arrive."

Elizabeth startled at this, turning her attention to the books. She turned the small binding over, searching for the titles. The first book had a title on the spine, but it was so small, Lizzy had to bring it close to her nose to read it.

*Memoirs of a Woman of Pleasure.*

Elizabeth gasped. "Lydia!"

"Shh, don't make a fuss. Jane might come back and hear you."

"Goodness, no," Lizzy said, turning away from the door as though hiding the books from prying eyes. "She would be utterly scandalized."

"But you're not, are you, Lizzy?"

4

Elizabeth paused. Was she scandalized? No. Not at all.

Shouldn't she be? Most certainly.

"Here, this edition is especially tawdry," Lydia said, snatching the book from Lizzy's hands for a moment. She parted the covers, took the pages between her fingers, and bent them just so, leaving a curve in the paper, and the edges to slope downward. As the paper moved, an image appeared along the edge.

It was a woman of ivory skin strewn across gold and blue blankets, a man on all fours over her, his tongue protruded, seeking between her legs. Despite the crass artistry of the image, the woman's expression was enough to make her heart race.

Lizzy gasped, swatting at the book with enough force to nearly knock it from Lydia's hands.

Lydia giggled, mischievously. "Oh, don't be like that. They both have such artwork. You'll love this one even more!"

Lydia lunged toward the second book, but Lizzy darted aside, hiding it from her sister's reach. Her face was burning, and though she was curious to see what sort of image the other book harbored, she didn't dare look at it with Lydia there to watch her reaction. She was far too embarrassed for that.

Embarrassed, and something else. She was excited.

Lizzy had heard of books like this, but never seen one firsthand, let alone read one. Now, it looked as though she might have some titillating reading to enjoy.

And perhaps learn from.

She'd never admit it to her younger sister, but she was terrified of going to bed with Fitzwilliam. Not because she didn't want to, but because she feared she might disappoint him.

At least these books might offer answers to her questions – questions she thought she'd never be able to ask anyone.

Lydia turned toward the window, opening the book to the middle and smiling. "My favorite scenes are in chapter seventeen. She has two men at once, and it is simply -"

"Lydia! There you are!"

They spun around to find Mrs. Bennet careening through the doorway. Lizzy snatched the book from Lydia's hands and tucked them both under her skirts. She quickly sat upon them, feigning complete innocence.

"Mother, I was simply wishing her well. Can't a sister do that?"

"No! Leave the poor girl alone, can't you see she doesn't need you fraying her nerves!"

Lydia made to protest, but Mrs. Bennet was already herding her back out of the room. It was clear Mrs. Bennet felt that if she wasn't allowed in the room with her daughters, no one should be.

Lizzy turned to face the mirror, pressing her fingertips to her cheeks as though she might stamp out the blush that still burned there. She could feel the hardcovers of the books under her leg, and as she listened to the voices retreating down the hall, Lizzy shifted to retrieve them.

She set one on her lap, the other in her hands. Glancing toward the door, Lizzy twisted the pages as Lydia had done, watching as the image of the naked woman came into view. Her legs were splayed open in some wonton pose and the man's expression was one of focus and determination. Lizzy felt a tingle between her legs, followed by a strange ache.

*Goodness, what was he doing to her?* She thought.

The ache didn't die away as she opened the book to glance at the words.

Lizzy laid eyes on the words, 'her tongue slathering his rigid phallus,' and she closed the book, nearly yelping in startled excitement.

She set the first book down and snatched up the second, hunching over this one with a sudden rush of tension in her stomach. If what Lydia said was true, this book would offer a truly remarkable – and inappropriate sight.

Lizzy took the pages between her fingers and twisted them. The image slowly came into view, and the ache between her legs quadrupled. This image was of a woman splayed open between two men, one kneeling over her head, the other between her legs. Again, her expression was one of lust and need, as she took the first man's erect phallus in her mouth. Lizzy lifted the book closer to the window to see the exact spot where the second man's phallus was plunging into the naked woman.

She swallowed, letting the pages slip back in place as she darted her eyes to the door. She felt as though the very curtains were prying into this private moment.

Lizzy crossed her legs, feeling the sudden thrill of hundreds of pages in her hands – hundreds of pages that might make her feel just as she did now.

Just as she sometimes did when she was alone in the bath, and she touched herself.

The notion that it would be another to touch her next – that Fitzwilliam would be the one to lay hands on her gave the ache between her legs new life, and suddenly, she felt a flood of moisture between her legs. Were it later in the month, she might've feared her monthly to be arriving.

Lizzy twisted the pages again and stared at the image of the woman and two men, then she snatched up the other book, quickly skimming through the pages.

*Was it Chapter Seventeen Lydia mentioned?*

"Mr. Darcy, you cannot go in there. It's bad luck to see her before -"

"Superstitious nonsense," Fitzwilliam said, his tone accented by the speed of his footsteps.

Elizabeth shot up from her seat as her husband-to-be approached, scrambling for a place to hide her tawdry books. Time ran out too soon, and she slammed them down onto the table, placing a handkerchief over them before turning back to the mirror to feign innocence.

"Mrs! Leave the gentleman alone," Mr. Bennet called.

"Am I the only one in this forsaken place who holds to tradition?" She cried.

Lizzy could hear her father consoling and scolding his

wife, and again their voices faded further down the hallway.

Elizabeth stared into the mirror, holding her breath as she listened for Fitzwilliam's arrival.

"I must tell you, your mother is in rare -"

Despite her efforts to feign calm, his mere presence demanded she stand, turning to face him as he marched into the room.

He met her gaze and went silent.

Lizzy searched for her proper upbringing, hoping to hide the giddy excitement she felt not just at the sight of her husband in his perfect tailcoat and cravat, but at the open-mouthed look he gave her.

Clearly, he was rather pleased with what he saw. "You look mesmerizing, Elizabeth."

The smile was involuntary. "My goodness, where was this gift with words when you first told me you loved me?"

It was his turn to smile. "I've been practicing."

He took another step toward her, and she almost recoiled. The tingling sensation between her legs was constant now, his nearness reminding her of what was soon to pass between them. This was their wedding day. Were he to demand it, he could kiss her, touch her, have his way with her as he pleased, and no one would be the wiser as to whether it happened before 'I do,' or not.

He came to tower over her, inspecting every inch of her face. Her whole body hummed with excitement – and trepidation.

"You and Charles both know better – you're not supposed to see the bride before the wedding."

He raised an eyebrow. "Is that so? And do you know why that is?"

"It's bad luck."

"No, it's an outdated notion invented during the ages of arranged marriages when the bride was hidden and veiled to keep the groom from changing his mind if he discovered his betrothed wasn't as lovely as he'd hoped."

He glanced down at the handkerchief on the table.

Lizzy fought the urge to lunge between him and the table. "That doesn't sound very romantic."

"Marriage rarely is."

She stepped toward the table, feigning a need for her veil, which still lay cast over the back of a tall chair.

He gave her a strange look. "Are you alright?"

She swallowed. "Yes, of course."

"Are you quite sure? I would normally expect you to scold me for such a callous comment."

"Ah, so you know full well how callous it was?"

He smiled. "I always know how callous I am. It's part of my charm."

She closed her eyes and bit her lip, pulling the veil up atop her head. Fitzwilliam stepped behind her to help, his chest pressing against her shoulders. She hadn't felt him this close before, not even on the ballroom floor.

He lifted the long drape of fabric over her head as she pinned it in place, then he let his hand graze down the length of her arm, his fingers lingering at her elbow.

Her whole body shuddered.

He didn't move away. "I can't begin to tell you how much I am looking forward to tonight, Lizzy."

The words were little more than a whisper, but she could feel his breath on her ear as he spoke.

No words in any dirty book could have the same power as that moment.

He pressed his lips to the top of her head and kissed her there, then he marched back across the room toward the door.

"I'll see you in a few minutes, then?" He asked, as though hinting at a worry she might change her mind.

She smiled, and he returned the gesture. Neither of them harbored reservations.

Seeing the purity of his smile made her heart swell all over again.

She was ready to be his Mrs. Darcy, and she couldn't wait to show him how much.

# CHAPTER TWO

## A Nervous Bride

The wedding was ended. Jane and her beloved were off to enjoy their honeymoon together.

Elizabeth stood in the parlor, her feet aching, her back stiff, and her stomach in a flight of nerves. She'd spent much of the afternoon accepting well-wishers and doing her best to deflect her mother's melodramatics. Her family certainly knew how to make a spectacle of themselves from time to time.

Somehow, Lydia and her espoused were docile in comparison. Even Jane threatened to faint just before the nuptials began.

Elizabeth Bennet was content to be done with the affair.

*Elizabeth Bennet*, she thought. *No. The former Elizabeth Bennet.*

She would never go by that name again. She was now Elizabeth Darcy, the lady of Pemberley, wife of Fitzwilliam - nervous in a manner she'd never been before.

Married. She was married to Mr. Darcy. She had a husband, and as of that very night, she would share a bed with a man who made her knees weak.

Elizabeth stood by the bookshelves in the corner of the room, the cool air of the windowsill leaving her bare arms chilled. She ran her fingers over the shelf to the hidden

10

treasures she'd tucked out of sight earlier in the day.

Lydia's gifts – the tawdry books. Elizabeth wanted to steal a few moments to read deeper into their pages, but she knew Fitzwilliam would be returning soon. She wouldn't have enough time to study their pages and learn just what it was that would be expected of her that night. She could glance at the naughty pictures and imagine, but what was it that the women in those images were doing? Was there direction in those pages? Might she find tips or warnings that she'd never by any means received by her mother.

*Thank goodness*, she thought.

Still, it might've been nice to know what she was getting herself into.

This was their wedding night. This was the night she would know the touch of a man for the first time. Not just any man; Fitzwilliam Darcy. The giant, brooding, stern-browed Mr. Darcy.

Elizabeth's stomach was in knots.

Yet, despite their coming home to Pemberley for their wedding night, Fitzwilliam had left her to her own devices, claiming the household required tending before he could retire for the evening.

What manner of nonsense is this? She'd thought, but she didn't say anything. Part of her wanted to get the terrifying notion out of the way, and the other part of her was grateful for the reprieve. If Lydia's excited tone of conspiracy was any warning, intimacy with a man might well be a wonderful thing.

Still, if her beloved Charlotte's letters were to be believed, married life was both dull and exasperating – and that included private moments.

Of course, Elizabeth couldn't imagine sleeping beside the insufferable Mr. Collins, let alone being intimate with the man. She wondered if his incessant blathering continued even when in the throes of passion.

Perhaps passion wasn't the right word, she thought.

Elizabeth did her best to settle into the parlor. She'd been in this room many times, even played the pianoforte for Darcy on more than one occasion. Still, though this was her home now, she'd never seen the inside of Darcy's apartments, never seen the bedroom she would share with him.

She didn't dare presume to go there without his invitation. Instead, she waited in the parlor as she would on any other afternoon before their wedding.

Darcy was taking a good time to tend to affairs of the household. Elizabeth still wore her wedding gown and felt silly as she caught sight of herself in the dark windowpanes.

*Goodness, Lizzie. Calm down*, she thought.

She pulled the veil off her head, setting it over the back of the settee and slumped down at the pianoforte. If she was to wait for her husband, she would make the best of the passing time. She'd yet to even bring her things from home, yet.

She touched a key, and the sound seemed to echo through the darkened house. Pemberley was quiet in a manner she'd never witnessed before. Elizabeth set her fingers to the keys and began to play; Beethoven. She was not as accomplished as some other ladies, but when she focused, she could sound rather soothing in a quiet house. She pressed the keys with the faintest touch, letting the music whisper from the instrument.

Elizabeth played the first three measures by heart before she noticed a change to the sound. Elizabeth glanced toward the door of the parlor and startled, the keys jamming beneath her fingers.

"Fitzwilliam! You startled me," she said, scolding.

He smiled.

Her stomach dropped to her toes.

He'd never smiled at her quite like that before. "Hello, my wife."

The tone was heavy with intention, and Elizabeth felt a strange pang between her legs. An almost ache that made her desperate to squeeze her legs tighter together.

"Keep playing," Darcy said, still standing in the doorway. His presence, and the sheer size of him, seemed to deaden the echo of the music.

"I don't want to disturb anyone," Elizabeth said, nervous to have him listen.

He smiled again. "I've sent everyone to bed or home. We have the house completely to ourselves."

Elizabeth swallowed. She thought of the corridors and long hallways, all quiet and empty. No one to hear her play. No one to hear anything at all.

"Elizabeth. I said keep playing."

They were alone. A man and woman – husband and wife – without chaperone for the first time since they'd met. She looked up at her husband, a nervous tension building in her spine, and did as she was told. She picked up right where she left off, still playing as best she could from memory. Darcy took a step toward her, his massive shape moving in the corner of her eye. She fought to focus on what she was doing, still trying to keep her legs clutched together against the ache. A moment later, her husband stood just over her shoulder, his hand grazing her shoulder.

Elizabeth shuddered at the touch.

"I can't begin to tell you how I've looked forward to this night," he said, leaning down to whisper in her ear. "To finally have you, every part of you."

Elizabeth stumbled on the keys and stopped playing. "Fitzwilliam -"

"I said keep playing."

She licked her lips, setting her brow a moment. She thought to protest this sudden stern domination. She wouldn't allow such treatment at any other time, yet here she was, somehow soothed by his confidence. It was as though she'd been given permission to simply be and to simply allow – whatever it was that may occur. She played on.

"Very good," he said, and his hand moved over her shoulder, his fingers grazing at her collarbone. He ran his fingers over the bare skin of her throat, then moved them downward.

Elizabeth gasped, stumbling on the keys again, but before she could speak, Darcy slid his hand down over the lace of her wedding gown and took hold of her breast, squeezing firmly. Elizabeth cried out, softly, her hands darting to take hold of his.

He bent down behind her, coming to whisper in her ear. "Mrs. Darcy. If you stop playing again before I tell you to, I'm going to be very cross with you."

Elizabeth turned to fight him, but his size alone stilled her.

Darcy appeared at her side, sitting the opposite direction on the piano bench with her. He shot a glance at the keys, then back to meet her eyes. He'd spoken without saying a word. Elizabeth felt her muscles tense all over. What did he mean by cross? Would he stop touching her? He'd certainly never raised a hand to her, or even raised his voice – she was certain that this man would never do her harm. Still, she recoiled from his gaze, a fiery blush burning across her cheeks.

She played on, her fingers tensing with nerves. Darcy leaned into her, his lips finding her ear and the crook of her jaw first, then the curve of her shoulder and neck. His lips were soft, but the touch felt like lightning traveling through her skin, down to the tips of her toes. She pressed her knees together again, fighting the rising heat between her legs.

His hand found her breast again, and his fingers deftly played at the fabric there, teasing the mound beneath. Her nipple hardened at the touch and sent waves and pain through her sex. She fought not to lose her place in the piece, but her throat couldn't contain the startled cry.

Darcy hummed softly to himself. "I cannot wait to get you out of this dress and see you properly."

Elizabeth held her breath.

"Have you thought of this night, Elizabeth?"

She blushed. Yes, she had. But how could she admit that to her husband. He'd think he a brazen trollop, wouldn't he?

She thought of the books tucked away in the corner of that very room, and averted her eyes.

"Because I have. Every night since the day we met. Thought of seeing the creamy white skin of your breasts. Thought of hearing the cries you'd make when I took you as my wife."

"Stop, Fitzwilliam," she whispered, barely able to form the words and keep her hands on the keys.

"Stop?" He said. "Did you just give me an order, darling?"

His hand squeezed her other breast, playing until this nipple hardened as well.

She gasped, softly, but nodded. "Yes."

He chuckled, leaning in until his lips were touching her ear. "I'm the one who gives orders, my petal."

Suddenly, his hand was at her knees, tossing her skirts upward until her legs were bared to the open air. Without thinking, Elizabeth grabbed at her skirts, pulling them back down to protect her modesty.

Darcy glared at her. "What did I say?"

"I know, but for goodness sake! You can't -"

"Play until I tell you to stop, or you will regret it. Final warning. Am I understood?"

The tone triggered something deep in her chest, and she turned on him. "When, sir, have I given the impression that I would allow you – or any man for that matter to order me around as you seem to feel entitled to do?"

He beamed at her, pressing his lips to hers with such force, it nearly knocked her off the piano bench. His lips played at hers, drawing her breath with each new kiss. Her anger evaporated, instantly.

"You wild thing."

"Wild? I will have you know, I am a lady in every sense - "

"Save for here."

The intensity of his look stilled her thoughts, completely.

"When we are alone – when we are together like this, I want your wildness. I know it's there."

15

Elizabeth searched for response. "Fitzwilliam – I have never been touched before. How can you think me wild?"

He smiled. "Because I see you. I know you."

Her cheeks burned. He didn't even know about her reading pursuits. She shook her head. "I fear you've seen something that isn't there."

He brushed a curl out of her face, tucking it behind her ear. "I know what I see."

Despite her previous anger, it faded entirely as he kissed her temple. "Now, as far as my giving orders, know this – I will never dare to order and demand. As your husband, I will be your equal in all things, all ways. Forever."

Elizabeth's chest grew tight. Somehow, this proclamation was drawing more emotion than their vows in the chapel that afternoon.

"But that is in our daily lives. When we are alone? When I have you in our marriage bed – you will submit to me."

She opened her mouth to protest, however much her body responded to these words. "And if I don't?"

He smiled. "Or I will make you. And you will love every second of it."

Elizabeth felt his hand at her knee, pooling the fabric of her skirts up into his hand. Then as he met her gaze, he slid his hand up beneath the skirts, his warm fingers grazing against her thigh.

Elizabeth whimpered in fear and something else – excitement. He hadn't just offered to take her in hand and lead her through this, he'd demanded it.

"Now play," he said, his lips grazing her shoulder.

A part of her wanted to protest, but a stronger part of her feared that her beloved husband might actually relent if she fought too hard.

She didn't want him to relent. She wanted to melt into him and be molded.

She wanted him to inspire an expression to match those of the women on the pages of her books. She wanted to know what inspired that ecstasy – that complete surrender.

She moved her hands back to the keys. They were shaking.

She started a new song now, a minuet by Pezold. She was three notes in when Darcy's hand slid upward, planting his whole palm against the smooth skin of her thigh, then pressing his hand down between her legs. His thumb was inches from her sex. She cried out his name, a pleading, frightened sound as she fought to continue playing.

"Good girl," he said, softly. "You play so beautifully."

He pressed his lips to her ear, whispering there as she fought to tighten her legs against his touch.

It was no use. A moment later, Darcy pushed his hand up fully, and his fingers found her sex. She gasped and squealed in near protest, almost standing up as she fought to pull away from him, but he held her there, his hand rubbing her aching sex, his other arm gripping her around the waist, holding her against him.

He rubbed softly, cooing in her ear. "I can feel how wet you are," he whispered.

Elizabeth gasped, her face burning. She whined softly, feeling as though she should fight this sensation, but his fingers pressed firmly to her, rubbing with intention. The ache in her sex was growing almost too intense to bear.

"Keep playing, my darling," he whispered.

Every sixth key was delayed or wrong, but Elizabeth did as she was told, Darcy's hold on her growing tighter with each passing moment. His breathing seemed to change, growing hoarser, faster, and he hummed and groaned his approval each time she cried out.

Suddenly, he reached further beneath her skirts, finding the waist of her petticoats and slipping his hand beneath. The warmth of his fingers found her sex anew, and he slipped his fingers into the wetness there, touching the most sensitive part of her with relish in his eyes. Elizabeth buckled from the sensation, her fingers losing their place on the keys completely. She reached down to grab his hand through the fabric of her skirts, clutching his shoulder with

17

the other hand as though holding onto him for strength.

"You stopped playing, darling," he said, grinning.

The words were foreboding in an indescribable way. She knew instantly that her failure to play was the invitation he'd been waiting for – that the tune was the only thing sparing her from his next assault.

"I'm sorry!" She cried, the words descending into an almost primal sound of trepidation and excitement. "I can't."

"How disappointing," he said, pulling her backward. "You leave me no choice, then."

"Please!" Elizabeth said, her stomach shooting into her throat with fear of what he might do.

Elizabeth's legs buckled, desperately trying to pull her knees together as Darcy slid his fingers further downward, then plunged them into her. Her sex was slippery and aching as his fingers drove into her there. Elizabeth screamed, forgetting the expanse of Pemberley around them.

"Fitzwilliam!" She cried.

Yet his fingers plunged deeper. Over and over again, a subtle sound of his hand slamming into her with each movement. She clung to him as he fingered deeper and faster, watching her face closely for response.

"You like it, don't you?" He said.

Elizabeth's mouth fell open, but she couldn't speak.

He smiled. "You love it. Well, my darling. You've no idea what's in store for you."

Suddenly he was up, towering over her on the piano bench. Her sex ached now with a need she'd never felt before. Darcy stood behind her, his fingers making quick work of loosing the buttons and ties of her wedding dress. A moment later, the garment fell loose around her shoulders, leaving her in her petticoats and shift. He plunged his hands down beneath the shift and took hold of her breasts, kneading them roughly.

"This is what happens when you disobey me, my love. I take you as I please. Do you understand?"

Elizabeth tried to make a sound, but could only lean back against him. Suddenly, she stiffened, startled by the hard shape beneath the fabric of his trousers.

He chuckled to see her response. "That's what's in store for you, Lizzie. I'm going to use every inch of you to please me. I've been waiting for this for too long."

He grabbed her face by the jaw and turned her up to him, then he kissed her deeply, sliding his tongue into her mouth. She cried out at the sensation, aching for him to slide his fingers inside her again. That moment of penetration was the only thing to soothe the pain between her legs, but somehow, as soon as he took them away, the pain returned with triple the force. She needed him. She feared him, feared what he would do, but needed him all the same.

"Do you want me, too?" He asked.

Her face flushed. She nodded, averting her eyes.

"Tell me," he demanded.

Elizabeth swallowed. "I do."

With that, Darcy grabbed her, pulling her up to her feet as her dress fell to the floor. She felt exposed, standing there in only her petticoats. Then a moment later, he ripped her petticoats off, leaving her standing there at the piano, naked.

Darcy pulled the piano bench aside and pushed her toward the keys.

She stood there naked and exposed as Darcy pulled the bench up and sat down.

He grabbed her by the hips and turned her toward the keys, roughly. "Play until I tell you to stop."

Elizabeth stared at him in desperation, a look she prayed conveyed her thoughts.

*What are you going to do to me?*

"Are you defying me?" He asked, as though daring her.

"No!" She said, a mix of terror and frustration battling in her chest. She feared what he'd do were she to say yes, but also wanted desperately to remind him that she would defy him – that she would always defy him.

"Good," he said, his hand sliding up the inside of her

thigh. "Lean forward and play, and don't stop until I damn well tell you to, do you understand?"

"What will you do to me if I do?" She asked, almost fearing the answer.

"Do you want to find out?" He demanded, and the tone was terrifying.

"No! No," she said, and swiftly found the keys to play a new piece. An easy piece – Fur Elise by Beethoven.

He hummed with approval at the music choice, then without pause, he slid his hand up between her legs, kicking her ankles aside to open her to him. His fingers slid up inside her again, this time three at a time. She felt her body strain against the sudden entry, and cried out in almost pain. He plunged them deep, nothing hindering him now. She fought to keep her hands on the keys as his fingers slammed up into her over and over, his knuckles pounding into her thigh and the lips of her sex as he pushed as deeply as he could. She felt her body stretch to take him, her sex growing hot as the knuckle of his pinky fingers slammed over and over into the most sensitive spot. She cried out, fighting to find the right keys, her knees growing weak, and her thighs trembling.

Suddenly, Darcy pushed the bench further back, yanking her by the hips until she was forced to fully bend over to reach the keys.

"Fitzwilliam, I can't - Oh god!" She screamed as Darcy sat down onto the bench, slammed his fingers up into her, and planted his face into her ass. Elizabeth's hands slammed onto the keys, completely losing the music as she tried to pull away.

This wasn't how a man was to behave! What was he doing to her? And oh god, what kind of woman was she to enjoy it?

"Please!" She cried, still trying to pull away.

A sound splintered the air of the parlor as Darcy's huge hand smacked her ass with the force of a tyrant.

She gasped, unable to scream. The sensation had stung

20

like nothing she'd ever felt before, and the shock of it left her speechless.

"Did I tell you to stop playing?" He demanded, his hand still planted on her ass, the sting of his touch emanating out in burning waves. Elizabeth's eyes began to water as she shook her head.

"No," she said, and she was almost on the verge of tears.

"Do as you are told, or face the consequences," he said, his hand suddenly moving in a gentle rhythm over her reddened buttock. The touch was soothing, gently caressing away the sting.

Elizabeth swallowed. "I don't think I can play when -"

"You'll do as you're told," he said, kissing the sore skin of her backside. "Or you'll suffer the consequences. Have I made myself clear?"

Elizabeth whimpered and returned her attention to the keys. Darcy's hand rubbed for a moment longer, then his fingers slipped down between her legs again and plunged inside, rocking her forward with each thrust. Elizabeth blinked against the tears, waiting in near fear for what he would do next.

Darcy's tongue found her ass again, darting and teasing at her as she cried out. He grabbed her hips, pulling her back to him, driving his tongue and his face lower. He flicked his tongue then opened his whole mouth to her, devouring her. She cried out, fighting against the sudden heat that was rising in her sex. Her legs were shaking violently, and she was barely able to hold herself up, but she kept her hands to the keys, fighting to make some kind of melody despite her whole body being under assault.

"Fitzwilliam!" She cried as her sex tightened around his fingers. She moaned at the sensation and lost all control of her legs, collapsing against him. Darcy caught her before she fell completely, lifting her up as he stood behind her.

"There we are, lovely. There we are." His fingers continued to move, drawing further gasps and moans as the wave piqued, then receded, leaving her helpless against him.

"You did beautifully – when you finally decided to behave," he said, his tone foreboding. He let his lips graze her ear, his breath warm against her.

Suddenly, he took hold of her hand and pulled it back behind her. He pressed her open palm against the front of his trousers, the pulsing shape beneath seeming to spring in response to her touch. She gasped, trying to pull her hand away, but Darcy kept it there, making her stroke him as his breath came, hoarse and hot in her ear.

"You feel me?" he said. "You've done that to me so many times, Lizzy."

She shuddered against him again, her ass sore as he pressed himself against her, pinning her hand between them.

She remembered the image from one of her books – a woman with a man's sex in her mouth. Lizzy wondered what he might taste like or if he'd be appalled at the notion of her touching him like that. Still, as he held her against him, she let her fingers knead the hard shape beneath his trousers.

He growled, softly – an almost startled sound. He stood to his full height and spun her around to face him, slamming her ass back into the keys. She tried to brace herself, but he was on her, leaning over her until the pianoforte groaned with the pressure of her ass on the keys.

Darcy suddenly turned, yanking the piano bench up behind him. Then he sat down in front of her, hooked his hand behind her knee, and pulled her leg up and over his shoulder. Before Elizabeth could protest, Darcy buried his face into the wet of her sex, pressing his open mouth to her with the force of a ravenous thing.

Elizabeth screamed, her eyes glancing toward the open parlor door, terrified someone would come and find her there, summoned by the unearthly clang of the keys beneath her. Yet even as the fear made her wary, her body melted in response to Darcy's forceful tongue. He darted it against her most sensitive place, playing with the flesh there as his fingers plunged deep. She fought to pull from him, her sore backside now pressed to the rough edges of the piano keys, but between her legs there was only pleasure. A warmth so hot, it was almost searing as Darcy forcefully turned his face from side to side, pressing himself to her with such force, she feared he'd drown there in the wet of her.

He hummed and groaned with relish, pushing her against the pianoforte in rhythm, the echo of the keys pulsing with his movements.

Suddenly he pulled from her for only an instant and spit in his hand. Before Elizabeth could move, Darcy's mouth returned to its work, licking and sucking at her with such fervor, she feared he might bite her. She heard an unfamiliar sound, a strange rhythm from Darcy's free hand. She craned to see, and spotted the red, throbbing shape of his cock in his hand as he stroked himself, madly.

His groans and hums grew faster, more furious with each passing moment. Elizabeth fought to watch him touching himself, the notion of him stroking himself giving a sharper edge to every sensation. She felt her mound quivering against his touch, her legs going weak again as the keys dug into her ass. She reached down, grabbing his hair to push him against her. He growled in response and was on his feet suddenly, his trousers open to display the massive, hard shape there, rigid and red with need.

"My darling, Elizabeth. I am not going to be gentle with you," he said, and the tone was so sinister, Elizabeth felt her knees buckle as he marched her across the room toward the settee. Elizabeth watched her veil fall from the back of the seat as Darcy threw her down onto her back and loomed over her. He pulled his britches down, kicking them off as he pulled his white shirt up over his head, displaying the pale, broad chest beneath. He was naked before her, towering there, the darker skin of his sex just above eye level.

"Come here, petal. Show me what you can do with that mouth."

Elizabeth's stomach shot into her throat. She stared at the massive shape of him as he pulled her upward, pressing her hand squarely on his cock. He wrapped her fingers around him, showing her how he liked to be stroked. She mimicked his movements, watching his expression for response. His eyes closed and his head lolled backward. The sight of it stirred something deep inside her. She'd made the powerful Mr. Darcy sigh.

She'd do anything to make that happen again.

Elizabeth straightened, bringing his cock as close to her face as she could, then without another word, she opened her mouth, tentatively taking him into her.

He grabbed a handful of her hair, pulling pins free as he did. She met his gaze, startled by the sudden forcefulness. His expression was mad with need and hopeful expectation.

Elizabeth felt almost mad with power.

She opened her mouth and took him inside as deeply as she could, tasting the sweetness of his skin, and catching the subtle hint of his musk. It was intoxicating.

She sucked, deeply, wrapping her fingers around the rigid shape of him as she did. He breathed hoarsely over her, watching her every move with desperation. She smiled up at him and he seemed to groan to see it.

Elizabeth released her hold to breathe, then sucked at him again. She was nervous, praying that her efforts were right – that they felt as lovely as he'd felt a moment ago when he'd let her know the touch of his mouth.

He clutched her hair tight in his hands, moving her back and forth to show her his rhythm, to coax her throat open as he plunged back into her mouth. She whimpered as he pushed a little too deep, and he recoiled, letting her take the lead again.

That instantaneous act of concern and patience was enough to make her fall in love with him all over again. However forceful and aggressive he may be now, the gentleman would always be there, putting on this show of force and power as he harbored the tenderest love just beneath it.

He would never hurt her. Not ever.

The sudden rush of affection was intoxicating.

She unleashed him, gasping for air a moment, but before she could return to her work, Darcy shoved her back onto the settee, planting his knee between her legs.

"My darling, you are perfection," he said, lowering himself down over her.

She felt her face flush, but soon felt panic settle into her bones as Darcy took hold of his massive cock and took aim at her sex.

"Oh god, Fitzwilliam!"

*I won't be gentle with you*, he'd said. Elizabeth's whole body tensed in wait of him.

He ignored her cries, pressing the head of his cock against her quivering sex. She was wet, slippery and ready to be taken. She knew this state, having touched herself more than once in fantasy and desire of this moment, long before they were wed. He would find no resistance. She was helpless to him.

Elizabeth pressed her hands to his chest, begging with her eyes for him to be gentle.

He gave a look that was somewhere between a grin and a glare. "Are you ready for me, wife?"

She gasped, but couldn't speak.

"You must tell me yes, my love."

"Please," she said, and it came in barely a whisper.

He grinned at her, pushing the head of his cock into her. Her body strained against him, a pinprick of pain shooting through her body as he pushed deeper.

She tensed, arching her back to pull away from him. "It hurts," she said, softly.

He glanced down at her sex, retreating just so. Then he pushed a little deeper. "Mmm, I know it does."

She turned away, afraid to hear the relish in his voice.

"Look at me, Elizabeth."

She did as she was told, afraid to disobey.

"Slap my face, darling."

Elizabeth's eyes went wide. She shook her head, terrified of what sort of punishment such an act would earn her. "I can't."

"Oh, I know you can, and you will. Slap me, petal. Slap me with all your strength."

Elizabeth stared up at him in trepidation and shock. Even with the coaxing tone of his demands, she was frozen with fear. He had one hell of a slap himself, and her ass still throbbed from it.

"Do as you're told or I won't take you."

Her mouth fell open in shock. Somehow this threat was far more distressing than his threats of forceful lovemaking. The notion of him hurting her with his cock was far less troubling than the thought of him not taking her at all. She wanted to – needed to feel him inside her. If he stopped now, she feared the ache of need would kill her.

Elizabeth took a deep breath, and with a terrified whimper, braced herself against his retaliation and slapped him across the face as hard as she could.

He plunged into her, his cock thrusting to the hilt, buried deep inside her as he turned back to face her. Somehow, the pain was bearable. Somehow the act of slapping his handsome face had distracted her enough to take him. Still, her body sang with pain, and she was left breathless under the weight of him.

"Mmm, that's my girl," he whispered into her ear. The sound of his voice was gentle now. Almost sweet, as though he was pleased to see her fury.

He settled his weight over her and moved with slow deliberation. Her body had molded to him in that initial thrust, but with a slow retreat, she felt the pain of him fade, leaving in its wake the fullness of him, moving in her, stilling that pain of need she'd felt since the moment he stood in the doorway of the parlor.

"My god, you feel better than I could've imagined, darling."

Elizabeth whimpered at these words, and Darcy plunged into her again, slow and deep, pressing his hips into her as he pulled her legs higher. He wrapped her legs around him and pressed her into the settee, driving his cock deeper with each thrust. He moved slowly, deliberately, watching her expression for response.

Elizabeth's mouth fell open as his body moved against hers, the pressure of him causing a friction in all the right places. She reached down, grabbing hold of his backside to pull him down into her deeper.

Darcy's eyes went wide and he grinned. "Oh, you and I are going to have a lot of fun, my petal."

With that, he doubled his speed, letting their bodies slap against each other with each thrust. Elizabeth craned to look at his cock, to see the hard shape of him disappearing into her, the dark tuft of hair framing the rigid shape of him mixing with the dark hair at her own sex.

Suddenly, he rose onto his knees, grabbing her by the hips and pulling her upward to meet his thrusts. It was almost too deep, and Elizabeth cried out. Darcy just laughed, rocking her there as his cock plunged deeper and deeper.

"You wanton thing, you."

Her head fell back and she clutched the back of the settee, fighting to hold on as he pounded into her.

"God, you've no idea what you've gotten yourself into, Miss Bennet."

She gasped, holding on for dear life as he plowed her over and over, his body slamming into hers.

"I'm going to take you every way you can imagine."

Elizabeth held her breath, a heat rising in her sex as his words came in hoarse bursts, the foreboding tone growing darker and darker.

She loved it.

"I'm going to make you behave in all ways. I'm going to make you scream, and cry, and beg for the most depraved desires you can imagine. And you will love it. I will make you love it."

She whimpered suddenly, the heat growing more intense by the second. He responded by doubling the force of his thrusts.

"I'm going to make you submit to my every whim, show you what a submissive wife you can be. Do you hear me, Miss Bennet?"

"It's *Mrs. Darcy*, you fool!" She cried as he lifted her hips off the settee to slam into her unhindered.

His eyes went wide, and he laughed, a look of unbidden affection on his face.

Elizabeth closed her eyes tight, feeling her body tighten around his cock. He growled, pounding into her as sensation became too much to bear. Elizabeth screamed, fighting to pull from his hands as her body seized violently. But he held fast, clutching her by the hips, a snarl crossing his lips. He pressed her down into the settee and bore down on her, pressing her into the cushions as her body convulsed, and she begged for reprieve.

The darkness in his eyes frightened her as he opened her legs wider, pummeling her sex with every thrust.

Darcy shuddered over her, thrusting deeply as he growled. He thrust again, grunting and howling with each convulsion. She could feel his seed pouring hot inside her, and she reached down to his backside, pulling him deeper. He moaned, bucked one more time, then stilled, his eyes closed as his mouth fell open over her.

Elizabeth clutched him to her, pulling him into her in a subtle rhythm, relishing in the sensation. Finally, he slumped down onto her, his face buried into the crook of her neck.

They lay there for a long moment, the warmth of their bodies causing their sweat to mingle on their skin. Elizabeth ran her fingers into Darcy's hair, brushing her thumb along the length of his sideburns.

His body rose and fell with each ragged breath he took. Elizabeth clung to him there, feeling his breath, his weight. Nothing had ever felt so right.

This man was hers. Fitzwilliam Darcy was hers. His touch, his body, his lust – they all belonged to her, and she could have them, whenever and however she wanted.

"My darling," he whispered, lifting just enough to meet her eyes and kiss her. "You were better than I could have imagined."

Elizabeth blushed, covering her smile with the back of her hand.

Darcy was up, groaning as he pulled from inside her. She felt almost cold to feel him pull away. He stood over her, running his eyes over her body.

"God, you are breathtaking," he said. Then he held his hand out to her. She took it, and without concern for their state of undress, Darcy yanked her toward the door of the parlor and led her down the hall, leaving their clothes scattered around the pianoforte.

They reached the doors to Darcy's apartments – their apartments, and he showed her inside. Elizabeth sighed at the sight of the four-poster bed, her body exhausted and ready to sink into the comfort there.

Elizabeth Darcy decided then and there that she would love married life.

# CHAPTER THREE

## *Scandalous Reading*

---

Elizabeth sat to her breakfast with a near constant burn across her cheeks. With each visit of her maid, Molly, Elizabeth had to stifle a grin and avert her eyes.

Would Molly know she was no longer a maid?

*Of course, she would, idiot. It was the week after your wedding, after all.*

Still, there was certainly no way for her to know just how ravenous her husband was. There was no telling that her beloved Fitzwilliam had thrown her about their bedroom for hours the night before, or every night since their wedding. And there was certainly no way she'd know that Elizabeth still felt the sting between her legs from their long hours of lovemaking even as she sat to her breakfast of scones with jam and clotted cream.

She sipped at her tea in silence, stifling yet another smile.

"Will the master be joining you, this morning?" Deirdre asked from the parlor door. Deirdre was the head of the housemaids and a formidable woman. She stood in the doorway in black dress and white cap, her broad shoulders nearly filling the space.

Somehow, being gazed upon by Deirdre's stern eye was nearly mortifying. This was not a woman she imagined having giggling conversations with about men, let alone about intimate details thereof.

Elizabeth shook her head. "No, Miss Deirdre. He's gone riding this morning."

He had certainly gone riding, an endeavor he claimed was the only way to draw him away from their bedroom that day. They'd rarely left it for a week.

Still, he threatened to have his way again as soon as he returned.

Yet again, Elizabeth averted her eyes from Deirdre.

Deirdre nodded and turned back toward the kitchens. She'd be there much of the day preparing afternoon tea.

Once her plate was clear, Elizabeth bid Molly thanks as she collected her tray. Soon, Lizzy would be alone with her thoughts – and the sting between her legs. The clatter of teacup and saucer echoed far down the hall, letting Lizzy know she was truly alone.

In a flash, she was up and across the parlor, sliding a heavy bookend aside to get to the hidden treasures behind.

Lydia's books.

This was the first time she'd had a moment truly to herself in several days. Elizabeth took one of them out, not daring to move away from the bookshelf as she opened its pages to explore.

*"Here she took my hand, and in a transport carried it where you will easily guess. But what a difference in the state of the same thing! . . . A spreading thicket of bushy curls marked the full-grown, complete woman. Then the cavity to which she guided my hand easily received it; and as soon as she felt it within her, she moved herself to and fro, with so rapid a friction that I presently withdrew it, wet and clammy -"*

Elizabeth snapped the book shut, her heart racing in her throat to have read such words. The notion that such intimate, tawdry details had been put to page was enough to set her heart aflutter, but the true cause of her scandal was

31

more pressing than that.

This passage was of two women.

Two women finding pleasure with one another. The mere notion confused and unnerved her, but she presently opened the book again to read on. She had to know what happened on the next page.

"Madam?"

Elizabeth startled so intensely that the book nearly flew out of her hands. She spun to face the doorway, tucking the book behind her as she faced Molly.

Molly's blonde hair was beginning to sneak out around the sides of her cap, and she kept her eyes down when she spoke. "A Mrs. Bingley has come to visit with you?"

The tone was almost questioning, and Elizabeth wasn't sure if Molly was afraid of her or if she was unsure of the guest's name.

*Mrs. Bingley.*

The sound of it was so very strange to her, but her heart lifted nonetheless.

"Yes, of course! Oh, how wonderful."

How wonderful, indeed. Her beloved Jane had come to visit, and not on any day, but on a day where they would both have learned the intimate secrets of married life. Elizabeth felt nearly giddy at the notion of having someone to talk to about her married life, and about the bliss it brought her.

Still, she certainly wouldn't be sharing these tawdry novels with her beloved Jane. She feared her sister might faint and never rouse at such reading.

Elizabeth tucked the book back into its hiding place and quickly snatched up another innocent tome, settling into her seat with it in wait of Jane.

The sound of her footsteps approaching in the hallway gave her butterflies. Suddenly, it struck her.

Of all the people in the world who would look at her and know without doubt that she was no longer a maid – Jane was at the top of that list.

The blush on her face must've been crimson.

Jane rounded the corner into the parlor and flung her arms around Elizabeth.

Elizabeth held her for a long moment, as though holding her would delay the moment where they would be forced to see one another and acknowledge that they'd both known men - biblically.

When Jane pulled away, her cheeks were the same color as Elizabeth's, but her expression was strange, somehow. Jane settled into her seat across from Elizabeth, and the two of them stared at the table between them for a long moment. Though Elizabeth was shy and almost embarrassed to acknowledge the events happening in her bedroom each night, she was giddy first. She wanted Jane to know the happiness she'd found in her still short marriage, and she wanted to know that Jane had found the same.

Yet, Jane's whole demeanor betrayed some strangeness. An embarrassed sadness, almost, and she couldn't look Lizzy in the eye.

When the quiet tension was too much for Lizzy to bear, she commented on the beautiful weather, suggesting they take a stroll.

Jane seemed grateful for the suggestion.

The grounds were luscious and perfectly kept, and the garden paths gave way to trails through field, meadow, and wood. They could walk for days and never cross their steps. Elizabeth hooked her arm in her sister's elbow, letting Jane know that she needn't speak.

They strolled along for several minutes, the sun peering through fast-moving clouds, warming Lizzy's dark hair.

When they reached the fountains at the far end of the garden, Jane sighed. "Where is your Mr. Darcy, this morning?"

"He's gone riding," Lizzy said, choosing not to elaborate on why.

"Charles has done the same. Has he been in a bit of a mood, as well?"

33

Lizzy furrowed her brow. "What manner of mood?"

Jane frowned. "Charles was rather – oh, I can't be sure. Frustrated? I fear I've displeased him, somehow."

"Oh, dear Jane. I'm sure that you couldn't possibly displease him. He adores you."

She touched her hand to her nose, and Lizzy saw the full extent of her emotion. "He did. I fear he won't for much longer."

"Why on earth would you think that?"

Jane gasped for air and unleashed a flood of honesty. Clearly, the privacy of the garden felt safer than the parlor within.

She explained that unlike Elizabeth, her wedding night had been clumsy and strange. That they'd laid together and attempted to make love, but the effort brought little pleasure to either, and Charles seemed to feel inadequate when he found her unresponsive to his efforts.

It was clear Charles knew as little about the act of lovemaking as Jane did.

This revelation stopped Lizzy in her tracks.

How had Fitzwilliam been so adept at the deed, when his best friend was oblivious?

Where had Darcy learned his way around a bedroom?

Jane went on to explain that they'd tried again more than once since, but each effort only ended in soreness and frustration, then fitful sleep.

"Jane, darling. It isn't your fault. You cannot punish yourself for a faulty start."

Jane wiped a tear from her eye and turned to Lizzy for the first time since she'd arrived. "Do you really think so? Was it the same for you? Is that why your Mr. Darcy is riding, as well?"

Elizabeth stared at her older sister, an ache pulling at her heart, and nodded. "See? You're not alone, my love."

Jane exhaled, and the weight seemed to visibly lift from her shoulders.

And settle squarely on Elizabeth's.

The two sisters walked along the path, conversing about mother back home, and being grateful to be away from the prying Bennet family eye. Lizzy couldn't imagine having to face her mother on the days following her wedding, let alone her younger sisters.

Save for Lydia, of course.

*The books*, she thought.

Perhaps, she could give one of those scandalous tomes to Jane. Perhaps, that would help her in her marriage bed.

Or perhaps it would change Jane's opinion of her, forever.

The two sisters found their way back to the parlor in time for an early tea, then Jane took to her room for an afternoon nap. Mr. Bingley would be following her to Pemberley that evening, and the two of them intended to stay for a couple nights.

Elizabeth was both pleased to know her sister would be near, but equal disappointed that her day-long stints of lovemaking would have to be put on hold. A good hostess doesn't neglect her guests in lieu of gazing lustfully at her naked husband.

Or does she?

Elizabeth watched out the window for a sign of her husband returning from his day's ride. He'd been gone longer than she anticipated, but she was grateful for the time with Jane. Grateful and curious. She wanted to know more of her husband's past – know how he came to be so skilled at pleasuring her, without having ever touched her before.

Perhaps, if she could decipher this, she could share the information with Jane.

Or perhaps, Fitzwilliam himself could endeavor to arm Charles Bingley with a better understanding of the act.

She instantly laughed to herself. She could already imagine Fitzwilliam's response to such a request.

"Absolutely not, I refuse," he'd say.

Then the true test of their marriage would begin. Would she be able to win him over, coax him to help her beloved sister? Perhaps there were deeds she could offer to tempt him? Deeds she might learn of in one of her tawdry books.

She smiled and made her way to the bookshelf again. This time she opened the title with the erotic painting of a woman with two men along the page edges. She skimmed through the pages, searching for words that would betray inappropriate scenes.

She found her prize in mere seconds, and within a few sentences, her whole body hummed with trepidation, wonder, and shock.

*"The first man splayed her open to him, his rod ready to cleave into that waiting depth. Yet, with the lubrication of a spit filled hand, slipped his waiting phallus lower still, teasing at her puckered ass. The Jezebel gasped, but held herself open to him as the second man teased the head of his cock to her other lips. She did take him there, wholly, gazing up with longing as her ass was filled with hard flesh."*

Elizabeth gasped, touching the back of her hand to her lips.

Two men at once?

Her whole body had responded, a throbbing ache between her legs where before it had simply been the sting of lovemaking. Now it was need. She was aroused in a manner that she couldn't rectify – and she was desperate to keep reading.

"Interesting choice of literature, I see," a voice whispered at her ear.

Lizzy threw the book onto the bookshelf, yelping loud enough to travel throughout the house. She spun around to face her husband who loomed over her now, smelling of horses, fresh air, and sweat.

She was mortified, desperate to hide the book from him, but he simply leaned over her, reaching for the black-bound offense. He lifted it to read the title, and when he found none, he smiled, twisting the pages to find the hidden painting thereupon.

"I'm sorry! It was Lydia's. She left them on our wedding day. I've kept them hidden away so no one would find them, but I – I was curious why they were so scandalous – why she would dream to give them to me. I just wanted to know. I was just curious."

Darcy opened the book to the pages she'd just been reading, and Lizzy felt her chest growing tight.

How cross would he be to find his wife reading such filth in his own house when he's out riding for the day?

He lifted his eyes to look at her, but there wasn't a hint of displeasure to his expression. Quite the opposite, in fact.

"Did you enjoy what you read?"

Elizabeth gasped. "I beg your pardon? Certainly not."

Fitzwilliam glanced to the door, and when he found it empty, pressed her back against the bookcase, lifting her skirts up with one hand, and before she could protest, he tore her petticoats aside, ran his hand up her thigh, and plunged his fingers between her lips.

He groaned, softly. "Your body disagrees with you," he said, sliding his finger through the wetness there, teasing her.

She gasped, trying to pull away from him as she thought of her sister being somewhere in the house.

He just smiled.

"Stop, Fitzwilliam. Someone might come in," she whispered, growing breathless.

"Then, we should take this literature with us to the bedroom, shall we?"

He took hold of her hand, and tucking the little book into his breast pocket, led her down the hall toward their apartments.

"Wait, Jane is here. She's said Mr. Bingley will be arriving soon."

"He's already here. We were riding together. Molly is running him a bath."

Elizabeth furrowed her brow. Knowing her husband had

been with Charles Bingley all day inspired a whole new slew of questions. Had Charles seemed changed to his best friend? Had he expressed his frustrations with him as Jane had with her? Did men discuss the private details of their marriages with one another or was that idle gossip for the lady's parlor, only?

The answers to these questions would have to wait, because they'd reached the bedroom door.

Elizabeth felt breathless, knowing the release she would feel from her husband's touch, and how desperately she needed it after reading the few pages of that book that she had.

Fitzwilliam released his hold on her, closing the door behind him. He turned back to her, reopening the book to skim the pages further. He shot her knowing looks with each passing moment.

She felt desperate and helpless. What would he do to her now?

"Did you enjoy this, Lizzy? And don't lie to me. I want to know the truth."

Elizabeth swallowed. "I don't want to answer you."

"For what reason?"

She searched for words. For fear that he would judge her too wanton for wedded bliss? To save the pretense of demure womanly graces?

If she didn't dare show the books to Jane, what would her husband say to hearing she found them exciting and titillating in ways she'd never imagined. She turned away, unable to say anything at all.

"Ah, come here, darling."

Elizabeth turned to find Darcy standing in front of a tall cabinet. He stood aside, gesturing for her to join him.

She crossed the room, still nervous to discover what he might do or say.

"I have a copy of this book, and many more like it," he said. "If you want to continue reading, I would love to know your opinion of their subject matter. See, I'm rather fond of such literature myself."

"You are?"

He smiled and opened the cabinet doors to her.

The contents within stilled her breath.

"I've been preparing for your arrival for weeks now," he said, a sly grin on his handsome face.

Within the cabinet was a treasure trove – dozens more books like the ones Lydia gave her, a painting along one of the cabinet doors with artwork that looked Japanese in origin – an image of a woman being pleasured by some manner of octopus. It set off that throbbing ache all over again.

Beyond that, she saw paddles, leather straps, whips, cuffs, belts, stretches of satin cord and rope, strange phallic looking objects, and shackles. Elizabeth took a step back, almost afraid to look further.

"You haven't read too far into this book, have you?"

She shook her head. "Only a couple passages."

He smiled. "I see. Well, I encourage you to explore further. This title is about a woman submitting to two men, at once."

She felt her face flush.

"And I see you liked what you read."

She turned away, willing herself invisible.

He chuckled. "As I said, beloved, I am going to demand your obedience in all things."

Elizabeth stood a little straighter, her fury rising despite the horror of being discovered with such books. "You, sir, cannot ask that of me! I am not meant to be some obedient little wife. I never was. You of all people should know that."

"Oh, I do," he said, pulling a long stretch of satin rope from within the cabinet.

Elizabeth recoiled, fear rising in her chest.

"I don't want to ruin the book for you, so I won't tell the sordid details, but every manner of thing you see in this cabinet is found in those pages. This and far, far more."

She swallowed.

"Now, I did marry you because you are my equal in every way. As my wife, I want the woman I fell in love with. Challenge me, test me, keep me guessing as you always have, but in the bedroom?"

He stretched the rope between his hands, pulling it apart with such speed, it made a sharp 'Thwap!'

Elizabeth chirped in nervous response.

Darcy grinned. "I also married you because I hoped you would share my passions, that you would indulge every fantasy you might possess, and when you and I are behind closed doors, you would learn to see me as your master, do you understand?"

Elizabeth swallowed. "But -"

"I want your unconditional trust. In all things. No matter what I ask, no matter what I threaten, I want to see complete faith in your eyes. Faith that no matter what I do, it will be for your pleasure, as much as it is mine."

Elizabeth felt her courage rising. "Really? That whip there? That's for my pleasure?"

Darcy glanced at the whip, then shot her a sideways look. "Oh yes. You will love it when I leave your ass red from it. You will love it when I slide the handle inside you -"

Elizabeth gasped, stepping away from him. Despite the trepidation she felt, her sex was pulsing with need – painfully so.

"I'm going to demand obedience, but I will not force you to do anything. I will make you submit, but when I do, it will be because you want to."

She felt something cold against her back and realized she'd walked back into the bedpost. She gripped it in her hands, as though for protection as much as support.

"And if you behave yourself, I might indulge some of these -" He waved the book at her with a wry smile. "- more scandalous desires of yours."

"I never said I -"

"Sh," he said, setting the book with the others inside the cabinet. "Am I understood?"

She swallowed, watching him run his fingers over the length of red cord in his hand. She fought to push the images each toy in the cabinet inspired from her mind, but with each new flash, her sex ached anew. She wanted it all. She wanted to see just what depraved things her husband would do with her. She wanted to feel the release of letting herself succumb in his arms – over and over. She wanted to enact all the sordid scenes from those books, and she wanted to do it without shame.

She took a deep breath and nodded.

"Good, now come here so I can tie your hands."

With that, Darcy crossed the room to her, cracking the length of rope as he approached with a wicked grin on his face. Elizabeth felt a pulsing between her legs, and with a knowing smile, dropped to her knees before her husband.

# CHAPTER FOUR

## *The Master of the House*

━━◆━━

"There's a letter for you, Missus."

Elizabeth stiffened at the breakfast table, excited at such news.

Molly hurried into the parlor, offering the letter to her on a silver platter. The gesture was almost comical to her, but she took the letter nonetheless.

The script was enough to forget any strangeness of her new life.

Who is it from?" Jane asked.

Elizabeth was busy breaking the wax seal on the back of the envelope. "It's from Charlotte."

"Oh, how lovely," Jane offered, but there was little actual mirth behind the words.

Elizabeth opened the letter, scanning over her dear friend's familiar script.

**My Dearest Lizzy,**

*I hope this missive finds you well. My heart both swells and races at the notion of relaying this rather astounding news with you, but as I feel it too powerful a message to share in something as informal as a letter, I am writing in the hopes that you might allow us to*

*visit you in your new home. I await your response with*
*bated breath and a hopeful heart.*

*Yours in earnest,*
*Charlotte Lucas Collins*

Lizzy cringed at the word – Collins. Still, she'd promised never to speak ill of her friend's choice to marry the clergyman, again, however averse she might be to the mere thought of darling Charlotte having to tolerate the man's incessant prattling at all hours of the day.

Charlotte was going to live comfortably and well, however unfortunate her marriage might be.

"What does she say?" Jane asked, startling Elizabeth back to the world.

She smiled. "Charlotte is coming to visit. I will have to write a response, promptly. Will you allow me a moment before we move to the garden?"

Jane assured her she was happy to, and Lizzy was summoning Molly back within moments, adamant that her response get to Charlotte as soon as possible. She felt almost responsible for Charlotte's marriage, and couldn't wait to offer her less trying company.

Lizzy couldn't imagine living in the constant company of Mr. Collins and the Lady Catherine de Bourgh.

And there was no measure to her curiosity to what manner of news Charlotte might want to share.

She and Jane made their way out into the garden, strolling and partaking in some croquet to pass the time.

The Bingley's planned to enjoy the hospitality of Pemberley for another two days, and Jane was still fretting over the bedroom activities she didn't dare engage in while at Pemberley.

Their husbands were together, somewhere in the neighboring grounds, and they didn't return to Pemberley until Jane and Lizzy were just finishing their tea.

Though Lizzy loved her sister's company, her dower

mood left Lizzy aching for the comfort of her husband's presence. She took her leave to find him, using the excuse of too much sun.

Darcy sat at his desk, scribbling away in his careful, cursive script. He was writing a letter to Lady Catherine, attempting to calm the fury she'd expressed upon hearing of the most recent scandal in the Bennet family. Darcy mumbled some choice words under his breath when he read her letter, but ever the dutiful nephew, he now wrote her in the placating language of a man who knows how to tame wild boars.

Elizabeth wondered what Lady Catherine would think knowing Elizabeth compared her to a wild pig.

Elizabeth snorted to herself.

"What are you chortling about over there?" Darcy asked, barely raising his head.

"Nothing," she said and returned her attention to waiting.

She wanted a private evening with her husband, and she'd been dreaming of it as she took a turn in the gardens. Darcy was out riding much of the afternoon and came home dusty and smelling of horses and wood shavings from the stables. The rough look of him had set Elizabeth off when she found him at his desk, yet Darcy had barely glanced up at her.

Elizabeth would have none of this.

She watched him for a long moment. "I've invited the Collinses for a visit."

This earned her a look. She knew it would.

"Did you now?"

"Yes. It seems she has some rather pertinent news to bring."

"And she couldn't share it in her letters?"

"No," she said, not offering anything further.

In their private moments the night before, Darcy had been nothing but a gentle lover. He'd caressed her cheeks, kissed her deeply, held her in his arms, and called her 'petal' or 'darling' when he was inside her.

Naturally, those delights were just that – delightful. Still, Elizabeth enjoyed the darker side to her husband. She liked the danger of when his voice dropped low, or when he threatened to drag her over to the cabinet where he kept his toys, paddles, ropes, and things. She was sure his approach to lovemaking was changed because of their houseguests.

The sound of lustful screams might not be the best lullaby for the Bingleys to hear all night.

Especially given Jane's troubles.

Still, she wanted to be dragged to the cabinet tonight, and she was ready to ask him, outright.

Yet, he was busy writing letters.

When Darcy finished the first letter and began in on a second, this time to his sister, Elizabeth sighed and rose from her seat. Making a point to draw attention to herself, Lizzy marched over to his cabinet and opened the doors. A moment later, she set a paddle, the one with the smooth handle that Darcy had teased her with, onto their bed. She set out a length of satin rope, but when Darcy didn't respond, she grew impatient and tied the stretches of silken cord to the bedposts. The room would be ready for him when he finished.

There was still a hint of sunlight outside as the evening wore on.

Elizabeth felt her heart race as her husband's shoulders rose. Was he done? Finally?

He cracked his knuckles, stretching out his fingers, then leaned back over the desk to continue writing.

It was as if she wasn't even there. Elizabeth exhaled out her nose, puffing up her chest as she stood by the bed. She wanted to draw Darcy's chagrin. She wanted to misbehave.

She loved seeing that sideways glance of his - the one that told her she'd set him off. That look had taken on a whole new world of meaning since she saw the contents of his cabinet. Would he be teaching her a lesson the minute they were safely behind a locked door?

Could she inspire him to ignore the concern for

houseguests?

Yet here they were behind a door that could easily be locked, and he was more interested in writing letters. That simply wouldn't do.

"Fitzwilliam," she said, finally.

"Yes, dear?"

"Are you quite finished?"

There was a subtle whine to her words, and Elizabeth scolded herself for it.

*Don't beg*, she thought. *You're not a beggar. You're his wife.*

Darcy barely looked up from his letter. "I am almost finished with this, but I will need to write to London afterward. Why?"

*Why?* She thought. *If he'd so much as look up, he'd know.*

Elizabeth fought to steady her nerves. Little more than a week of marriage, and he still gave her butterflies in her stomach. She stood by the window watching him, suddenly almost embarrassed by the display of paddles and nonsense across their perfectly made bed.

Elizabeth held her breath. "I demand your attention," she said.

Darcy straightened slightly, shifting to look at her. A moment later, he stood.

Elizabeth almost recoiled. Fitzwilliam Darcy could fill a room when he wanted to.

Darcy shot her a look, the tiniest hint of a smirk on his face. "I see. I'm keeping you waiting, am I?"

The sly grin sent that same familiar pang through her sex. He crossed the room slowly, letting each step linger. When he drew close, he smelled of wood shavings and horses, still. He pushed her up against the windowsill, the ridge of it digging into her backside. She shimmied against him, glancing back at the bed and all the wonderful things in store.

His lips were dry from thirst, and his hands were warm. He wasted no time slipping a hand up the front of her dress, squeezing her breast as he kissed her. Elizabeth squealed at his touch, but then hummed into his mouth, still wanting to welcome him. He pried her knees apart and pressed himself between her legs, then kissed her deeply.

She was ready for him in every way.

He broke from their embrace, suddenly, and Elizabeth watched in shock as Darcy crossed the room back toward his desk and sat down.

"Where are you going?"

Darcy sat down in his chair, took up his pen, and leaned back over the paper to write. "As I said, I must finish this, then write to London. You will have my attention when I am done."

The tone was stern, as though he spoke to an unruly child.

Elizabeth was furious. She didn't make him wait for her, or turn him away, or say, 'later.' And now here he was, treating her like some nuisance he had to tolerate.

Was this a part of his punishments? Was she being punished now by being ignored?

This would not be tolerated.

*You may be the master of this house, but I am not your servant,* she thought.

Elizabeth glanced toward the bed and the chosen toys she'd laid out for him.

He hadn't touched the paddles. He hadn't hoisted up the riding crop to threaten her. He'd never used the riding crop before. Why hadn't he stopped to inspect her offering?

Elizabeth stood there for a long moment, staring at her beloved husband, and began to feel neglected.

A mere week after their wedding day. Perhaps, she was spoiled, but she didn't care.

Elizabeth turned for the bed and marched quietly across the room. She took the small stretch of red, satin cord from the bedpost, working as quickly and quietly as she could.

She took a moment to look at her husband, his head leaning back for a moment as he stretched his fingers, his white shirt loose around his shoulders as his arms slung at his sides, giving a comfortable sigh. His shoulders were the widest part of him, framed perfectly by his billowing white sleeves and vest. He sat there silent, his eyes closed. She took only a moment to decide.

If he wasn't ready to punish her without reason, she'd give him something to punish her for.

She moved to the back of his chair to take his hands. He started at the sudden touch, craning to look back at her. Elizabeth pulled his hands back to the wooden slats of the chair and wrapped the bright red cord around his wrists.

"What are you doing, woman?"

The tone almost stilled her, instantly, but she stayed the course. "Nothing," she said, looping the tie around his other wrist before tying the first knot.

He straightened. "I wouldn't do that if I were you."

She moved swiftly, nervously. His tone was soft, but his temper was up. Even if he softened his tone for her, no matter how sweet his manner, he could frighten. She knew what she was doing would get her in trouble, especially given that he'd already told her he was indisposed.

Their hours in the bedroom – he'd made it clear how he wanted her to behave in the bedroom.

"You are my equal in the world, Elizabeth, but behind locked doors, I am your master in all things. In private, you trust me implicitly. You give yourself to me, implicitly, and I will always reward you for it."

Yet, here she was, their bedroom door shut, and she was not minding her master.

He would be furious.

She couldn't wait. She knew this might be too dangerous a way to try him. Still, she was soon finished tying the second knot, affixing his wrists to the wooden slats.

It was done; he was helpless.

She stood up and came around to the front of the chair to face him. His shoulders seemed broader now with his arms trapped behind him.

He glared at her and gave a tug at his wrists. "Are you trying me, Elizabeth?"

She set her jaw, nodding. She let each word ring with purpose. "I demand your attention."

Darcy took a deep breath. "You're making demands of me, now?"

She tugged the skirt of her dress up to her hips and kicked a leg across him. He straightened, but she settled into his lap. His face turned up to her, his eyes growing dark in that sudden shift of intention, from blind frustration to intimate menace. And it was menace; a dominant will that rendered her every time he touched her a certain way, the quiet warning that she would be his, however he wanted, whenever he wanted. She feared he might be too angry to want her, but as she settled over him, she felt the hardness of him and knew such worries were needless. That menace returned to his eyes now, but when he pulled at his wrists, the knots held fast. However furious he was, his dark eyes betrayed the same desires she harbored.

Then why did he refuse? She wondered.

He couldn't grab hold of her, toss her off, or pull her closer if he liked, couldn't throw her onto the bed or smack her backside. All he could do was strain beneath her as she began to move against him in familiar rhythm.

His body responded, instantly. He growled, his words barely a whisper. "You don't want to do this."

She smiled, touching her nose to his, searching his face. "Oh, but I do."

He tugged at his wrists again and glared at her. She giggled at the sight of it. She was going to be punished when he pulled free. She would be punished, and love every second of it.

"Untie me," he said.

"No."

She shifted over him, grinding down into his lap as the muscles in his shoulders strained. He was working at the knots around his wrists; he would get free in time, but for now she would enjoy these moments, feeling the solid warmth of his body and the involuntary ripples of pleasure that played across his face.

"Woman. Untie me now, or you will regret it."

She laughed, nervously, dragging her nails up through his hair as she rose and fell over him. He was hard beneath her, his breathing shallow and hoarse, but his brow was set with a glare of warning. She lifted herself enough to get to his belt and unfastened it, pulling his britches open and down over his hips as much as she could.

"This is what happens when you neglect your wife for Charles Bingley," she said. "Now, lift yourself up."

"You can't be serious. Bloody untie me. Now, Elizabeth."

She tugged at the waistband of his britches, ignoring him, and they slipped down to where his backside was squarely planted on the chair. He refused to budge, leaving his cock hidden beneath fabric. She stood before him, meeting his glare with one of her own. Then she reached for his ankles, grabbed the hem of his britches on each pant leg and pulled them out before him. He swore under his breath, but the garment slid down a few inches. She gave another tug, causing him to lurch forward in his seat, and the garment came free from beneath him. She pulled his britches off, then knelt before him. He sat there in his wooden chair, arms useless, eyes burning into her, threats and frustration spewing from his lips, but as she pushed his knees apart and moved closer to him, the words stilled.

This was what she'd read in her tawdry book – a woman touching a man like this, using her mouth to please him. She'd thought to do it before – wanted to – but she hadn't dared let Fitzwilliam see just how wanton she could be.

She wondered what he would taste like.

His expression fought her with every glance, but his body sprung to meet her. Elizabeth kissed the inside of his thigh, moving her hands upward. He tensed to her touch.

When he spoke, it was a whisper. "I'm going to punish you for every second of this."

"Promise?"

With that, she took him in her mouth. He groaned.

His skin was smooth, stretched taut across the grand shape of him, and he barely tasted of anything, save for the subtle lingering of salt.

She could feel him straining above her, but she kept her focus on her work, letting her lips play across the smooth skin of his sex, slick from her mouth. He gasped when she took him wholly, sucking as deeply as she could. He was far too big to take further, but she'd read of women capable of opening their throats to fully accommodate large men.

Perhaps, she could try.

She shifted upward, opening her mouth as wide as she could and fought to take him. An instant later, she was gagging and had to pull away to catch her breath.

Well, that didn't go to plan.

He fought against the knots, and she was sure he would come free, but she had him helpless for now, and she attacked him with the fury of a woman on borrowed time. When he came loose, he would take over, grab her and throw her wherever he pleased, and though there was a chance he might simply leave her there, aching with need as punishment for her behavior, she hoped she knew him well. She hoped he wasn't one to walk away from her.

She hoped he was as helpless to his passions as she was finding herself to be.

Elizabeth grazed her nails against the sensitive skin of his balls, listening for the soft hiss of pleasure. Darcy had taken her in hand on their first night together, his fingers curled in her hair, softly coaxing her. He wasn't cooing now. He was silent, fighting with the ropes that held him as he tried to withstand sensation.

She ran her tongue up the length of him, looking up to meet his gaze. His brow was set in stern warning, but his lips were parted. He enjoyed watching her.

He jerked suddenly, and she fought not to recoil in trepidation.

She glanced back toward the bed and the paddles and toys that lay there. Her stomach shot into her throat. Would she love every second of her punishment as he'd warned her before? Would he use those things to give her pleasure as he promised, and how on earth would getting her backside paddled bring her pleasure?

It frightened her just enough to elicit nervous giggles, and make her heart pound in her ears.

She'd take the punishment over being ignored, thank you very much.

She took him in her hand, stroking him as she played her tongue against the sensitive skin of his balls. He hummed his approval, despite himself, trying to hide it with a growl. Her heart leapt at the sound.

Suddenly, his arms lurched forward. She jerked up, bracing herself for his assault. It didn't come. Though the tie had loosened, he wasn't yet free.

She moved with new fervor, wanting to torture him as long as she could. She made quick work of untying her stays, then lifted her dress up over her head. She stripped off her shift and petticoats, kicking them across the room.

He tugged at the tie again and his arms inched outward. Darcy's face was set in frustration and warning.

She had moments, if not seconds.

She straddled him, reaching down to take him in her hand and direct him.

He glared up at her. "My god, you're going to pay for this."

She smiled, sliding down onto him, feeling him slip into her with ease as she lowered herself into his lap. He tensed, gasping softly in tandem with her. She settled onto his lap, the full length of him sheathed inside her, and she began to rise and fall there on him. He'd had her atop him in the previous weeks, demanding that she ride him like some steed as he lay back on the bed. It left her legs wobbly and made her feel self-conscious and unsure, but it had felt simply wondrous.

It felt even better now.

He yanked at the tie and the telling sound of fabric tearing lit a fire in his eyes. He was almost free. She ran her hands through the tendrils of his hair and lifting his face to her, kissed him.

He bit her lip. Not enough to draw blood, but enough to hurt.

Elizabeth jerked back. "You scoundrel!"

"I warned you."

Despite the sting of her lip, she continued to move over him. His angry expression wavered, but held. He wouldn't give in to sensation. He turned his head down and clamped his open mouth over her breast, biting her again. She grabbed him by the hair, pulling his head back. He chuckled in a manner that would haunt her.

"Nothing will prepare you for what I am going to do to you, Elizabeth."

Her stomach shot into her throat. She felt as she had on their wedding night, when first he'd appeared with the red cords, fixing her wrists to the bedposts as he had his way with her. He'd been gentle that night.

He wouldn't be now.

She moved faster, pressing herself closer to him, their noses touching. She could feel his breath, hot against her lips, growing sharper and shallower as she moved.

He smirked. "You're doomed."

"I know. I still want you to kiss me though, damn it."

He glared at her, straightened in his seat, and did just that, piercing his tongue into her mouth. She shuddered and cried out at the sensation. This offering of reciprocation, like some tiny act of submission from the most dominant man she would ever know rendered her helpless against him. She wanted his hands free now, she wanted to be taken in hand and given whatever punishment or reward he might see fit. She simply wanted to be his. She sighed into his mouth, rising and falling over him as he kissed her.

The movement was sudden and upending as his fingers dug into the soft flesh at her hips. She shrieked, and he launched her off him and onto the bed. Elizabeth held her hands out before her as though she might be able to hold him at bay. He stood there, towering over her, the satin cord dangled from one wrist, flayed strands of satin hanging at the other. He'd torn the thing in two.

Darcy glared down at her, and Elizabeth felt a new sting of need between her legs. She'd recognized the look. He was coming for her.

"Fitzwilliam," she said, her voice almost pleading now as the punishment approached.

"Master Darcy!" He growled. Then, he barreled down onto her, taking hold of her hair as he guided himself into her again.

Elizabeth cried out against the sudden force of him.

"Is this the punishment you wanted?" He asked as he thrust into her with such force, her insides buckled. She tried to scream, but he clamped a hand over her mouth, lowering his lips to her ear. "Shh. No need to scream. You knew exactly what was coming to you."

He thrust again and again, holding her beneath him, helpless to him, battering her insides with force in juxtaposition to his gentle whispers. She cried out against his hand, trying to gasp for air, but he held her there, watching her face as he punished her, not with paddles and whips, but with his body. She could feel the heat in her sex rising, feel the way he slammed into the right places, urging her on and on. Her legs clamped around him, but his movements didn't slow. She was coming close to release and there was no more she could do about that than free herself from his grasp.

She closed her eyes tight, feeling tears slip down her cheeks and into her ears, and held her breath.

"That's right. Come for me, you vexing thing," he whispered into her ear. She seized beneath him with such violence, he loosed his hold on her mouth, letting her scream, pinned beneath him. He drove into her harder and faster, as though punishing her now for her release. The wave crested, began to recede, but with the fervor of his

54

movements, started anew, and stronger. She reached for him, wanting to touch his skin, pull him onto her, but he saw the movement and grabbed her wrists, pinning them over her head.

"How does it feel? Wanting to touch me and being denied."

She cried out in near pain and frustration.

"How does it bloody feel?"

"Please!" She cried, her head craning back.

He pounded into her now, grunting and growling with each thrust. She recognized the sounds of his coming end.

She tore her hands from his grasp, reaching down to clamp her hands over his backside, pulling him into her, pushing herself up to meet him. He met each movement with another more powerful thrust.

She dug her nails into his ass. "Is that all you have for me?" She said.

His went wide.

Before the words could even pass her lips, she braced for impact. He clutched his fist in her hair, and roared. She could barely catch her breath as she came again, this time the sensation searing like gunpowder through her sex, splaying out into her limbs and her belly. He shuddered over her in unison, feeling the warmth of his seed inside her. He convulsed, pressing his forehead to hers, his breathing hoarse on her face. Then he slumped onto her, his face buried into her hair.

They took a moment to catch their breath, silent. She draped her arms across his back, playing her fingernails at his smooth skin. He hummed softly in appreciation.

"I should tie you up more often," she said.

He lifted himself up, slowly, then met her gaze. The stern glare was enough to strike fear in a Roman. She giggled beneath him.

He rose to his feet, leaving her skin cool from their sweat and the absence of his warmth. "Believe me, if you do, the punishment will only be worse."

She smiled, watching him collect his britches from the foot of the bed.

"Is that meant to deter me?" She asked.

He shot her a warning look and bent to pick up her dress from where it fell, rumpled on the floor.

"No, on the contrary, actually."

Elizabeth sat up in the bed, staring at her husband. "No? What do you mean?"

Darcy stepped into his britches, pulling them up and tucking his still half erect cock under the fabric before tying them. "I mean, I have no intention of deterring you from this – vexing behavior."

"You don't?"

"Not at all."

Elizabeth crossed her legs at the ankles, feeling a rush of wet between her legs in the wake of their lovemaking. "You confuse me so, Fitzwilliam."

He took his time tucking his shirt into his trousers, smiling to himself. "Well, Elizabeth, if you were to behave as you are told, I would have no cause to punish you. And I do so love to punish you, darling."

Elizabeth felt tingling in her sex to hear him say this. "Really? Why didn't you tell me?"

Darcy stopped by the desk, shooting her a sideways glance. "I didn't think I had to. I didn't exactly marry you for your demure, submissive nature."

Elizabeth felt her face flush. "But I thought you wanted obedience. Isn't that what all of this is about?"

Darcy's eyebrows shot up and he paused. "Well, in some manner, yes. But then again, there's nothing quite so satisfying as having a powerful woman reduced to a whimpering, quivering mess at the mere threat of the paddle. But what good is a paddle if you never give me reason to use it."

Elizabeth shifted to the side of the bed, her cheeks burning. "I don't whimper."

Darcy met her at the side of the bed. "Oh yes, you do. I

make you whimper."

He took hold of her, pulling her onto her feet to meet him. She barely reached his collarbone, but he leaned down to kiss her, his hands slipping down the curve of her back to tease at the cleft between her buttocks. She squirmed, pulling from his arms, and crossed the room, collecting her dress from the chair where he'd lain it. She shot a sideways glance toward the desk and the waiting letters he still meant to write.

"You know, for someone who keeps threatening the paddle, you've barely looked at them when we're together."

Suddenly, he slapped her ass hard, the sting of it causing her to yelp as she scurried out of reach. He returned to the desk as she began to get dressed. "Sounds like someone is curious."

Elizabeth rubbed her stinging backside for a moment, then stepped into the dress, smiling at him.

"Elizabeth. Where is my inkwell?"

She couldn't help but snort in a stifled laugh. "What? I certainly have no idea."

Darcy turned and shot her a familiar glare. Her backside burned from the fading pain of his last assault, but she felt that same familiar rush between her legs.

"Elizabeth."

"Fitzwilliam, if you can't find something, it isn't my duty to miraculously produce it. I'm your wife, not your maid."

He ruffled his hair and exhaled. "Bloody hell."

She smiled and turned for the door, but he was on her before she could escape. He wrapped his arms around her, hoisting her off her feet, and marched her across the room to the bed. "Riding crop it is, then."

Elizabeth squealed as he hoisted up her skirts.

A soft shuffling sound in the hallway outside their door stopped them both. They stared wide-eyed at one another, waiting for the sound to return. When it didn't, Elizabeth lifted herself off the bed.

"Surely, it was just Molly," he said, but his tone was

wavering. Whether it was Molly or no, neither of them ever intended for Molly, or anyone for that matter, to hear them in their private moments. The trepidation of his tone was soon replaced by a stern look of indignation. His concern for Molly's virtue had given way to frustration that she'd come to his chambers at all.

Elizabeth quickly finished dressing, shooting Darcy warning looks as she scolded his rising temper.

"Don't blame the maid for hearing us. It's our own fault for being so brazen in the middle of the day."

"I've every right to be brazen, it's my bloody house, isn't it? And I certainly pay the woman's wages. I'll not be shamed by her prying. I will not."

He was doing his best to rally anger, but Elizabeth could see through it. He was embarrassed for the maid and felt helpless. What better way to diffuse shame than to replace it with anger.

Elizabeth scurried back to his desk, pulling his inkwell back out from the nook in the windowsill where she'd hid it. "Here, you sit to those letters of yours. I'll go see to Molly. It will all come out in the wash."

"Meddlesome. Simply meddlesome little -"

"Stop. It's a matter of weeks since our wedding. Surely, maids can come to expect such things from their master's bedroom doors."

"An hour before tea?" He said, exasperation ringing loud in every word.

She hushed him, leading him back to his desk. "Write your letters and forget this silly disruption. I will see you in the dining room."

He groaned, softly to himself, but did as she bade him, slumping into his chair and taking up his quill.

Elizabeth turned for the door, fighting to still her racing heart. However steadfast she tried to appear to Fitzwilliam, she was nearly mortified to think poor Molly had heard them.

Clearly, Molly was due a nice bonus in her wages this

month.

Elizabeth opened the bedroom door and stepped into the hallway.

"You're still getting the riding crop later," Fitzwilliam called softly from his desk.

She spun around to face him, but he hadn't even lifted his eyes from his letter.

She couldn't help but smile. It was almost enough to diffuse the roaring fury in her belly. Elizabeth turned down the hall and headed toward the parlors and the main house, standing as straight as ever she'd stood before, her chin pointed skyward. She'd never been so desperate to seem a lady.

She marched down the hallway, the oriental runner soft underfoot. She passed one of the small reading rooms and startled to find a figure standing at the bright open windows. Her stomach leapt into her throat, but she stopped, turning back to meet the woman and smooth any ragged edges left by the inadvertent eavesdropping.

"Did you need to summon one of us, Mol -"

Elizabeth stopped, stricken.

The figure standing at the window gazing out at the grounds was not wearing the dowdy dress of a long-time maid.

Jane.

Neither woman spoke or moved for a long moment. Finally, Elizabeth took a step toward her sister, watching the glowing blonde curls, golden in the light from the window. Before she could speak, Jane shifted, turning to look at Lizzy over her shoulder. Her expression was one of nervous misery.

There was no question now. She'd heard them.

Jane frowned. "Why isn't it like that for me?" She said.

Elizabeth's heart broke. "Oh, my dear Jane."

# CHAPTER FIVE

## *The Saddest Sister*

❦

"I refuse, outright!"

Fitzwilliam was moving about the bedroom, a whirlwind of obstinate displeasure.

"How can you say that? He's your dear friend – there should be no trouble in such a -"

"You want me to breach the subject of Charles' bedroom activities, clearly proclaiming that I know them to be severely lacking, all in order to assure your sister gets a proper rogering?"

"Fitzwilliam Darcy!" She said, startled to hear such language from her noble husband. Despite herself, she found it almost endearing. Elizabeth closed her eyes, frustrated. "He doesn't know what he's doing, Fitzwilliam. She tells me he literally inserts himself, then they both lie there prone until she's nearly suffocating, and they give up and go to sleep."

Fitzwilliam stifled a half laugh. "That can't be true. He's not a simpleton."

"No, of course not, but neither was I. The only knowledge I had of lovemaking was from a tawdry book I received mere hours before our wedding. Perhaps, you could give him one of these books, couldn't you? Isn't that how you learned?"

He turned to face her, giving an impatient look. Still, his fury was wavering.

60

Elizabeth paused. Somehow, she could see quite clearly in that wavering that the books were not where he learned his craft. She didn't want to think on it further.

Not yet.

"Even if I gave him such a book, his opinion of me would be altered. Permanently."

"Yes, but his marriage would be, as well. This isn't just for Jane. If he is such a dear friend, don't you want him to be happy?"

"His marriage is none of my business, woman!"

Elizabeth glared at him.

"Why don't you give the book to Jane. Let her breech such a subject with her husband."

"Oh, yes. His virginal wife comes to him with a copy of *Fanny Hill*, and you think his opinion of *her* won't be altered?"

"My opinion of you wasn't altered," he said, and she stopped.

No, but it was clear he'd had more experience with such tawdry tomes. It was quite clear to anyone who heard Jane's sorry story that Charles Bingley had no knowledge of lovemaking, whatsoever.

Fitzwilliam tossed the book onto his desk. He'd been pacing with it in his hands since she handed it to him.

Elizabeth didn't speak, her mind had been racing since the moment she asked this of her husband. She knew what she asked was no small task. She knew it could well alter the man's opinion of Fitzwilliam, but seeing Jane's grief – hearing her confess that she feared it was her fault their marriage wasn't as satisfying and passionate – it was enough to make Elizabeth cross the river Styx to ask Hades himself to talk to Charles Bingley about his husbandly duties.

She owed it to her darling sister to at least try.

"Haven't I done enough meddling in your sisters' marital affairs for one lifetime?"

Elizabeth pursed her lips. A part of her wanted to scold him for this comment. It almost sounded as though he wanted to hold Lydia's melodrama against her. Yet, when he met her gaze and saw the hurt in her expression, he softened.

"Fine."

Elizabeth's eyes went wide. "Pardon? Oh, do say it again!"

"I'm not going to speak to him, myself. I won't subject either of us to that manner of humiliation -"

Elizabeth opened her mouth to protest, but he raised a hand, stilling her.

"- but I know someone who I can trust to do it for me. And I'm certain this gentleman won't care in the slightest about Charles' opinion of him."

"Who?"

Fitzwilliam turned to her, a soft glare to his expression. The look said, 'I'm warning you, do not press, or I may well change my mind.'

Elizabeth lunged toward him, throwing her arms around his neck. "Thank you, you beautiful, wondrous thing, you."

"Yes, yes. Of course, I'm wondrous when I cater to your whimsies, but I assure you, Lizzy, this will not become routine. Do not ask this sort of thing of me. I am a private man, and I intend to remain that way."

She swallowed, still clinging to him as her turned toward his desk. "I will need to write a letter requesting he visit. I don't dare put these words to something as permanent as pen and ink."

"Whatever you think is best, darling. God, you marvelous man," she said again, throwing her arms around his shoulders as he sat at his desk. He pat his hand on her arm, dipping his quill in ink.

"Don't think for an instant that you won't be repaying me in some way, Elizabeth, dear. I assure you, I will come to collect."

She smiled, hoping the debt would involve ropes and sighs. "Whatever your heart desires."

He shot her a sideways glance, a slight smirk to his lips. "Good, now for the love of God, please go downstairs to meet the carriage when your family arrives and help Deirdre plan our Dinner. The last thing I want today is to have your mother bursting into my bedroom. She's just the sort of woman to go throwing cabinet doors open to snoop inside."

Elizabeth gasped, her mouth hanging open to argue with him, but as he leaned over the desk to begin his letter, she stopped herself.

He wasn't wrong, and even she was a little unnerved to receive the letter that morning, announcing her family's plans to join the Bingley's at Pemberley for a visit.

She wondered if the letter was simply delayed, or if her mother had specifically sent it late in order to remove any chance of Elizabeth refusing them.

Not that she would refuse her family's visit, but still. Having Jane in the house had put a mild damper on their marriage activities, but having Mr. and Mrs. Bennet in the house, with Kitty and Mary in tow would be like dumping a torch in a pig trough.

She made her way down the stairs to find Deirdre.

The carriage arrived an hour before tea, and Mrs. Bennet was in rare form.

"How delightful to find all of my girls under one roof again!"

"All but one, darling," Mr. Bennet corrected her.

"Well, of course, but who expects Lydia to make time for the rest of -"

"So good to see you, sister," Kitty said, rushing forward to give Elizabeth a warm embrace.

It almost startled her. Kitty had never been the most agreeable character in the household, only outdone by the tempestuous Lydia. Yet, her hair was perfectly curled and pinned, and her smile was genuine. Elizabeth was pleased to see it.

"I'm so pleased to get to spend time at your lovely home. Mother says you might allow me to come stay from time to time?"

"Catherine! Now's not the time. We've just arrived. Let

your sister breathe, for once," Mrs. Bennet said, giving Kitty's elbow a pinch.

Kitty winced and pulled away, shrugging to Elizabeth. Lizzy just smiled. "I'm sure we could find room for you."

Kitty beamed as Elizabeth turned her attention to Mary.

Mary had never been the most charming or beautiful of the Bennet sisters, but she smiled wide to see Elizabeth, and the smile brought a new light to the dark-haired girl's face. Clearly, Mrs. Bennet had taken good care to braid and pin Mary's hair for their visit. She looked quite lovely.

"You look well, sister," Mary said, mirroring her own thoughts.

"Thank you, Mary. I'm so happy to have you here. Fitzwilliam is indisposed at the moment with letters, but I wondered if while mother and father take a rest that you and Kitty might enjoy an afternoon ride. I can have Angus prepare horses for us. The grounds are simply beautiful."

Mary smiled, offering an almost curtsy as she declined the offer. "Thank you, Lizzy, but I think I'd much prefer to settle in with a book before tea. Might I pester you to show me to your library?"

Elizabeth smiled. "Of course." Even with their mother's clear attention, Mary hadn't changed.

"I would love a ride, sister," Kitty said, fighting the familiar urge to hop in place, excitedly as she and Lydia often did when they were together.

Molly bustled about each member of the Bennet family, stealing away their coats as the carriage pulled away down the drive. The air outside was crisp, but not too cool. Elizabeth thought it a lovely notion to take a ride.

And a nice change. She smiled to herself.

*See, Fitzwilliam. You're not the only one who can take to the hills all afternoon.*

With the Bennets comfortable nestled into Pemberley's various corners, Kitty and Elizabeth were each coupled with beautiful mares from the stables. Kitty was riding a beautiful brown horse named Helvetica, and Elizabeth rode her favorite horse, a tall, white mare named Mist.

She had half a mind to take Fitzwilliam's favorite horse, Zeus, but he was a far grander and faster creature than she was used to.

The two Bennet sisters rode along the paths, cutting through small corners of woods, but keeping to the open space. Given the expanse of the grounds, it was quite possible to ride for hours and never lose sight of the magnificent house in the distance.

Despite her love for Pemberley, Elizabeth was ready to explore further afield.

"Shall we cut through these woods, here, then?" Lizzy asked her younger sister.

Kitty's eyes widened as she glanced down the darker wooded path. "Oh, shall we? It looks rather foreboding, doesn't it?"

There was an air of conspiracy and excitement to her tone. Much like Lydia, Kitty loved getting into trouble.

"Where does it go?" She asked.

Elizabeth shrugged. "I haven't the faintest idea."

She needn't say another word. This was enough for Kitty. Her sister took off down the path, riding at a canter into the woods. Elizabeth quickly gave Mist a soft kick in the side and rode after her.

The two of them slowed after a while, sauntering along on their horses as the path rose over a wide ravine below.

"Have you spoken to Lydia at all since the wedding?" Kitty asked, her eyes trained on the path ahead.

Elizabeth thought of the last time she saw Lydia, and the filthy books she shared. "I haven't. I'm sure she's off somewhere regaling someone with the news that she was the first Bennet sister to marry. Again."

Kitty stifled a laugh.

Elizabeth didn't bother to share that just a day or two after her wedding, she'd received a letter from Lydia requesting an allowance of three hundred pounds per annum.

Fitzwilliam had simply loved that bit of news.

Of course, she only shared it after writing back that there would be no such allowance incoming.

They reached the edge of the woods, coming out to a small field. A cottage was tucked into the hillside nearby, its fading garden spilled over the stone wall in a lovely splay of green and faded reds.

The two sisters rounded the corner of a small pond just as Kitty clucked softly to her horse, pulling the reins to keep her from trudging headfirst into the water for a drink.

But Helvetica had other ideas, and before either sister could protest, the horse plunged into the water as though jumping a log in the midst of a fox hunt.

Elizabeth watched helplessly as Kitty toppled off Helvetica and landed headfirst in the water. An instant later, she reappeared, her yellow dress clinging to her, a lily pad sliding down the side of her head.

It took all of Elizabeth's will not to laugh. She dismounted as quickly as she could, rushing toward the edge of the water.

"No, no, madam. Allow me," a deep voice spoke from nearby, and as Elizabeth watched from the shore, a tall man in black coat and britches marched out into the pond, offering a hand to poor Kitty.

Kitty was a mess, fighting to pull the tendrils of water plants from her skirts and hair, but as soon as the tall man opened his hand to her, her whole demeanor changed. Her face turned bright red, but she took his hand.

He helped pull her back toward the shore, turning right back for the water to retrieve the willful horse who now stood happily munching on shoots by the water's edge.

He turned back to them, high-stepping back through the pond to return Kitty's horse to her. He held the reins out to her and finally removed the wide-brimmed hat from atop his head.

Elizabeth could see why Kitty was blushing.

"Are you quite alright, Miss?"

"Bennet," Kitty said, blurting out the word as though it

burned her tongue.

"Miss Bennet," he said, offering her a rugged, but youthful smile. "How lovely to make your acquaintance. I'm James Farnsworth. I live at the vicarage just there."

"A vicar?" Kitty said, incredulity in her voice.

Elizabeth leapt to speak, hoping to cover her sister's rather blatant affection for the young vicar. "Mr. Farnsworth, we indebted to you. Thank you so much for coming to our rescue."

"Ah, I imagine Miss Bennet didn't need rescuing," he said, and Kitty blushed all over again.

"You're not like the other vicars I've met," Kitty said, and Elizabeth took hold of her arm.

"Come, sister. Let's get you back to the house and warmed up. You'll catch a death."

"Would you prefer to come inside, here? How far is the ride home?"

"Yes!" Kitty blurted out.

Elizabeth glanced away, trying to hide her eye rolling. "Pardon my rudeness. I'm Mrs. Darcy. We've come from Pemberley through the wood there."

"Oh, yes. Quite a ride. Please, that's rather far to chance in this weather. Do come inside and warm yourself before you head back."

Elizabeth glanced at her younger sister, then at the vicar. They would most certainly be missing tea.

Fitzwilliam would kill her for leaving him to dine with her mother alone.

Kitty turned a pleading look on her, and Elizabeth softened, not because of her sister's sudden ardor for the handsome vicar, but because she truly worried after her sister's well-being. The gray clouds had rolled in, and were the sun to come out, they'd be under tree cover for much of the ride.

"We hate to impose," she said, forcing out the proper, polite response.

"I insist," he said, smiling wide at Kitty. "Come, I have a

fire already going. Was about to sit down for some tea."

Mr. Farnsworth took hold of both horses' reins and led them all toward the quaint little cottage.

***

"Wasn't he handsome? Wasn't he simply the most handsome man you've ever laid eyes upon?"

Kitty had been unable to contain herself since the moment they were out of Mr. Farnsworth's earshot.

"And such a gentleman, wasn't he? Offering me his coat and blankets – and the seat closest to the fire? Such a gentleman."

Elizabeth didn't respond. Her sister didn't need her to. Still, she was smiling as she listened. Somehow, Catherine's whole demeanor had changed in the many weeks since Lydia left Longbourn, and now Kitty was bearing the positive effects. She was a proper lady now, not willful and childish as Lydia had always been.

She was a woman – and she was absolutely smitten.

"I'm so happy you invited him to Pemberley. Do you think he'll come? Would tonight be too soon to call? When do you think he'll call on us – you, I mean, of course?"

"I can't rightly guess."

Kitty sighed. "Oh, I can't wait to see him again. We could go riding again, tomorrow, couldn't we? Only this time, I won't fall in the pond. Goodness, how mortifying. Intolerable mule, this horse."

"I don't know. Seems to me our darling Helvetica did you a favor."

Kitty beamed. "Do you think so? You're so right. He was just so lovely. And wasn't a lovely home. I've never been inside a vicarage before. It was cozy. And it smelled so nice."

Kitty prattled on for the entire ride back to Pemberley.

Despite the dramatic events of their ride, Elizabeth only remembered how long they'd been gone when they rode up toward the stables. Mrs. Bennet was wailing her way down the drive before Angus could take the horses from them.

"We thought you'd died! Where on earth did you disappear to? Good grief, look at the state of you," she said, laying eyes on Kitty.

Kitty seemed deaf to their mother's squalling as she let herself be led into the house, a constant smile chiseled on her face.

"What is wrong with you, silly girl?" Mrs. Bennet asked as they turned up the stairs. Mrs. Bennet was insisting on a nice warm bath.

Elizabeth thought that a fine idea as she made her way up the stairs, herself.

There was no sign of Fitzwilliam in the downstairs, and she could hear Mr. Bennet and Mr. Bingley talking in the library.

Elizabeth turned toward her apartments, passing the quiet parlor as she went.

A soft gasping sound slowed her steps as she walked.

It was a soft, female voice - someone was in the parlor.

Elizabeth approached the doorway slowly, coming to stand just outside. She peeked into the familiar space and found Mary curled on the settee.

She was sobbing, a small, black-covered book in her hands.

Elizabeth gasped.

It was Lydia's copy of Fanny Hill.

*Oh dear god, how had Mary found it?*

"Mary, darling. What's wrong?"

Elizabeth hurried across the room, settling onto the settee beside Mary. She waited for Mary to scramble, hurrying to hide the offending book, but she barely moved, bringing a free hand up to her eyes to wipe away her tears.

Elizabeth reached for her sister's hands, pulling the book from her.

Mary let her take it.

Elizabeth frowned to see her sister in such a state. Had the scandalous nature of the book somehow harmed her.

69

She knew some women were simply unnerved by the idea of intimacy, let alone filth.

"Come now, darling. What's wrong? It's just a book."

Mary shook her head. "It's not, though. Is it?"

"Pardon?" Elizabeth, turning to look at the still open pages. She skimmed a line and instantly knew which scene her sister had been reading.

The opening love scene – the scene between two women.

"Oh, Mary. Don't let it trouble you. You've read hundreds of books with far more troubling scenes than this."

"It didn't trouble me, it – it's -" she stammered, unable to complete her thought.

Elizabeth looked down at the book again, running her finger over the pages. A notion struck her, and suddenly her beloved, but difficult sister, Mary, made some strange new sense.

"Then, what's wrong, Mary? Why has it made you cry?"

Mary wiped her eyes and finally met Elizabeth's gaze. "If it happens in books, does that mean – could that mean there are women who -"

"Women who desire other women?" Elizabeth said in a low, calm whisper.

Mary gasped, fighting another bout of sobs. "Yes?"

Elizabeth felt a sting at her eyes as she smiled at Mary. "Yes, sweetheart."

Mary threw her arms around Elizabeth, crying into her shoulder. "Then I'm not alone," she whispered, and Elizabeth dropped the book on the floor and held her sister as tightly as she could.

# CHAPTER SIX

## *How Many to Tea?*

———✦———

The house felt alive with the Bennet family bustling about in its rooms, and soon the days turned to weeks. Despite Fitzwilliam's proper upbringing, he was growing less and less enamored with his houseguests with every morning he was awakened by his wife's mother, wailing some new protestation to her disinterested husband.

He had far better notions of how he'd like to be woken up each morning.

Elizabeth found them tiresome after a short time, as well. Unlike their first week together, Fitzwilliam's forceful, aggressive lovemaking approach was quelled almost entirely by the constant bustle of Bennet sisters. They'd made love, of course, but he certainly hadn't shown her the riding crop as he once threatened.

He hadn't so much as threatened a smack of the hand across her ass.

Though, to be fair, she hadn't deliberately misbehaved, either. Neither Darcy wanted to chance Mr. or Mrs. Bennet snooping in the hallway outside their apartments. Being overheard by poor Jane was enough to mortify Elizabeth for a lifetime.

Thankfully, Mr. and Mrs. Bennet had finally made their way back home, followed closely by the Bingleys. Mary was content to go home with them, but Kitty didn't dare leave.

Elizabeth found her standing at the parlor window, gazing

out at the ground as she always did. Elizabeth frowned.

She was still hoping for a visit from the rugged Mr. Farnsworth.

"Are you trying to manifest him with your stare, dear Kitty?"

Kitty startled, glancing over her shoulder. "Don't tease."

"I'm sorry. Still, I'm rather surprised he has taken this long. It isn't proper to accept an invitation to call, then not do so."

"Surely, something must be keeping him away," Kitty said, her eyes still trained on the view outside.

"Surely," Elizabeth said, but her conviction was by no means a match for Kitty's.

Molly scurried in to set the first pot of tea on the table, but before Elizabeth could sit down, Molly curtseyed to her.

"You've a visitor, Missus. Would you like me to send Mrs. Collins up to have breakfast?"

Elizabeth gasped, darting for the door. She scurried down the stairs to find Charlotte settling her cap and coat in Deirdre's arms.

"My darling Charlotte!" She said, lunging for her friend. Despite their trials after Charlotte married Mr. Collins, Charlotte remained one of her favorite people placed on this earth.

"Lizzy," she said, squeezing Elizabeth tight.

Elizabeth felt the layers of Charlotte's warm dress pressing into her stomach, but as she pulled away to suggest Charlotte change to something more comfortable, she saw the true cause of the extra girth.

Charlotte was heavily pregnant, now.

Elizabeth's eyes went wide, and she threw her arms around her friend again. "Oh, Charlotte! What a blessing?!"

The words were out there, and they'd been truer than most things she'd ever say, but still, the mere idea of what placed Charlotte in such a predicament made her want to shudder.

"It is so nice to be out in the world."

Elizabeth smiled, glancing for the door. She felt the need to brace herself for the coming greeting of Mr. Collins.

"He's not here, Lizzy."

She turned back to her friend, her eyebrows raised despite her manners. "Oh, that's such a shame. You traveled all this way alone?"

Charlotte handed the last layer to Deirdre, and the matronly woman was gone a moment later, leaving the two of them to speak in private.

"Don't think poorly of me, Lizzy, but I simply had to get away. You've no idea how constant the noise is in Hunsford."

"Oh, I've an idea. Come, Kitty is upstairs. We were just about to have some breakfast."

Charlotte groaned, softly, in hungry approval, and they made their way upstairs. Elizabeth fought the urge to speak ill of Mr. Collins. The notion that he'd allowed his very pregnant wife to travel from Rosings Park all alone soured her opinion of him even further.

They settled in for their breakfast of eggs, sausage, and scones. Charlotte shared news of Lady Catherine, saying Anne didn't seem to be fairing too well as the seasons shifted. Elizabeth was sad to hear it.

All during their breakfast, Kitty remained by the window, gazing out at the overcast day.

"What shall we do today? You're certainly in no state for riding, but would you fancy a stroll a turn around the garden? Perhaps, Fitzwilliam would humor us in a game of cards. With Kitty, we'd have a full four."

Charlotte simply shook her head, eyes closed. "No, dear Lizzy. I hate to disappoint you, but I fear I might be in need of a rest."

Elizabeth stood up, instantly fretting over her friend. "Of course, of course. The house is rather empty as compared to the past few weeks. You're welcome to take any room you please and stay as long as you like."

Charlotte gave her a sideways glance. "Don't tempt me."

Elizabeth shot a look toward Kitty. Though Charlotte was her closest friend, she'd never seen Charlotte throw propriety aside when they were in company. The true honesty was always spared for when they were alone.

Elizabeth hooked her arm with Charlotte's and led her down the hall. They were just a few yards down the hallway when Elizabeth spoke again. "Well, darling, what was it that you wanted so much to tell me in person?"

Charlotte placed her hand over her belly and sighed. "The midwife believes I may be having twins."

Elizabeth's mouth fell open, but it wasn't her that responded. "And the parson let you travel alone?"

They both turned toward the open doorway and found Fitzwilliam standing just inside, a collection of letters in his right hand.

"He had pressing matters at the parsonage. I was happy to leave him to it."

Darcy harrumphed, then turned down the hall and walked past them.

Elizabeth closed her eyes, frustrated with her husband. Still, she shared every ounce of his sentiment.

Mr. Collins wasn't the most popular fellow with either of them.

They rounded a corner in the hallway, and Elizabeth gestured to the first bedroom door on the right. It had high open windows and they cast a beautiful glow across the space. Still, Elizabeth made quick work of untying the bed curtains as Charlotte slumped down on the bed and began the arduous task of trying to remove her boots.

"Had I known I'd get this big so quickly, I might've pushed him off."

Elizabeth gave Charlotte a scandalized look. It wasn't because the conversation offended her, by any means. It was the foreign nature of hearing such words from Charlotte's lips.

Apparently, pregnancy was stripping her of her well-bred propriety.

Or perhaps, she simply enjoyed the freedom of speaking with another married woman.

"Twins? Goodness, I can't imagine."

She moved to the floor at Charlotte's feet, loosing the laces before Charlotte could make a second attempt. She pulled them off the poor woman's feet, feeling a swell to her ankles.

"It's a blessing. The midwife assured William that intimacy was simply off the table for the next few months. Even suggested I be allowed to have the bed to myself."

Elizabeth frowned. "Is it so bad?"

Charlotte leaned back against the pillows. "No. Tedious, but not bad."

"I'm so sorry."

Charlotte gave a half laugh, waving the thought away.

Elizabeth made her way around the bed, untying the bed curtains as she went. "I shouldn't gossip, but Jane is having trouble with her husband, as well."

"Oh, no. That can't be. She loves Charles."

"Well, of course -" Elizabeth said, but she stopped. The same frustration and exasperation she'd felt at first hearing Charlotte's wedding news cause bubbling back to the surface. "Perhaps, it could be better. I have some – if you'd like, I have some books that might -"

Charlotte shook her head. "Oh, darling Lizzy. I don't want it to be better. I'd hate to tell poor William how much I prefer the swollen ankles and the ache in my back to the thought of being touched."

Elizabeth slumped down on the edge of the bed, her shoulders sagging.

"Don't fret. If I'm being honest, William has grown on me. He's kind, generous, aims to please in all things, but truth be told, my desire to be a wife never equated to my wanting to be wanted."

"Would you feel differently if you'd married a man you loved?"

Charlotte got a distant look in her eye and smiled. "I

haven't the faintest."

Elizabeth left her friend to her sleep and made her way back toward the parlor. Fitzwilliam was hovering in the hallway near their apartments, his back to her. She reached for him, grazing a hand over his shoulder.

"Is she well?" He asked.

Elizabeth felt a swell of affection at his tone of concern. "She is. I imagine this might be the first quiet moment she's had in months."

Fitzwilliam exhaled in a half laugh. "I don't doubt it. I've just written Lady Catherine again, this morning. We shall see if enough time has passed for her to forgive and forget."

Elizabeth slid her arms under his, wrapping them around his torso. "I'm sorry there's still tension, there."

He smiled, glancing over his shoulder at her. "I'm not. I wouldn't trade for anything."

Elizabeth didn't look up at him, but she held him a little tighter. "She's having twins, they believe."

"My god," he said, softly. "What you women endure."

Elizabeth turned her head, pressing her cheek to his shoulder.

A soft cough alerted them to the presence in the hallway. Molly stood there with her eyes down.

"Yes, Molly?" He said. His tone with Molly was always similar to his tone with Georgiana. He took extra care to soften his edges with these younger women.

He did not, however, take such care with the Bennet sisters. Elizabeth didn't blame him.

Bennet women didn't mind sharp edges.

"You've received a message from the village," she said, holding out a small envelope.

Fitzwilliam took it, giving Molly a nod to dismiss her, and she disappeared back toward the stairs. He turned the envelope over, tearing the edge with his thumb before glancing at its contents.

He stiffened in her arms.

Before she could ask after the letter, Fitzwilliam

straightened, turning to look down at her. He wasn't smiling, but the look was warm. "I have to take a ride into town. I should be more than a few hours. I'll return before tea."

Then, he leaned down to her, pressing his lips to hers in a lingering kiss. She slipped her arms around him again and held him there for a long moment, making him kiss her again. "Is it something urgent?" She said, trying to hide her worry.

"No, no. It's nothing to trouble yourself. I've been waiting several weeks for this. We'll speak of it, later."

He offered one more kiss, then disappeared down the hall.

Elizabeth watched him go, smiling when he glanced back at the top of the stairs.

She'd hoped he would.

She blew him another kiss, and he smiled. Then he was gone.

Elizabeth found Kitty at her familiar post, staring out the parlor window. Still, there were two less scones on the platter. At least she'd eaten.

"Would you like to go for a stroll? I cannot go far from the house, as I want to be near if Charlotte needs me, but perhaps the fresh air might distract you."

Kitty frowned.

"Should I have gone back to the vicarage – to see him, I mean. Do you think that would've been inappropriate?" She asked as they circled the grounds for the third time.

"Yes, I do," Elizabeth said. The air was crisp, and the sky was turning a darker gray by the second. Their stroll would be cut short if it began to rain. It was a miracle Kitty hadn't fallen ill after their riding mishap.

*Thank you, Mr. Farnsworth*, Elizabeth thought.

"Why, though? Why wouldn't it be appropriate?"

"Because he didn't request you come to call."

"But he seemed so keen to…"

She drifted off.

Kitty was smitten. She was thoroughly smitten, and though Elizabeth didn't dare share this thought, she'd gotten the impression that Mr. Farnsworth thought rather highly of Kitty, as well.

"Catherine Farnsworth has such a lovely cadence to it, doesn't it?"

"Oh, stop it, Kitty. You're such a silly girl."

"I know it, but he was so lovely, Lizzy!"

Elizabeth squeezed her sister's arm, laughing as they reached the corner of the house. The familiar rhythm of gravel undercarriage wheels startled them both, but it was Kitty that took off for the drive. She reached the path and craned to see the carriage that was rolling up to the front of the house.

Elizabeth marched up to join her, refusing to run as her younger sister had.

The black carriage had a familiar look to it – a hired carriage, rather than one the rider owned. They both stood watching as the driver hopped down from his post and opened the door to his fare.

Lydia Wickham climbed out of the coach, dressed head to toe in mourning black.

Elizabeth's heart dropped to her toes. "Oh god, no."

"What? Lizzy, what's wrong?"

But Elizabeth didn't answer, she took off toward the front of the house, watching Lydia as she marched up the front steps of Pemberley, oblivious to her sisters' approach.

"Lydia!" Elizabeth called.

Lydia spun around on the top steps, laid eyes on Elizabeth, then Kitty, and the two younger Bennet sisters both shrieked in glee to see one another.

Yet, before Lydia could rush to meet Kitty, she took Lydia's arm, turning her to meet her gaze. "Tell me it's not true?"

"What's not true?" She said, a tone of irritation to her voice, but it swiftly changed back to giddiness as Kitty threw her arms around Lydia, and they embraced.

"What's happened to George?"

Whatever scandal George nearly brought to the Bennet family, he'd been a good friend to Fitzwilliam once upon a time, and he'd even managed to earn Elizabeth's favor before she'd learned of his desperate behavior. The thought that Lydia might be a widow so soon after their desperate union – well, it broke her heart.

Lydia released Kitty, a look of indignation on her face. "I am not his keeper, sister. He does as he pleases."

Elizabeth's mouth fell open. "Is he alive?"

Lydia rolled her eyes, then looked down at herself. "Oh, of course. Yes, he's alive. He's just not my husband anymore."

With that, Lydia turned for the doors of Pemberley, she and Kitty walking arm in arm.

Elizabeth stood there for a long moment, dumbfounded. She wished desperately that Fitzwilliam was home. If only he'd heard this bizarre exchange.

The carriage driver mounted the carriage behind her, bidding her a farewell before riding off, leaving her standing there in the empty drive.

"Mrs. Darcy?"

She startled, spinning around to find a hunched figure teetering on the other side of the drive. He was wearing a familiar black suit and white collar, but his lovely posture was now bent by the crutch under his arm.

Mr. Farnsworth was looking worse for the wear, and he was sporting what looked like a broken foot.

"Oh goodness, what happened to you, vicar?"

He forced a smile, leaning onto his crutch as he made his way across the drive. Elizabeth lunged toward him, offering her arm, but he waved her away with a thank you.

"Please forgive me for taking so long to come to call. I tried to make the journey the very next day, but it seems your sister and I share a poor luck with horses, as my mare threw me some distance from my house. I broke my leg, and the doctor only now said I was fair enough to travel."

"Oh, Mr. Farnsworth, you poor dear. How long have you been walking?"

"Not long. Not too long."

Elizabeth walked alongside him and quickly knew him to be lying through his teeth. Poor Mr. Farnsworth was hobbling like an elderly man. He must've been walking all morning.

"I do hope I haven't come at a bad time. I saw the carriage. If you've company, I can come back another time."

"Absolutely not. You will stay for the evening. I'll have our driver bring you home in the morning."

"Oh no, Mrs. Darcy. I couldn't possibly."

Deirdre appeared in the doorway, coming down the steps to offer an arm, as well. This time, he took it, letting the two women help him up the stairs.

Elizabeth was fighting the urge to laugh. Kitty had been doing so well in Lydia's absence, when her baby sister arrived, she feared Kitty would regress to the obstinate difficult creature she'd always been, but now that Mr. Farnsworth had arrived?

Poor Lydia would be finding herself old news, very quickly.

"Molly, go summon Catherine, would you please?" Elizabeth asked as they entered the house.

Molly took one quick look at the man, spotted the white collar, and smiled. "Yes, missus."

With that, she was gone, darting up the stairs toward the sound of giggling girls.

Deirdre offered to take Mr. Farnsworth's coat, quickly suggesting that they take tea in the dining room downstairs.

Elizabeth smiled to the head maid. "What a thoughtful idea. Yes, please, Deirdre. That would be fine."

"Yes, mum," she said, turning to head for the kitchen. "How many to tea?"

Elizabeth stared at her for a moment, then glanced toward the stairs. "Quite a few, it seems."

80

# CHAPTER SEVEN

## *The Unwitting Widower*

———❧———

"Come now, sister. It's the nineteenth century. Women are leading their own lives."

"Leading their own lives? You're married. You are married."

"No, I was married. I'm a widow, now."

Elizabeth rolled her eyes, slumping against the back of the settee. She was grateful Fitzwilliam was home in time for tea. He was still settled into the dining room with Kitty and Mr. Farnsworth, offering the two a chaperone as they proceeded to get on like a house on fire.

"You can't be a widow if your husband isn't dead."

"Who needs to know?"

Elizabeth sighed.

"This is not unheard of, Lizzy, dear. There are women who divorce in other countries."

"You're not divorced, either."

"Exactly, I'm simply no longer bound by the confines of married life. George understands."

Elizabeth pressed her hand to her face, unable to look at her sister. She wasn't wrong. Lizzy had heard of women separating from their husbands and living as widows, despite their husbands still being in the world. It was an option for women who simply could not remain in unhappy marriages, and in some cases, preferred by both husband and wife.

She wondered how blissfully Mr. Wickham agreed to this arrangement.

"Of course, he does. You were so desperate to marry that man – that scoundrel of a man, and here you are less than a year later?"

Lydia shook her head, giving Elizabeth a patient look. "I never wanted to marry George."

Elizabeth's mouth fell open. "What nonsense! You ran away with him."

"Yes, I ran away with him. I wanted to enjoy him without our mother breathing down my neck. He is truly spectacular in the bedroom, but I've had other officers with similar gifts. He isn't the only man of his breed, I assure you. We only married because Darcy offered him such a generous – ehm, dowry? We decided wedded bliss with some money lining our pockets was better than drifting from tavern to tavern without."

"I cannot believe this. You must be mad."

Lydia laughed to herself. "Perhaps, but I'm happy."

"Was this your decision? You left George?"

She shook her head. "No, it was a mutual decision. We're both open to pursue our own interests."

"You're mad."

"I am not!" She said, and the spoiled child Elizabeth grew up with was there for anyone to see.

Lydia seemed to catch herself, settling back onto the windowsill. "I have plenty of options. Do you know how much a woman can expect to receive as a mistress to one of the wealthier noblemen in London."

"Lydia!"

"Oh, stop. I've seen you reading those books I gave you, I know you're not so easily scandalized."

"The contents of those books are behind closed doors. They're something one keeps in their private life. You're

82

talking about living openly as a mistress?"

"Well, not openly – not outside the Spring Festival, of course."

Elizabeth furrowed her brow. "Pardon?"

"The Spring Festival. Lady Carrington's Spring Festival. It is the absolute event of the season – at least for ladies such as myself. You wouldn't believe the things wealthy people get up to."

"Ladies who want to let a married man have them in exchange for an allowance?"

Lydia smiled. "Mistresses. Kings and Lords have taken them for centuries. In fact, King Charles II gave his favorite mistress a palace. She bore him children."

"This will kill mother."

"Mother will never know, Lizzy. Well, she'll know I'm no longer married."

"It's going to kill her."

"Ah, both of you are too prim for your own good."

Elizabeth grabbed a sugar cube from the tray before her and threw it across the room at her sister. "Too prim?! I knew that Wickham was a bad influence on you! I knew he was a scoundrel!"

Lydia laughed. "You think he made me this way, sister?"

The tone stopped Lizzy's words. She met her sister's gaze and saw a look of patient pity.

"I was this way before I met George. George has his struggles, but he isn't the scoundrel you think he is. Well, he is – but he has his reasons."

"And he's the kind of man who would accept a separation from his wife, demand payment to marry her -"

"Lizzy. I was the one who demanded money to get married. He had nothing. What good is an officer if he can't give you a comfortable life?"

Elizabeth stared at her sister, the whole world changing around her. "I can't talk about this anymore."

"Listen, just – when the invitation comes, go to the Lady Carrington's. You'll see I'm not the only woman of my kind

– of our kind."

"What does that mean?" She said, indignantly.

"Women who enjoy pleasure. Adventurous, wealthy women. There are many aristocratic women living a life of leisure and pleasure, and there are even more men happy to supply it. You'll see. In fact, if you've been enjoying those books I gave you, I think you'll love it."

Elizabeth stood up from the settee, ready to end the conversation. "Thank you, but I've no interest in being some gentleman's mistress."

"Of course not. You'll bring your husband. You can both enjoy the Festival together. And you can finally live out that fantasy of two men at once that you secretly harbor."

"Lydia?!" Lizzy shrieked.

The sound of a man coughing behind them startled her around.

Fitzwilliam Darcy stood in the doorway, his brow furrowed. "I'm sorry to disturb, darling, but your friend Charlotte has called for you."

Elizabeth felt her face burning, but she hustled out into the hallway, hurrying to join her friend.

Elizabeth's heart was racing as she helped Charlotte get her house shoes on. Then she led her to the parlor to take her belated tea.

"That was the best sleep I've had in over a year," she said.

Lizzy couldn't even look at the food as Charlotte ate. She was mortified. Her husband had heard Lydia's comment of two men at once. She'd never admitted that desire to Lydia. She'd never so much as let Lydia see her read the books, yet somehow, Lydia had read her.

Was it when she saw the painted image on the page edges of the second book? Was Lydia just saying things to humiliate her? Had she seen Darcy appear and chose to speak then, deliberately mortifying her?

How cruel was Lydia truly capable of being?

"You seem lost. Everything alright?"

Lizzy startled, turning to meet Charlotte's gaze. "Yes. I'm

sorry. I don't mean to seem far away."

"It's fine. I slept half the day away. You don't owe me an apology."

"May we join you?"

Lizzy turned to find Kitty and Mr. Farnsworth in the doorway of the parlor. It almost surprised her to find the vicar with Kitty. Oftentimes, the gentlemen would retire to the library after they took dinner, but Darcy was preoccupied with something.

Lizzy was certain she knew just what it was.

How could she express to her wonderful husband that he was enough? How could she assure him that Lydia's comment was utter rubbish?

Especially, when it wasn't.

They sat up for another hour, talking and playing cards.

There was still no sign of Fitzwilliam.

Despite the rather pleasant company – Mr. Farnsworth was a surprisingly funny man, and a wonderful conversationalist – Elizabeth excused herself when Charlotte was ready to head back to her bed. The gentleman that Mr. Farnsworth was, he made his way to bed at the same time, refusing to insult Kitty by suggesting they be together alone. Lydia was nowhere to be found, but Elizabeth didn't half much confidence in Lydia as a chaperone to her just barely older sister.

Where was Lydia? She wondered.

Elizabeth made her way down the hallway to her bedroom, a knot twisting in her stomach as she approached the door. She was sure Fitzwilliam was harboring some strange distress, but she didn't want to put it off any further. She would face him, and if he asked, she would be honest.

Good lord, how could she be honest?

Yes, I love that story. Yes, I love that picture of the woman in the throes with two men. Yes, the notion of being ravished like that keeps me up some nights.

How could she admit that and not hurt his ego?

She'd read chapter seventeen well over thirty times, often

accosting her husband in the moments thereafter, seeking the release of her husband's body and touch to find relief from the ache that story caused in her sex.

She stopped outside her bedroom door, listening within for a sign of Fitzwilliam and closed her eyes.

She sighed.

*How could Lydia be so awful?*

Fitzwilliam was sitting back in his chair by the window, a small glass of brandy in his hand. By his posture, it was clear this wasn't his first glass.

"My darling? We missed you after supper."

He shot her a look, then took another sip. "I wasn't feeling particularly social, this evening," he said, pouring back the last sip from his glass.

He stood up then, startling her. His gait was loose, swaying slightly as he stepped. He wasn't drunk, but he was comfortable.

"Please, let me apologize. I hate that you had to overhear such a -"

His eyebrows shot up, and she stopped speaking. He watched her for a moment. "What is it I overheard?"

Elizabeth's face flushed. "Lydia's comment in the parlor, this afternoon."

She kept her eyes averted in wait of a response, but when none came, she looked up to find her husband smiling at her.

The smile was familiar – and it made her whole body respond.

"I had an inkling of your interest."

"You didn't!"

He raised his brows and smiled. "The pages were getting a little worn somewhere around Chapter Seventeen last I saw."

Elizabeth gasped, spinning on the spot to turn her back to him.

His fingers grazed down her spine, sending a shudder through her that nearly swept her legs out from beneath her.

Thankfully, Fitzwilliam was close enough to lean on, his chest solid and warm.

"Don't turn away, darling. I want to see you," he said. His voice had dropped to that low place, the tone that warned her of his desire – that he would want her. She pressed back into him, inviting him.

"If that didn't trouble you, why were you so early to retire?"

His arms were around her waist, but at this he pulled away, walking across the room toward the bed. He slumped down on the side of it. "Your bloody sister and that bastard, George."

"Fitzwilliam!"

"I won't apologize. I'm in the privacy of my own home, I'll speak as I please."

Elizabeth moved across the room to her husband, settling onto the mattress beside him. "I know. It is just ludicrous."

"Is it? Then, why was I not in the least surprised?"

"Did Lydia tell you?"

He shook his head, lying back onto the bed. "No, George did."

Elizabeth stiffened. "George? When did you speak to George?"

He exhaled. "This afternoon in the village. He was my errand."

"You went into town to meet George Wickham."

"That I did."

"And you didn't tell me?"

Fitzwilliam opened one eye, glaring at her sideways. "I'm telling you now, am I not?"

She swallowed. He wasn't angry. He was a dreamy warm kind of inebriated, and the sleepy look to his eyes was most endearing.

"If you were going to tolerate his company, why not invite him to the house?"

"Oh, I did. He thought it best to let Lydia hold court, given their new *arrangement*."

He took his time with the word, letting her hear just how ridiculous he thought it.

She sighed. "You must be quite angry."

He reached for her, not opening his eyes, and pulled her down onto his chest, cradling her against him. "No, not angry. I thought I knew well enough the sort of man George was. Knowing some of that was your sister's doing – I'm not so hard against the man. We spoke at length. There were old wounds to reopen – and perhaps heal."

Elizabeth didn't speak. Instead she waited, hoping her husband might continue to open up to her.

*The wonders of Brandy*, she thought.

"I almost pitied him. Seems he may have met his match in your sister. Perhaps she knocked sense into him."

Elizabeth smiled, rubbing her cheek against the fabric of his shirt.

He squeezed her arm, grazing his fingers over her skin until the hair stood on end. "I expect a proper show of gratitude, you understand."

Elizabeth lifted her head to glare at him, startled. "What on earth for?"

He gave her a feigned patient look. "The whole reason I summoned him here was for you – for your dear Jane's troubles."

Elizabeth sat up, pulling from him to turn and face him. "Do explain. What does poor Jane have to do with Mr. Wickham."

"Well, I certainly wasn't going to give Charles lovemaking guidance myself, Lizzy."

"Oh, you scoundrel," she said, rising to her feet and crossing to the vanity. "I asked *you* to help. You!"

"Yes, and I did."

She turned to protest this, her stays only half untied, but he stopped her.

"I know Charles better than you, my love, and I know George better than I'd like some days. Charles would not have taken this well from me. He would've known Jane

88

spoke of their intimate moments to you, and he would've been wounded. This way, Wickham can invite himself to Netherfield, and as unprovoked as anything else he does, he can offer unsolicited advice. From George Wickham, it will sound like simple bragging or prying, but in the end, George will be able to get through, because George has no qualms with impropriety. And whatever your opinion of Charles, he knows George an expert when it comes to women."

"And not you?"

She turned to see Fitzwilliam smile at this. "Not me."

Elizabeth wanted to maintain her frustration, but she saw the sense in his logic. He wasn't wrong.

And in the end, if her darling sister could enjoy her marriage better because of the scoundrel, Mr. Wickham, then it was well worth it.

Fitzwilliam's touch startled her as his hands wrapped around her waist. She hadn't heard him approach.

She sighed, losing all will to fight him as he crossed his arms across her belly and pulled her into him.

"So, Chapter Seventeen is your favorite, then?" He asked.

Elizabeth watched her face burn red in the mirror.

# CHAPTER EIGHT

## *Two Scoundrels*

⊰•❈•⊱

Elizabeth stood in the parlor listening to the clock tick.

After weeks of hosting various Bennet family members, their guests had found their way homeward.

Charlotte insisted on traveling home alone, but in the end, Mr. Farnsworth offered to go along as her chaperone. Lydia was heading home to Longbourn before making the trip to London for the month, an invitation Elizabeth didn't pry any further into. The only reason Lydia managed to convince Kitty to come home as well was inspired by Mr. Farnsworth having his own travel plans to attend to.

He would be away in Edinburgh for the month to visit with family and welcome his first niece. Charlotte was lucky enough to be on his way.

She was sure he'd exaggerated Charlotte being on his way, but he was a vicar, and it seemed he understood Elizabeth's concern for her friend traveling alone.

Elizabeth liked Mr. Farnsworth quite well. A nice change after Lydia running away with an officer of ill repute.

Still, hearing Fitzwilliam's tone when he spoke of his old friend had almost softened her.

Seeing Lydia galivanting around as a merry widow helped soften her opinion, as well.

Despite his horrendous behavior, she had rather liked

George Wickham – before she'd discovered what a scoundrel he could be.

One would think having the house to themselves again would be a joy.

Yet, Mr. Darcy was nowhere to be found, something Elizabeth was rather distraught over, and Pemberley was feeling frighteningly quiet on that Sunday evening. The servants were all to bed, and she was alone.

Elizabeth stood by the tall windows watching the road outside for Darcy's coach. He'd promised he'd be home for bed. She had needs that only her husband could fulfill.

She'd gone out of her way all morning to be willful and headstrong, behavior Darcy both loved about her, and loved to punish her for.

And she loved to be punished.

She'd hoped so desperately that he would take out the paddle again tonight. Her backside was barely sore from their last long, brutal lovemaking session. Darcy had barely thrown her around the past three nights while they were making love. He'd been all but tender, even gentle.

That was lovely and fine, but a lady needs a little adventure if she's going to be cooped up in the estate all season.

"Damn it, Fitzwilliam," she said under her breath, tucking her half-read book back into the bookshelf.

She'd be tearing her own corset off this evening.

Elizabeth marched her way up the stairs and turned down the long hallway toward their apartments. The house was exceptionally dark and quiet, but it was nothing unusual for a Sunday.

She spotted a crack of blue light from her apartment doors down the hall and stopped, her stomach tightening at the familiar sight.

There hanging from the doorknob was a red scarf. She took a breath and blew out through pursed lips, touching her stomach with an excited, trembling hand.

She knew what the red scarf meant.

Elizabeth's heart was racing. The red scarf meant Darcy

had every intention of punishing her tonight. She stood there for a long moment, surprised she hadn't heard her husband come home. He would already be in the bedroom. The ropes would be tied to the bedposts, the paddles and riding crop lain out along her vanity for her to choose how she wanted to be spanked.

Elizabeth stifled a giggle. She was going to be brave tonight and finally choose the cat o'nine tails. Her backside was soothed enough to handle it.

Yet, unlike the previous nights when Darcy left the red scarf on the doorknob, he hadn't announced her fate with foreboding, sultry tones. This time he'd slunk into the room in the dark. This time she wouldn't know from where he'd come. The fact left her nearly breathless.

Elizabeth knew this game well, they'd played it before on the road. Darcy had hidden his face, pretending to be her coach driver, then when they were far afield, he leapt into the carriage under the pretense of a robbing highwayman and took her roughing, his hand clamped tight over her mouth as she screamed.

Tonight, she was to make her way inside knowing that Darcy was somewhere within, hovering in the shadows, waiting to pounce, to pursue, and chase her down to take her wherever she succumbed in the empty expanse of Pemberley Estate.

She loved this game as much as he did, and though her arms and legs began to shake with excited fear, her sex responded as though Darcy had caressed her thigh.

"Fitzwilliam?" She called. He wouldn't respond, but it made her feel better when she was afraid. It was an unspoken pleading; *please don't torture me too long.*

Elizabeth took the last couple steps toward the door glancing in every direction, jumping at the movement of shadows on the floor, cast there by trees in the garden outside. She could hear her heart pounding in her ears, hear every breath she took, each sounding more ragged as she made her way down the hall

"Darcy? Please tell me where you are!"

She stood in the upstairs hallway, each doorway on the north side open and dark. She swallowed and made her way down the hall, slowly. She found herself afraid to glance into the rooms, afraid she would see a dark figure silhouetted against the windows. The first time they played this game, she'd made her way up the stairs only to turn and see a figure at the other end of the hall, standing still in the dark, watching her. She'd called his name, screamed to him, begged him to stop it, all while her heart raced, and she braced herself for his attack. He'd stood there in silence for several seconds before suddenly taking off down the hallway towards her, chasing her into the washroom and having his way with her on the floor. Elizabeth stopped outside their apartment door, glancing back down the hallway, excited and terrified that she might see this figure again.

He knew she loved to be scared, loved to be chased. There was something so arousing about being afraid, all while knowing she was safe.

Elizabeth stared down the dark hallway, willing her eyes to adjust to the dark. The touch was so sudden, she hadn't time to scream. An arm wrapped around her abdomen, grabbing her as another hand planted soundly over her mouth. She tensed in his arms, feeling the heat of his breath against her ear. She shivered and fought to catch her breath, but something was strange. The way her backside pressed to his thighs, the way his cheek felt against hers. She shook against his grasp. He only squeezed her tighter and chuckled.

Elizabeth froze.

"Be a good girl, and I won't hurt you."

Elizabeth jerked against his embrace. Shoving her shoulders into him, tearing her head from side to side to free her mouth from his grasp. She tried to scream out, slamming her elbows back into his side, but he was solid and strong – and he wasn't her husband.

"Fitzwilliam!" She screamed, but his hand planted over her mouth again before the word could escape. Suddenly her feet were dangling beneath her as Wickham lifted her and carried her into her bedroom, into the bedroom she shared with her husband. Oh god, where is Darcy? What if he's hurt?

Elizabeth screamed and bit at his gloved hand, kicking her legs into his shins and writhing in his arms, but he held her like some child's doll, his fingers digging into her ribs as he fought to keep his hold. She would fight him. She would fight with every breath. Please God, let Darcy be alright.

Wickham shoved her down onto her bed, and she flipped over onto her back, kicking her legs at him to fight him off, her skirts billowing with each frantic movement. She screamed now, wishing to God Sunday wasn't his day. Wickham simply grabbed her ankles and pinned them down, climbing onto the bed to straddle over her. She lashed out, reaching for his masked face, fingernails bared and ready to tear skin through the black fabric tied over his face. She'd mark him, damn it. He wouldn't leave here unscathed. She swung a hand up toward him. The gesture was stopped short by a strong hand around her wrist. Then the other. Suddenly, her assailant had four hands. She struggled against the weight of his large frame and the pressure at her wrists. Then, she felt the presence of the second man at her ear, holding her down on the bed, drawing close to her face with sudden purpose. The covered face pressed to her ear, whispering in a gentle tone.

"Say you wish it to cease, and it all ends."

The last of Elizabeth's screams loosed in a ragged exhale. She shook against the mattress, relief surging through her body as she pressed her cheek to her husband's masked face. Her body shuddered beneath the unknown man, her throat sore from desperate wails, but she was safe.

"Darling?" Darcy whispered into her ear. "Shall we cease?"

Elizabeth looked up at the masked stranger, his broad

94

frame poised over her, lying in wait of her consent.

She took a slow, shaky breath, and her words betrayed all her lingering fear. But beneath that, an ache of curiosity and need. My god, what would her 'yes' bring? She turned to face Darcy. "No. Don't stop."

He moved, instantly, reaching for his mask and tearing it off. "Goodness, she is feisty, isn't she?"

Wickham slid his hands up her stomach toward her breasts, letting his fingers frame them. She whimpered against the touch.

Wickham chuckled. "She nearly tore my head off."

"Mmmm, I think she needs to be taught a lesson, don't you?"

Elizabeth writhed beneath Wickham's weight, her wrists still pinned to the mattress by her husband. Suddenly, he took hold of her breasts through her dress, squeezing them intimately. She gasped.

Darcy reached down and tore her stays open, leaving her shift bared beneath. He tugged the garment up and over her head. Wickham grabbed the fabric of her shift and tugged it down, baring her breasts to the cool air. Darcy grabbed her jaw in one hand, then grabbed her breast with the other, groaning in appreciation.

"Get off, scoundrel. You can't very well fuck her like that!"

Elizabeth gasped. She loved to hear her husband talk like that. She cried out as Wickham lifted himself off her, and Darcy tugged her off the bed and onto her feet. She stood there in her loose dress, shoes and stockings still on, and Darcy hooked his arms through her elbows, pinning her arms behind her back.

"I have her. Let's see what she's hiding under all this nonsense."

Wickham lunged to the edge of the bed and tore down her shift over her hips. Wickham groaned at the sight of the dark patch between her legs, drawing his face close to her thighs as he tore off her shoes, then her stockings. She was naked and helpless, her back against her husband's chest, a stranger's masked face just inches from her thighs. Wickham blew onto her skin, and she felt goosebumps spring across every inch.

Darcy kicked a foot against her inner ankle, knocking her leg aside, then the other, leaving her standing there with her legs wide apart.

"Well, get on with it. Make sure she's ready for us," Darcy said.

Elizabeth gasped, turning her face into Darcy's neck as Wickham laughed to himself. "Don't mind if I do."

He bit the end of his glove and tugged it off, one finger at a time, tossing them across the room before dropping to his knees in front of her. She squealed in fear and excitement, knowing how wet she was already. His fingers drifted up her bare thighs, and he pressed his thumbs against the lips of her sex, prying them apart just enough to bare the wet within. Then he pulled the mask down, too fast for her to see his face, then pressed his face into her pussy, lavishing her with his tongue. The action wasn't tentative or timid, but forceful and almost mean. He was devouring her, wrapping his arms up around her backside as he buried his face between her legs. She screamed, losing the use of her legs as Darcy held her up, egging on Wickham as he worked.

"Oh yeah, she likes that. Don't you, darling?" Darcy took hold of her face, turning her to him as he spoke. "You like getting devoured, don't you? Makes you wet, doesn't it?"

She shook her head against his grasp, but he held her there. "Don't fight me. Fighting will only make it worse."

Wickham pulled from her and pulled his mask off completely, revealing a head of brown hair and a clean-shaven face. He was handsome, glancing up at her with sleepily lustful eyes. He pressed his thumb to the most sensitive part of her sex and moved from side to side as she squirmed. Then he was on his feet.

She knew him.

"Wickham!" She screamed, struggling against her

husband's arms. "You scoundrel!"

The old rival of her husband smirked down at her. "Pin her down."

Darcy obliged, throwing her onto the bed. Darcy moved to hold her shoulders in place as Wickham grabbed her legs.

"No, no. Put her to work. Make her suck you while I get her ready."

Darcy groaned in agreement and Wickham spread her legs before him, pressing a hand to her throat in warning as he slid his fingers inside her. She shrieked at the sensation, turning her face away as he watched her, intently. She turned to find Darcy stripped from the waist down, climbing onto the bed at her head. Then he moved over her, straddling her face, bringing his balls closer, his hard cock bobbing just inches from her mouth.

"Give me her legs!" Darcy hissed, and Wickham obliged, chuckling as he hoisted her legs to Darcy's waiting hands. He grabbed her calves and pulled them up to his sides, leaving her spread eagle and helpless, her ass in the air. She squirmed, trying to pull free, but before she could, Wickham slid his fingers inside her again, deep. She felt him wriggle them inside, pressing in rhythm. She gasped, no longer able to see him beyond the sight of her husband's sex above her.

"Be a good girl down there, or you'll be punished," Darcy said.

Elizabeth turned her face into Darcy's thigh, fighting to still her cries as Wickham slid his fingers into her. His touch was gentle, but purposeful, working to please her.

Darcy reached down and squeezed one of her breasts, humming with relish. "Those balls won't lick themselves," he said.

She fought against the urge to move her hips with Wickham's fingers, show him what she needed. Suddenly, Darcy growling.

"Alright, bitch. If you won't do as you're told —" Darcy swatted Wickham's hand away. "You're not doing it right. Let me show her what happens when she doesn't behave."

Wickham's fingers retreated, and Darcy shifted his weight over her. Suddenly, her husband's fingers slid between her legs, then inside her, and unlike Wickham, he knew damn well how to make her scream. He drove them into her with such force and speed that her back arched and she fought to reach down and still his hand. She screamed, but he did not slow, punishing her for her disobedience with the very thing he knew she loved. She cried out against his touch.

"Will you behave, woman?"

She shook her head, and he moved harder, Wickham pushing her legs wider apart as she screamed.

"You're going to behave!"

"No!" She cried.

Darcy moved with sudden purpose, turning himself above her so he was now straddling her chest, his cock hard against her jaw.

"Suck it."

She shook her head, turning her face away from him. He grabbed her by the hair, pulling the carefully pinned braids free as he forced her head back to meet his eyes. He gestured back to his rival and Wickham's fingers found their prize again, this time matching the intensity her husband had shown.

Darcy leaned closer to her, whispering in a warning tone. "Suck it and suck it properly, or I'm going to let our old friend here fuck your ass."

Wickham? He'd let Wickham have her like that? They'd played such games in the past as husband and wife, but the thought of the handsome, rakish scoundrel Wickham knowing her body like that – it unnerved her. And yet she felt the rush of arousal between her legs at the thought.

She swallowed, aching to defy him, to see just how far he'd go tonight if she pushed. He smiled down at her and despite the urge to fight, she opened her mouth.

He pulled from her before she could take him, returning to his previous post, holding her legs up for his friend as he straddled her face. "Open up."

She did, and he lowered himself down to her mouth, letting her suck at his balls as he groaned his approval.

"Mmm, what a good girl? Show her what happens when she behaves."

Wickham lowered his mouth to her and slid his tongue against her aching pussy. She needed to come, her body shaking with anticipation of both release and the mystery of what they would do to her. Darcy stroked his cock as he lowered to her mouth, pulling away every so often to tease her or to let her breathe as Wickham's tongue worked.

"How does she taste, Wickham?"

Wickham – bloody fucking Wickham – hummed, and she shuddered at the sensation. "She tastes like she needs to be ravished."

"Oh, she will be," Darcy said.

Darcy released her legs, letting them fall to the bed, and rose from over her. Before she could brace, he grabbed her under the arms and pulled her off the bed, her body falling onto the floor at his feet. He turned her there to face him as Wickham stood up behind her.

"I think she should reward you, don't you?" Darcy said, his eyes betraying a wicked smile, though his expression remained ever stoic.

Wickham smiled down at her and began to unbutton his britches. Elizabeth swallowed as Wickham pulled his cock out for her to see. He was long and rigid, the veins pulsing just under the skin. He stroked himself there, just a few inches from her face.

"I'm telling you, you're in for a fucking treat," Darcy said, smiling at the man he once thought of as an enemy.

Wickham shot her a smile again. "I can't wait."

Wickham reached down, took her hand, and placed it on his cock. She felt the hard shape in her fingers, the smooth texture of his skin, the lines and divots of every inch. She let her fingers move against him as her husband took her other hand and wrapped it around his own cock. She glanced up at Wickham, took a breath, then took him in her mouth. He groaned, resting a hand on her mass of hair.

"My god, man. You speak the truth! Dear god," Wickham moaned, his head falling back.

Darcy chuckled. "I taught her well. Still, I think she can do better. Fuck her face."

Wickham paused, then took her face in his hands, and began to move himself in and out of her mouth. She obliged, opening to him. She gave him control over the rhythm and depth, letting her tongue lap against him in her mouth, then spitting on him when he gave her a moment to breathe. She stroked his cock, now slick from her mouth, and watched his head fall back again. Then she turned to her husband and squeezed him firmly in her hand before sucking him deep and fast. He gasped, clutching her hair in his hand, his hips moving with her.

She moved between them, giving each her attention, stroking one as she worked the other. They took turns whispering their appreciation, conferring with one another. Her pussy was quivering with need now. The way they spoke of her, of what they would do, of how they would fuck her; her body was ready, even if her mind still faltered.

Finally, Darcy pulled from her grasp, grabbing her by the wrist and pulling her onto her feet. He pushed her toward the bed, letting her kneel on the edge of it.

"Why don't you lie down, George?" Darcy said, and Wickham chuckled as he fell back onto the bed, spreading his legs before her.

Darcy pushed her down on all fours. "You keep sucking him like a good girl, and I won't go too hard."

Elizabeth cried out softly as Darcy pressed the head of his cock against her, then plunged in. Her pussy was too wet to give resistance, and he moaned openly as their bodies met. Wickham's cock was inches beneath her, but as Darcy took her from behind, she could do little more than brace herself. He took his first deep thrust, then another slow one, then began to find his rhythm. Elizabeth held her breath, waiting for her body to conform to his size. She felt pressure at the

100

back of her head, pushing her down toward the bed as he sometimes did. This time he was pushing her to the rigid shape beneath her.

"You don't want me to get rough, do you?"

Elizabeth opened her mouth and took hold of Wickham, sucking at the head of him as her body rocked back and forth with Darcy's thrusts.

Wickham brushed her loose hair aside, watching her as she sucked him, as she fought to keep herself steady against the hard pummeling of her husband's cock. He drove deeper, slower, letting each thrust sting as she whimpered against the hard shape in her mouth. Then he returned to his fast pace, his breath growing hoarser with each passing moment. Elizabeth braced against him, his fingers digging into her hips. Suddenly, she heard the sound of him spitting into his hand. The sudden pressure at her backside startled her.

"Fitzwill – ungh!" She cried out as Darcy slid a finger into her ass.

He chuckled, sliding his finger in and out gently as he plunged his cock into her. There was no use trying to please Wickham now, her full attention was drawn to her husband's touch. "Fitzy, please!"

"Shh, we have to get you ready, don't we?"

"No!" She cried. He'd said he would let Wickham have her ass if she misbehaved. She hadn't misbehaved, and she was prepared to argue that point.

Darcy slid a second finger into her, and her body began to shake. He reached down, grabbing her around the throat and pulling her upright, her back against his chest, her ear to his cheek, his fingers still inside her, pushing deep, moving in fast rhythm just the way she liked.

He smiled, letting his teeth graze against her ear. "No, she says? No?"

"Please," she said, breathlessly.

He kissed her cheek and whispered so softly, she barely heard him. "Shall we cease, darling?"

101

She took a deep breath as his fingers stilled, but his cock continued to pulse into her. She spoke for only Darcy to hear. "I'm scared."

"You know I would never hurt you, but if it's too much, say the word and it all stops."

She let him hold her there, looking down at the long frame beneath her as Wickham stroked his cock in wait. She wanted this, wanted every piece of it, and her heart was pounding in her chest now with excitement as much as fear, but could she do this? Actually let men have her this way? Elizabeth swallowed and when she spoke, her whisper was as quiet as his had been. "No. Don't stop."

Darcy pulled from her, letting her fall toward Wickham. Darcy stood up from the bed, rounding it toward the nightstand. She knew exactly what he was going for.

Wickham held his hands open to her. "Come here and ride me, beautiful."

She glanced to Darcy despite everything, still seeking his permission.

He glared at her. "Do as you're told, woman."

Elizabeth turned to face Wickham, crawling toward him obediently, straddling over him. He wriggled down from the pillows, lying flat beneath her. She held herself ready above him and as he pressed the head of his cock against her, lowered herself down onto him.

Wickham took hold of her ass, pulling her and pushing her to learn his rhythm. It was similar to Darcy's, but with a rocking swing that left her body pressed against him in a surprisingly pleasant way. He pressed down on her hips, grinding and rocking her on him as his hips thrust upward. Wickham's cock was longer and narrower than Darcy's, and favored a lean to the right. He knew just how to use it, too, and Elizabeth began to feel a warmth rising in her sex that would soon get out of hand.

She startled at the sudden cold of Darcy's hand sliding up the cleft of her buttocks. His fingers were slick with oil, slathering her in preparation of him. She recoiled at the touch, throwing herself onto Wickham as sudden trepidation returned. She held her breath for an instant, then cried out as Darcy's fingertip slipped into her ass, again. He didn't go deep, just enough to let her feel him, to play at the pleasure centers hidden there. He was teasing her, almost tickling her, letting Wickham carry her through with his steady, purposeful rhythm. Soon, Darcy, slid another finger inside, deeper now. Then another.

Suddenly, he chuckled. "Sounds like she's ready."

Wickham smiled, and only then did Elizabeth realize she'd been moaning.

Wickham shifted beneath her, moving his legs to accommodate Darcy behind her. Elizabeth held her breath, pressing her face into Wickham's chest. Anything solid to hold her steady. She could say 'no.' She could stop it.

She didn't want to.

Darcy's cock pressed against her, a familiar sensation despite the newness of Wickham beneath her. She felt Wickham's fingers entwine with hers and squeezed his hand with grateful purpose.

Darcy's cock slipped into her slow and steady. She gasped, bracing herself. He retreated, then pushed again as Wickham stilled beneath her, letting her take Darcy unhindered. Darcy pushed again, deeper this time, but still hardly halfway. He would let her get used to him before he fucked her. He always took his time when he had her this way.

He pulled out again, wholly, letting her relax and recover, then pushed, sliding deeper now, filling her. She gasped, finally taking a breath as Darcy pushed all the way in. There was no pain, no discomfort, just a sense of being so full she couldn't move. Darcy squeezed her ass, pulsing gently there, letting her feel him inside her. He hummed to himself, a groan deep in his throat as he appraised her ass, and relished in the way she felt. She knew the sound well.

"I think she's ready."

Wickham squeezed her thighs and raised an eyebrow. "I

think you're right."

Wickham began to move again, bucking beneath her as Darcy held fast. Wickham still held Elizabeth's hand, but he released it now, taking hold of her legs as he moved her and with her. Elizabeth was holding her breath again when Darcy finally took hold of her hips and began to thrust into her. His movements were slow and shallow at first, but as Wickham rocked her on his cock, she began to breathe - and moan. The sensation was unlike anything she'd ever felt. The tension of every muscle in her body, her legs shaking, the familiar sensations of being taken both ways, but now feeling them coincide, combine to this whole other sensation, all while Wickham's unfamiliar body moved beneath her. Both men were thrusting into her, their fingers digging into her hips, into her thighs, holding her, pulling her against them as they sought their own pleasure. Elizabeth planted her hands into the mattress and took them both, turning her head to see Darcy. She caught sight of her reflection in the dark bedroom window and cried out. She could see Darcy behind her, his body moving, the muscles in his arms and legs taut with effort, and beneath her, the lean lines of Wickham's tall frame. She watched the two men struggling beneath her and behind her, a lustful voyeurism, as though seeing the act made the sensation stronger. She watched, whimpering softly as Wickham continued grinding, the friction of his movements making her warm and desperate. She reached down between her legs, pressed her fingers to her sex and watching their reflection, stroked herself.

Darcy suddenly grabbed her around the shoulders, pulling her upright against him. She cried out, the sudden movement making her thoroughly aware of the two men inside her. He pulled her against him, taking hold of her throat as he met her eyes in the reflection.

"I see you watching. You like what you see, don't you, you filthy creature?"

She pulled against the hand at her throat, but stilled as

Darcy reached down to her sex, taking over her efforts, and began playing at her the way only he knew how. He pinned her against him, thrusting into her there, stroking her pussy as he forced her face toward the reflection.

"I want you to watch us defile you."

She moaned, the force of his thrusts lifting and dropping her onto Wickham's cock as Darcy stroked her. She could see his body, see the expression on his face, the heavy eyes, the swollen lips, open and wet, his brow set as he watched her, and made her watch him. She cried out.

"You love this, don't you? My darling whore."

She cried out again, trying to shake her head, but he only thrust faster. Her muscles began to tighten and spasm.

Wickham groaned in appreciation. "You feel that? I think she likes getting ravished, don't you, sweetheart?"

She growled, but didn't speak.

Darcy tightened his grip on her jaw. "Say it. Tell me you love it."

Her cries were growing louder, more shrill as her body responded to the wealth of sensation. Her head fell back onto his shoulder.

"I want you to come all over his cock."

Elizabeth screamed as Wickham suddenly joined Darcy's forceful movements. The two men leveraged themselves to thrust fast and forceful. Elizabeth felt her pussy tighten, then her whole lower body as she shuddered there against Darcy's chest, letting him hold her up as she screamed, gasped, then held her breath.

"That's right, come all over his cock like the well-trained whore you are."

She succumbed with such force that her body convulsed, held upright by Darcy alone. Darcy slowed his thrusts as did Wickham, then as the wave subsided, Darcy tugged her off Wickham, pulling her gently onto her knees.

"I think she owes us a debt of gratitude, wouldn't you say?" Darcy said.

Wickham smirked. "Absolutely."

Darcy pushed her down onto all fours again, her face inches from Wickham's cock, now slick from her.

"Now, clean up your mess."

Elizabeth smiled up at Wickham, and he groaned at the sight. Then she took him in her mouth and sucked him with purpose. The timidity and fear was gone now, giving way to free lustful expression. She could taste herself on his cock, but beneath that was the early sour taste of his seed; he was close. She sucked him and stroked him, bracing against Darcy's thrusts as he continued to pound into ass, his breath getting ragged. Wickham took her by the hair, gripping it gently, then she felt the surge as he came, his seed spilling into the roof of her mouth, filling it with the taste of him.

Wickham gave a shuddering exhale and she reached back, trying to hold onto Darcy as his thrusts grew sharper. He reached down, grabbing her face and turning her up to him, making her meet his eyes as he came deep inside her. He held her there, driving into her again and again, slower each time, until he took a deep breath and retreated.

Darcy tossed her down onto the bare part of the mattress. Her legs were undone, her hips and thighs a gelatinous mass of aching, quivering exhaustion. Darcy slumped back onto the mattress as Wickham rose from the bed. Darcy soon followed.

Wickham grabbed his shirt, mask, and gloves and buttoned himself before glancing to Elizabeth. "You're a lucky man, Fitzy."

Darcy shot him a look. "I know."

Darcy lunged onto the mattress with such speed, Elizabeth flinched. He pressed his hand to her throat. "You were so good, we might have to steal back to your chambers another night."

Elizabeth covered her face.

When she lowered her hands, both men were gone, fulfilling the guise of the game by stealing away after doing their dark deed.

Elizabeth lay there a moment, the prickle of drying sweat

106

on her skin. She rolled toward the edge of the bed, testing her legs as she stood, and made her way to the bedroom door. She stopped at the doorway, still fearing further surprise, and peeked out into the dark hallway. It was empty.

Elizabeth slipped back into the apartment to find their wash basin full of now tepid water. She took up a small washcloth and began to clean herself. The bedroom echoed ominously in the dark, but she was no longer afraid. The spell was wearing off; that glorious spell. She replayed moments of the night and felt her sex sting with arousal all over again. She would replay this night and abuse herself forever, and she knew it. She ran her hands over her face, her body shivering at sensation and memory. The bedroom door creaked open. She was barely turned around before the figure appeared at her shoulder. She turned to face Darcy as he took a fresh cloth from beside the basin, dunked it into the water, then proceeded to run it down between her legs, teasing her with it.

She gasped, still too sensitive for touch. She quickly took the rag from him under the guise of wanting to touch him back. He let her stroke his cock with the warm cloth, humming softly in appreciation.

"Our Mr. Wickham is gone, but I don't think I can leave without having you a second time."

Darcy lifted her leg to open her to him, pressing his hard cock against her as she clutched him, her legs barely strong enough to keep her upright. As he ran the head of his cock into that slick place, Elizabeth smiled, then gasped as he slid inside her again.

# CHAPTER NINE

## *The Awakened Woman*

Elizabeth stifled a moment.

She'd caught very little sleep the night before, tossing and turning in her empty bed, re-reading the same page over and over in her book. Fitzwilliam had been gone for several days, leaving her to lay awake at night thinking about him – and the events of the last night they spent together.

Darcy had brought Mr. Wickham to their bed. He'd not asked her permission beforehand, not consulted her. Elizabeth stopped herself at these thoughts. Darcy warned her that their bedroom adventures would always be exciting, and even frightening at times, but he would never do anything that wasn't for her pleasure above all else.

Then he brought Wickham to their bed in a night of feigned danger and earth-shattering lust, letting a man who'd betrayed them both know not only Darcy's bed, but his wife. Wickham and Lydia's marriage having disintegrated, Lydia leading a life of leisure at the kind charity of various wealthy patrons – and Elizabeth was sure, her own husband's charity, from time to time.

Mr. Wickham was free to do as he pleased.

Elizabeth had scolded Fitzwilliam after their tawdry night together with Wickham – how could you? After what he did to Lydia? After what he did to Georgiana?

Darcy assured her Wickham's purposes were as a tool, nothing more. That there was no better man who not only knew his way around a woman's body, but who Darcy could happily throw out after his purposes were served without concern that he'd demand further knowledge of his wife.

Darcy paid the man handsomely for wedding the youngest Bennet. If he'd burned through his funds, it would not be Darcy's concern.

"And naturally," as Fitzwilliam reminded her. "I recall you thought him rather handsome at one point in time."

That had certainly drawn her ire, however true it may be.

Yet, before she could wholly scold him for his comments, he was leaving – drawn away from Pemberley in quite the state, leaving Elizabeth to remain with her fury – and her lingering desire.

Elizabeth physically huffed at the memory of those words.

She was livid and frustrated with her husband, but in truth, the worst crime Fitzwilliam had committed was not bringing a rake into their bed, but making quite sure that Elizabeth loved every second of it. So much so that she thought of it in the quiet moments before bed, aching for her husband's return to Pemberley so she could exercise her demons on him.

Elizabeth sat in the parlor listening to the clock tick in wait of her husband's return. He was due that afternoon, having collected his Aunt, the Lady Catherine, after her trip north to the Highlands with Anne in an attempt to aide her finding a reasonable husband. From Darcy's account, his cousin Anne was not a willing participant in this whirlwind husband hunt.

How long was the ride from Rosings? She wondered. Or more aptly, how long would Lady Catherine keep him before letting him take his leave and return to his wife at home.

"Lady Elizabeth?"

Elizabeth startled on the settee, nearly dropping her book onto the gryphon-like creatures woven into the oriental rug.

"Yes, Patricia?"

The young maid curtsied at the door, bowing her head in a reverence Elizabeth still wasn't quite accustomed to. She wondered how dear Patricia would think of her Lady Elizabeth if she knew she'd taken the lustful advances of two separate men just a few nights prior.

She shook her, fighting away the thought.

"The Master is in the study. He's awaiting you to attend him."

"In the study? Did he not know well where to find me?"

Patricia's cheeks went rosy, but she did not answer. Elizabeth sighed, rising from her perch with a huff before turning for the door to seek her husband. How long had he been home?

And how long must she maintain this look of indignation before she could beg her beloved Fitzwilliam to have his way with her?

She let Patricia lead her down the hall until they reached the closed study door. Elizabeth gave Patricia a polite nod and waited until the maid was well out of earshot. Despite her excitement to see her husband, she still feared there might be residual anger between them – even if she felt her heart skip each time she thought of the deed that drew her ire in the first place.

Elizabeth turned the doorknob and opened her mouth to call for him, but stopped dead in the doorway. A figure stood in the study, framed by the light of the high windows beyond, cutting a figure so fine it took her breath away.

Fitzwilliam stood there, his skin pale and perfect, bare-chested, wearing nothing but a set of hose, a sporran, and a kilt. He blushed suddenly, having clearly hoped he would have another minute before he was discovered, turning to face her as he finished fastening the second of the two buckles about his waist. He reached for the nearby chair, snatching up his dress shirt and pulling it over his shoulders as quickly as he could. Elizabeth just stared at him for a long moment, confused, but smiling.

"Don't look at me like that." Darcy said, a blush creeping across his cheeks.

"What is this?"

He sighed, looking down at himself for a moment before finally pulling the dress shirt back down from his shoulders. She was his wife, after all, he didn't need to be bashful with her.

"Lady Catherine's idea of a thoughtful gift."

"A kilt?"

Darcy harrumphed softly, tossing the shirt over the back of a chair as he planted his hands on his hips. "Precisely. Said she'd seen a fair number of gentlemen wearing them in the Highlands and simply had to procure such a garment for her beloved nephew. Made me wear the nonsense all afternoon."

Elizabeth fought not to laugh as Darcy lightened his voice in a nasal impression of his rather stern Aunt Catherine. She couldn't help but laugh, it was so rare that Darcy let himself speak of her in such a fashion.

"I had hope to be out of it before Patricia summoned you, but I am having trouble with these foolish buckles."

He reached for the small pouch at his groin, flicking it aside with an annoyed touch, only to have it fall right back down into place.

Elizabeth shut the study door behind her, watching him wordless for a long moment as he stood there, his broad shoulders perfectly mirrored by the flare of the kilt pleats. Elizabeth smiled. The Lady Catherine had some strange ideas, but this one was truly special.

He was wearing the Stuart colors, red with green, his sporran black and silver with three horse hair tales. His hose sheathed his beautiful calves in black, tiny ribbons on each side, a small ornamental knife tucked into the left sock. He finally turned and met her gaze. He grinned at her, sheepishly rubbing his hands up the back of his neck as she took in the sight of him, frozen in the doorway.

The way a man looks at his wife when she appears in white on her wedding day; she was sure that was the way she was looking at Fitzwilliam. Not just in his kilt, but shirtless in his kilt.

She opened her mouth to speak, staring at him. It still took a moment to find words.

He watched her face, his own smile growing wider by the second. He was blushing, which made this swell of affection only stronger.

"How long have you been home?"

He exhaled out his nose, opening his arms in exasperation as though she was only now seeing the state of his dress. "Only a matter of moments. I wanted to settle myself before I came to you. Was concerned I might receive a scolding, which I wanted to at the very least be wearing trousers for – given the severity of last time."

"You deserved it."

He smiled and seeing that she was apparently glued to the spot. He took a step toward her, and she flinched just so. He chuckled softly as he came for her in the doorway, slipping his hands around her waist to pull her in. "I know." He buried his face down into the crook of her neck, inhaling her as he pressed her into the study door, his arms around her waist. "I've no excuse."

Elizabeth felt the smooth touch of his skin under her fingertips and lost all memory of frustration. All she remembered was the lust she harbored each night as she fell asleep. "Are you quite certain this kilt wasn't a ploy to weaken my resolve?"

He straightened, towering over her in feigned offense. "This ridiculous thing? You can't be serious!"

Elizabeth looked down at his bare belly and the perfect line of hair that ran down from his navel, disappearing beneath the waistband of the tartan fabric.

She ran her hands up over his shoulder blades, relishing in the touch of every inch of his bare skin. "Were you planning to toss me a couple cabers, really make an impression?"

He laughed, pressing his forehead to hers as he pulled her against him. He began to pull her into the study, exaggerating each step with a lean as he rubbed his hands up and down her spine, cupping her ass and giving a good squeeze. She slid her hands down to grab his backside as well, feeling the curve of his ass smooth under the torrent of wool and pleats.

"I'm still angry with you, Fitzwilliam?"

He smiled, pressing his nose to hers. "I know. I should have consulted you first, darling. I will not make the same mistake again."

"Don't you dare," she said, giving his backside a good squeeze.

His eyebrows shot up. "What?"

"Apologize. These tactics are simply unfair."

She took another step into him and he dropped back onto the settee, leaving her standing there over him, his hands reaching for her hips, inviting her to straddle him. She stared down at him, part of her mind still fuming at him. She could remember the sensation of both men inside her, remember the way they'd played every inch of her body with such forceful expertise. She'd never protested. Not one had she thought to stop them. Wickham was a handsome fellow, but a scoundrel nonetheless. Now, she looked down at her beloved Mr. Darcy and recognized the look of a scoundrel in his eyes as well. It aroused her only further.

He tugged at her hips, pulling her over him. She did as he asked, wriggling her knees against his hips, settling herself there, his chin level with her breasts. He grabbed them roughly, squeezing them together through the layers of fabric before tugging the neckline of her dress down enough to see the fabric of her corset, shielding her nipples from him. He leaned in and kissed the mound of her breasts, exaggerated by his rough hold on them. She laced her fingers into his dark hair and gave a soft tug, urging him to turn his face up to her. She held her breath a moment, fearing the repercussions of such an act with a husband as dominant and powerful as Fitzwilliam Darcy.

He looked up, smiling with such joy, it crinkled his nose.

She felt her face flush at the sight of that smile. "Goodness, you'll be my ruin."

He gave an eyebrow wiggle. "In a good way, I hope."

He wrapped his arms around her, their mouths close, open, inviting, but still teasing with sharp inhales, his arms pulling her against him in a familiar rhythm.

He kissed her throat. "I see my dear Aunt isn't the only one affected by this ridiculous garment?"

She spoke softly, lost in the way his arms felt. "I can see her appreciation."

"How, pray tell?"

"Because you're the most beautiful thing I've ever seen."

Her heart leapt at the sight of him, not a man in a kilt, but Fitzwilliam. It felt as though her heart, which always sang a familiar song, found its harmony and sang a thousand times louder when she saw him - like he'd been made for her. It always did after he'd been away for a time.

She pinched his earlobe gently between the knuckles of her fingers, feeling the almost invisible hairs that grew there, fair and soft. He hooked his fingers under the hem of her skirt and tugged it upward. She didn't protest, rising to accommodate. He ran his thumb over her belly button and she curled into herself involuntarily, his touch causing the muscles beneath his fingers to spasm and clench in ticklish protest.

He cupped her breasts, squeezing again, pressing his open mouth to one and biting her through the fabric of her dress.

"We have a problem, here," he said, still kneading her breasts in his hands.

She raised an eyebrow at him and he quickly matched it, looking back up at her with a wry smile.

He reached down and hooked a finger beneath the corset hem. "Your choice of clothing. How many times have I told you, you should always be naked?"

She laughed and he pushed her over, guiding her onto the couch. He didn't follow, instead remaining where he sat, reaching up under her skirts to pry her petticoats and underthings free. He wasted no time as he rose to his feet, leaving her there on the couch before him, her skirts up exposing her bare legs. She relished the look of him as he rose over her, his sporran swinging gently against her knees.

"Ye ready to be ravished, lass?"

Elizabeth curled into herself laughing, pressing her hands against his stomach as he leaned down over her. "My, my. I might make you speak in that accent more often."

"Oh, aye? Ye like that?"

Elizabeth beamed. She loved to see Darcy flash that wicked, playful side.

She let her fingers play up over his chest, running her fingertips over his nipples, feeling the tiny bumps harden to her touch. She lifted herself just enough to flick her tongue against one, responding to his groan with a gentle suck before moving to the other. He slid his hand between her knees, forcing her thighs open as he lowered himself over her. She felt the wetness caused by just seeing him when she walked in, and a tingle shot up through her belly in anticipation of his touch. His fingers found that wetness and he groaned, finally kissing her, clamping his mouth over hers and piercing her with his tongue. She sighed into his open mouth as his fingers explored her, moving against her and in her in ways only he knew how. Soon she felt the gentle tickle of the horsetails on his sporran against her thigh, his erection lifting it from beneath the kilt. She glanced down at him and giggled again. He followed her gaze and raised his eyebrows at her, inspiring more laughter. She grabbed him by the ears, her heart swelling with affection, and kissed him again, locking her legs behind him to pull his full weight onto her. He obliged, his fingers still at play. She wriggled her hips against his movements, thrusting herself upward, an unspoken invitation that he acknowledged with a rumbling sound deep in his throat.

"Would ye like me to get to it, then?" He asked. She stifled a nervous laugh, the chill of anticipation and desire traveling warm and fast out over her thighs and her stomach. She ached to feel him. He slid his fingers into her, forcefully slamming them deeply over and over, watching her face as he did. She wailed in response. She clutched at him, pulling at his backside, wordlessly begging.

He chuckled softly. "Be patient, love. I'll ravage you, forbye."

She couldn't help but laugh. "Did you just say forbye?"

"Aye, I did!" He beamed at her. "I've known a fair number of Scotsmen in my day, love."

She smiled again, but quickly tensed as he slid his body down the length of her and settled his shoulders between her legs. He grabbed her by the hips and pulled her to the edge of the settee, lowering himself to his knees on the floor. She let her legs drift together, but he stopped the motion with a firm hand, returning his fingers to their work. He kissed the inside of her knee, letting his stubbled chin rub against her skin, then his lips, parted and soft, inhaling as he ran them across the inside of her thigh, drawing closer to her. She knew protest would be met with firm disapproval, but still, her thighs tensed with anticipation. He planted a hand against her thighs, pushed them high over her, baring her ass to him, and slapped her backside so hard it rang off the walls. She screamed, feeling the sting subside beneath his palm as he caressed the sore spot.

"Don't make me bend you over my knee."

She blushed, and he gave her a quick eyebrow wiggle, then stifled her laugh with his mouth, clamping it down on her sex with such purpose that it shook her whole body. She felt his tongue dodging to and fro, soft hums escaping from his throat with every shiver or spasm he caused her. She wanted to watch him work, her fingers curled tightly in his hair, his brows furrowed slightly with focus. Every few moments he would release her, open her to him with his fingers and envelope her in warmth again. She let her hips rock beneath him, urging him onward, letting him know how right he felt. He'd learned to play her body like an instrument, knew how to tune, how to strum her to make her sing. He'd been a natural at this since the first time he touched her. She gripped his hair in both hands, pulling him against her, letting the pressure of his mouth carry her. He growled against her with appreciation and she melted under the warmth of his tongue. He kept his rhythm a moment longer, letting her orgasm subside before releasing her. He lifted his eyes to meet hers and she felt her smile in her bones. He returned it, a wide grin.

He stood up, towering over her as she lay there on the settee. He grabbed one of her feet, then the other, pressing them against his chest as he dropped onto his knees on the settee, his sporran pressed into the back of her thighs. She rest both legs over his shoulders as he leaned over her, forcing her thighs up against her belly. He reached down to pull the kilt aside. It didn't cooperate.

"Good grief!" He protested, shifting again to no avail.

She laughed as he fumbled with the pleats and sporran, far more intent on falling back into place than defying gravity and standing upright long enough for him to properly service her. She gave him a gentle push. He obliged, lifting his weight from her legs.

"Take it off, handsome."

He crinkled his nose and pouted a moment. "Are you sure? That won't break this spell, will it?"

She shook her head, vehemently. "Not in the slightest. You're magnificent in the nude, as well."

He grinned at her and stood up suddenly, determined that if he was going to take the thing off, he'd do it at light speed. Darcy had matters to attend to, clearly. He rushed across the study as the buckles came loose, and turned the lock in the study door. They were free of worry now.

"Slowly, damn it!" Elizabeth hissed.

He froze with his hands on the second buckle. He glanced up at her, eyebrows raised.

"Take it off slowly," she said again, smiling.

He chuckled, obliging. "Oh, who's making demands now?"

She ran her toes across his bare chest as he approached before crossing her legs at the knee. "I am."

She felt her smile overtake her whole face as Fitzwilliam smirked at her, one eyebrow cocked. He glared at her, then began swaying his hips slowly, offering a swagger and a rakish smile, turning slowly in a circle as he unlatched the sporran and tossed it aside. Then he lifted the kilt with a flick of his hands, letting her catch a quick glimpse of his backside before unbuckling it. It came loose in a tidal wave of plaid as he held it over his cock, leaving his hips and belly bared. She wriggled there on the couch, squirming with excitement and laughter. He beamed at the sight. He held the fabric out in front of him, shimmying it from side to side, keeping himself from her view. She growled at him, stifling giggles as he took a step toward her. Then he flung the kilt over the back of the settee, stood astride, legs wide apart, cock sprung at attention.

She laughed so hard that no sound would come from her throat. He finally lunged down onto her, replacing her legs over his shoulders as his hips pressed her into the couch.

"You ready for me, love?"

She nodded. He ran the head of his cock over her, finding her wet in wait, and plunged home without pause, impaling her there under him. She cried out as he drove deeper than her body could handle, but he didn't slow, nor lessen his force. She knew this was how he meant to take her by the

118

position alone. He used the bulk of his upper body to push her legs ever higher, directing himself as deep as he pleased with her helpless against him, save for her cries. And she did cry out, though not in protest. Despite the forceful nature of his lovemaking, he smiled at her with such affection, and she returned it, gasping with each thrust. After a moment of holding her there, helpless, he rose to his knees, pinning her thighs to his belly as he thrust into her, continuing to have his way. He ran his hands over her thighs, reaching down to squeeze her breasts, all the while cooing to her softly, even as she braced with each thrust. He began to lean into her again and her insides tensed with anticipation. He squeezed her breasts, running one hand over her stomach. She took the opportunity and wrapped her legs around him, yanking him down onto her and grabbing his backside in both hands. She pulled him into her as he groaned.

"Oh, is that how it is?" He asked.

She smiled, her breath catching in her throat as his body and her body met with heat and movement in such a way to make her toes curl. She gasped and pleaded with him to keep going. He smiled wide. He whispered to her, filthy compliments and gentle threats. She dug her fingernails into the soft flesh of his buttocks and he glared at her, growling. Exactly the reaction she wanted. His movement tripled in both speed and force and he pressed his weight on her, pinning her there under his powerful hips. She began to moan in rhythm to his thrusts, begging him onward as he braced a foot on the floor, his thigh lifting her own upward. She pulled his face to hers, clamping her mouth on his with desperation, tasting herself still on his lips. He obliged, and she could feel his quiet grunts vibrating in her mouth. Her legs shuddered suddenly and he pressed himself on her wholly, his cheek to hers, his breath hoarse in her ear. She clutched him by the shoulders, begging him, 'Don't stop, please,' knowing how close they both were. She held him to her, desperate for closeness, for oneness. His grunts grew louder and she felt a sudden swell of power in her arms, knowing that even if he were to stop now, the movement of her hips, the pressure of her hands pulling him into her would carry him through. She turned, pressing her cheek to his shoulder, crying out in desperation, and when that didn't quell the rising need to absorb him, to combine with him, she clamped her teeth down into the soft flesh of his shoulder and bit him. He roared against her cheek, leaning down to bite her back. She felt his teeth, his warm mouth on her shoulder, his back arching over her as he did, and she shuddered, her legs falling slack at his sides, clutching him to her as his thrusts grew stronger. Then he shuddered, still thrusting several more times as he spilled inside her.

He lifted himself, pulling away with slow precision, and slumped there on his knees. He ran his hands up her thighs as he took a deep breath.

He pressed his cheek to her leg and kissed her knee.

"Are ye satisfied with yer service?"

She laughed, nodding. "Yes, very much."

He paused, his cheek still pressed to her knee. "I'm sorry I upset you, love."

She sighed. How powerful it was to hear the massive Master of Pemberley soften his tone to apologize to her – his wife.

He took a slow breath and blew it out through pursed lips. "I thought about it afterward, how rash and senseless it was to let him have you the way that we did. What would I have done had you become with child or -"

"Shh," she said, frowning as her husband's expression changed.

He took a deep breath. "What can I do to make it up to you?"

Elizabeth smiled. "You don't need to -" She paused. "I enjoyed it, Fitzwilliam. Very much."

Fitzwilliam smiled. "That makes two of us."

They sat in silence for a long moment. "Would you have us do it again?"

Fitzwilliam's eyes grew wide. "With adjustments? Yes. Can't have the scoundrel believing he's welcome at Pemberley whenever he likes."

"Of course not."

"Imagine if he thought himself welcome when I'm not home – how that would look."

Elizabeth cringed violently. "You don't think he would?"

He scratched his head. "I don't put anything past the scoundrel. I invited him into our bed because he was once my good friend – and if I'm honest, he was my introduction to the – ways of intimacy. I knew he would be discreet, and I knew he'd be amenable to the pursuit. I also knew he'd never threaten my marriage. There's no man I fear you leaving me for than George Wickham."

Elizabeth smiled. "Well, then I don't know what can be done."

Darcy stared at the floor for a long moment, his brow furrowed in thought.

"What is it?"

"Well," he said, a smile creeping across his face. "If I recall some previous discussions with the scoundrel – there may be something rather enticing. Another option."

Elizabeth perked up, lifting herself to sit behind him. "What other option?"

Fitzwilliam glanced over his shoulder at her and the wickedness in his eyes made her legs tingle. "Oh, I'll let it be a surprise, darling. Give me a week or two, then we'll find out together."

She smiled, locking her legs behind him and pulling him down onto her. She squeezed him so tight, he groaned. He squeezed her right back. She held him there, grateful to feel the return of his weight and warmth. Forgiveness was involuntary with this man. He could have it, always, and he didn't need to ask. She kissed his jaw, nodding.

"Goodness, the mystery will drive me mad."

"Don't worry. I'll be here to distract you," he said, giving her backside a firm squeeze – the kind of warning squeeze that told her he had spankings in mind.

He pressed his nose to hers, gave her soft surface kisses, and searched her face, his breath slowing with each passing moment. She ran her hands up and down his back, scratching lightly at his smooth skin. He moaned in approval, the vibration of it tickling her ear.

"I know you must have a busy day planned, but will you stay with me for a time?" He asked.

She took a deep breath, trying to hide the surge of joy she felt at these words. "Of course."

She opened her arms to him and he came to her, kissing her collarbone, then her jaw. He pressed his nose to her temple, inhaling slowly before running the tip of his nose into her hair. "Do you feel adored?"

She shivered slightly and squeezed him as tight as she could. She wanted to latch onto him then like a barnacle on a ship's hull and never let go. She nodded, nuzzling into his cheek. "I do."

He took a handful of her hair and turned her softly to meet his gaze.

"Because you are, Elizabeth."

She smiled, and the marrow in her bones sang. She nodded.

"Good. Are you ready for another go?"

She stared at him, eyes wide, but before she could respond, he pulled her up onto him, making her straddle him on the couch, his gorgeous thighs taut beneath her, easily holding her weight. He held her tight against him. He was hard again, a mischievous look in his eyes. He pulled her down to meet the warmth of his kiss just as she lowered herself onto him, smiling as he groaned with approval.

# CHAPTER TEN

## *An Invitation for Mr. Darcy*

---

The letters arrived with tea, a familiar flourish in the letter z to let Elizabeth know exactly who this greeting was from.

She smiled, licking butter off the tip of her thumb before tearing the wax seal from the paper.

*My dearest sister,*

*I am writing to tell you I will be unable to venture to Pemberley before the end of this month as I planned. I will write again when we are free to make the trip. I have so much to tell you, but until then, know that I understand now. I truly understand.*

*Yours in wedded bliss,*
*Mrs. Jane Bingley*

Elizabeth smiled.

Jane didn't need to say another word. Dear Mr. Wickham had done his duty, and it was clear in Jane's elation that her darling Charles was a quick study.

Elizabeth thought of how to best thank Fitzwilliam.

The thought of thanking Wickham flitted through her

mind, but she instantly pushed it aside, ignoring the curious tinge of heat at her throat.

Molly collected the empty plates and discarded butter knife, and as she lifted them from the table, the second letter toppled onto Elizabeth's half-eaten plate of finger sandwiches. Molly scrambled to fix it, but Elizabeth waved to her, smiling.

"I have it, Molly, dear. You run along and have something to eat yourself. The master won't be finished for another half hour."

Darcy was mulling over some of his accounts that afternoon, and Elizabeth couldn't bear listening to him huff in frustration.

He was by no means having money troubles. In fact, some of his more recent investments and business ventures in the city had offered a substantial return. Nonetheless, he loved to groan over the rising cost of grain or the carriage fair for her family's visits.

Molly made her way back out into the hall, leaving Elizabeth with her cucumber sandwiches and the strange letter.

The Esteemed Mr. Fitzwilliam Darcy

Elizabeth furrowed her brow as she inspected the flourished script. It was a feminine hand, there was no question. She turned it over to inspect it and found a set of initials and a seal.

**_C.E.C._**

Elizabeth stared at the envelope for a long moment. *Who on earth?*

As she touched the wax seal, the fold of the envelope lifted – it was open.

Elizabeth glanced toward the hallway, then back to the envelope. However wrong it was of her to read her husband's letters, she couldn't deny the jealous sense of invasion that this woman's handwriting brought her.

She lost her battle with propriety and pulled the card from the envelope.

Elizabeth scanned the words, her eyes growing wide with repeat reading.

She was on her feet and marching down the hallway in a matter of seconds.

Fitzwilliam was sitting at his desk, his jacket slung over the nearby settee and his shirt sleeves unbuttoned and rolled up his forearms. Despite her fury, she paused at the sight of him. She always loved it when he looked comfortable.

Fitzwilliam looked up from his ledgers, and the smile instantly faded from his face.

Clearly, Elizabeth's feelings weren't easily concealed.

"The Lady Carrington requests your presence at her annual Spring Festival?"

Elizabeth held the letter aloft, not a whit of concern for having read it.

Fitzwilliam closed his eyes and made the same huffing noise he did when he read his ledgers.

"Why are you receiving an invitation to Lady Carrington's Spring Festival?"

Her tone was high, almost shrill, and though she tried to lower her voice, the words slipped out in squeaks of distress. She wasn't proud of it, but she didn't care. She wanted answers.

"Do you have any notion as to what Lydia told me about this event? She told me that wealthy gentlemen gather at this affair to find themselves mistresses! Can you imagine?"

"Is that all she told you?"

"Pardon me? She didn't need to speak further on it – I was made well aware what this Festival is about. Now, why are you receiving an invitation?"

"Because I receive one every year."

Elizabeth's mouth fell open, and the envelope fell to the floor. Fitzwilliam was on his feet and making his way around the desk toward her before she could find her wits to respond.

"You – what do you mean? This isn't your first invitation?"

He stooped to pick up the envelope, turning it toward her to show her the unbroken seal. It was a gentle chiding for having opened his letter. A part of her was relieved to see he wasn't angry.

The relief evaporated in the wake of her returned fury. "Why would Lady Carrington invite you to such things? Does she think you're in want of a mistress? Is that why she would -"

"Lizzy," he said, bending to wrap his arms around her waist. She wanted to fight him – strike him, perhaps, but the touch of his arms around her instantly cooled her fury. This wasn't the touch of a man who wasn't happy with his wife.

Then why would he be invited?

"I'm afraid you won't want to hear the answers to these questions."

Elizabeth's stomach began to churn, but she stood a little taller. "Then I must know."

He leaned into her ear and kissed her there. She didn't respond.

After a long moment, he sighed and released his hold on her waist. He held his hand out to her, waiting for her to hand him the envelope.

She did.

"George was the first I'd ever heard of Lady Carrington. He'd encountered tales of her celebrations and banquets, and he wanted to experience them for himself. I naturally balked at this nonsense, but somehow, that fool managed to get himself invited to one of these soirees."

He held the envelope up, waving it through the air with a disinterested flourish.

"He wrote of nothing else for weeks – how spectacular it was, how wondrous, how beyond his wildest imagination. I dismissed him, of course. Even when we were close, he was always an excitable fellow. Then, when he returned to Pemberley to visit father, he took me aside and – well, he told me everything."

Elizabeth stood by the desk, watching her husband lean

against the window. He spoke of his youth as though it were a century ago.

Elizabeth sometimes found it difficult to imagine her Fitzwilliam as a frivolous youth.

She took a step toward him. "What did he tell you?"

Fitzwilliam took a deep breath. "That the events at Lady Carrington's home are little more than wild, endless orgies."

She stopped moving, fighting to still the sudden surge of excitement and wonder she felt. "No, what a foolish thing to think you'd believe -"

"Oh, it wasn't a lie, darling. That's exactly what her gatherings are."

She swallowed, holding his gaze as he turned to watch her. "How do you know?"

He gave a half smile. "Because I let him convince me to attend."

Elizabeth's mouth fell open and she fought the urge to scold him. She'd wanted to know her husband's secrets, but now, as she was suddenly met with them, she wanted to close her mind to the thoughts and pretend them untrue.

Yet, there was no denying what she'd known since the first night Fitzwilliam touched her.

She wasn't the first woman he'd ever touched.

Now, hearing that he'd attended some lascivious gala with any number of willing ladies – it made her chest tighten.

She closed her eyes, trying to press the thoughts away.

She could hear him coming before the warmth of his hand grazed over hers. "Beloved. Are you cross?"

She inhaled through her nose, trying to steady herself before she spoke. "I'm not cross, no."

"Are you upset?"

She exhaled and opened her mouth, but no words came.

"I was not romantically involved with anyone else. I never even considered another woman before I found myself beguiled with you."

"Beguiled?" She said, a half laugh fighting to break through, despite the ache in her chest.

"I have enjoyed the company of other women, almost all of them in George's company. You were the only woman to have my heart."

She stiffened, startled by this revelation. "Wait. You've taken other women with George?"

He closed his eyes and exhaled. "I have."

She shook her head, staring up at him in shock. "You say that as though you're describing what you ate for tea, today."

He raised his brows. "Well, if I'm wholly honest, I've done far more tawdry things with you, darling."

She glared at him. "Tawdry?"

He grinned, wrapping his arms around her waist, as she tried to push him away. "What? You don't agree?"

"Stop!" She said, her voice rising in volume.

He released her, straightening to his full height. For a moment, his presence filled the room.

"Tell me what you've done at these parties. I want to know."

He tilted his head just so. "I don't imagine that's true, darling."

"Whether it is true or no, I demand you tell me everything. I must know."

"Must you?"

"Yes," she said, her stomach tight with a strange mixture of grief and excitement. She wanted to know the happenings of such events, but the notion of hearing his answer – of knowing whatever she heard would be from first-person experience.

She feared she wasn't ready for his answer.

"Let's see. I was a young man, at the time, so the Lady took a special interest in me. I witnessed husbands who wanted to observe as their wives were ravished by other men, sometimes more than one at once. I saw wives and husbands both slipping from their chambers at night to slip into their lovers' rooms – as though swapping wives."

"No," she said, scandalized.

128

"Oh, yes. I've been told the first few celebrations were for that purpose, alone."

Elizabeth sat in the leather chair by the corner of his desk, folding her hands in her lap. "And you? Were you slipping into the chambers of other men's wives?"

Fitzwilliam took a deep breath, his chest puffing up just so as he did. Then, he exhaled and moved across the room, crouching down to meet her gaze, taking her hands in his.

"I took part in threesomes with George, more than once. The women were either married or happily not. Some were particularly smitten with George, some simply wanted to partake in two young men. Still, the woman to take my innocence was the Lady herself."

"You've bedded Lady Carrington?"

He squeezed her hands. "I believe every man who arrives at the celebration on their own does at one point or another."

She swallowed, taking the envelope from his hand. She stood up from her chair, leaving him crouched there, and walked across the office.

She stopped in the doorway, looking down at the flourish of the letter in his name on the envelope. "I will send our RSVP, then."

"Pardon?" He said, lunging to his feet.

She turned on him, giving him a steely gaze. "Do you protest?"

His eyes went wide, and he flailed his arms a moment, as though looking for something in the room to answer for him.

"You speak of your time at these events as though they're nothing for me to be concerned by, yes?"

"Yes, but that doesn't mean I have any intention of -"

"Then, I would like to see for myself."

Fitzwilliam lunged forward, taking her hands in his. "My darling, you don't understand. Those books you enjoy – they're nothing compared to some of the things that go on in these circles. These are the same people who enjoy dungeon clubs in London or -"

Her stomach shot into her throat, not out of fear or nervousness, but excitement. She raised a hand to stop him. "Enough. I've made my decision. You will attend with me, and that is final." The notion that her tawdry books might truly come to life – that she might witness or even take part in such acts set her body ablaze. Were she not trying to make a dramatic exit, she might've demanded her husband's touch at that moment.

She turned back for the door, ready to put her foot down when he protested.

Yet, he didn't say another word.

She stopped just outside the door, glancing back to find him standing by his desk, watching her. Though he was trying to hide it, there was a glimmer of a smirk on his handsome face.

# CHAPTER ELEVEN

## *An Uncomfortable Carriage*

———◆———

"You needn't be so dower," Elizabeth said, but she didn't turn from her window. She'd been watching the world go by outside the carriage in silence for well over an hour.

"Oh, needn't I?" Fitzwilliam said.

He was in a mood.

"No. It's not as though we will see her while we're there. You said so yourself."

"I said no such thing."

Elizabeth turned on her seat to face him, her jacket catching on a corner of the window as she did. "The single attendees are housed in a separate wing, wasn't that what you said?"

"Yes, I did."

"And we will be housed in the married couples' wing, yes?"

He sighed. "I do not need you to give me a lesson on the finer workings of Lady Carrington's house. As you refuse to let me forget, I *have* been there before."

"As you say."

She turned back to the window, her back a little straighter, now.

A long moment passed, the rock of the carriage and the road beneath them their only companion.

Finally, he sighed. "Really, Elizabeth. You've invited your

131

most unfortunate sister to a bloody orgy – that we're attending, no less."

"Unfortunate?! Oh, I should box your ears for that."

"Am I wrong?"

"Yes! Lydia is by far my most unfortunate sister, and you haven't said one word about her attending this extravaganza."

He stifled a half laugh. "She doesn't concern me. Mary, on the other hand, is difficult in a whole other way."

"Difficult, perhaps, but not unfortunate, and I demand you take that back."

"I'll do no such thing."

"Take it back, or you will be the only gentlemen not invited to my bed this evening."

His eyes went wide, and he glared at her. "Do you think that funny?"

She held his gaze, but her heart was racing. "Take it back."

They held each other's gaze, his jaw set so squarely, it seemed to quiver.

She held her ground, half expecting him to grab her, tear up her skirts and spank her.

Or worse, refuse to touch her.

He'd never done the latter. Perhaps, that's why she feared it so desperately.

"Fine. She isn't the most unfortunate. She can be a little – unseemly at times."

Elizabeth gave a forced laugh. "You're one to talk."

They rode along in silence again, and Elizabeth feared her last comment may have upset him. And not in the same way any other snide comment might do, but in his center. She feared she'd hurt his feelings.

She glanced his way, waiting for him to look back at her. When he didn't she opened her mouth to speak. The words took a moment to form.

"I didn't know what else to do. She's not like Lydia and Kitty. She doesn't have the same ease with people."

His head shifted at this, as though he'd thought to look at

her, but didn't. "That sounds unfortunate to me."

"If what you say about this event is true – my hope is that she might find others like her."

He openly laughed.

She fought not to react. He was trying to push her buttons. "She deserves happiness, Fitzwilliam. You can't say you don't think so, too."

He shot a look toward the far corner of the carriage. His brow was still furrowed, but he didn't speak. He leaned back against the seat. "Then I hope she finds some lovely woman to ruffle her feathers."

Elizabeth's mouth fell open, but she didn't speak.

Fitzwilliam caught her looking out of the corner of his eye. He smirked. "I saw my copy of *The Ladies of Port Solace* on her parlor table when she stayed with us."

*The Ladies of Port Solace* was a French book translated by a man of the name H. B. Gardener. The entire story was one love scene after another.

There wasn't a single male character in the entire book.

"You know she took it with her when she left. That was mine, I'll have you know."

Elizabeth smiled. His tone had softened.

"One of your favorites, was it?"

He looked away. "It had its merits," he said, reaching his hand across the bench seat to her leg. He squeezed her thigh, letting his fingers slip down between them.

She sighed, opening her legs to him.

Just as his fingers grazed against her, the carriage jostled beneath them.

"Coming up on the estate, sir," the driver called from above them.

Fitzwilliam pulled his hand away, as though someone had walked in on them.

Elizabeth's stomach shot into her throat. The excitement was overwhelming and terrifying. Somewhere deep, she wanted to run, beg the driver to turn the carriage around and let Mary arrive alone and unencumbered.

133

The sudden trepidation caused a sudden rush of frustration, and she refused to let it win.

The turned to her husband, grabbing hold of his hand, and thrust it back between her legs.

His eyes went wide, and in an instant, he was on her, the two of them feverishly seeking each other in the mere moments before their carriage would pull up to Kenilworth House.

# CHAPTER TWELVE

## *Mr. Darcy's Secret Service*

---

Fitzwilliam knew the lighting of these halls well. He'd come to the home of Lady Carrington more than once in the past. He'd even made the trip on one of her yearly Spring celebrations, but this was the first year he would be taking part.

Spring celebrations took on a very different meaning at the house of Lady Carrington.

He recognizes the quality of each light sconce – the rich velvet walls, the long oriental runners that lined the floor. Every hall was the same, their differences hidden in the paintings on the wall, and the wild sounds coming from the closed doors as he passed.

Lady Carrington's Spring Celebration drew the aristocracy from all over England and Scotland. Fitzwilliam was sure one of the Earl's downstairs had come all the way from Scotland, his middle-aged wife smiling from beneath her Venetian mask.

The celebration was still in full form downstairs, but it was upstairs that many of Lady Carrington's guests would make their way tonight, often sneaking into the rooms of their lovers, all to Lady Carrington's full knowledge.

He knew this well. He'd witnessed it himself more than once. Still, this year was different. This year, he'd been called upon by the Lady herself.

And he was nervous.

The Lady was in the room at the end of the hall, she'd assured him and he walked past several doors, some silent, others betraying the gasps and cries of couples within fully enjoying each other's company. His freshly shined black leather shoes were silent on the pristine carpet. He'd worn his best for this evening, a deep navy blue and perfectly tailored. He'd padded his pocket with a kerchief to match the silk cravat, both a subtle purple hue – the Lady's favorite color, if he remembered correctly.

He'd taken the extra steps. It was a rare honor to be chosen as the Lady's companion for an evening – or an hour. Whatever his world was like at home, when he was in Kenilworth House, he was at her beck and call if she so demanded.

She'd demanded. He stepped up to the final door and tried to ignore the knot in his stomach. He raised his hand to knock, and stopped to arrange himself one more time, for good measure – buttons set, kerchief square, cravat straight. He ran his hands over the back of his hair, freshly shorn for the occasion. For this woman, he would arrive in peak condition. She would expect no less.

He rapped his knuckle against the door and listened. After a moment, there was a soft shuffle inside. He swallowed.

The door opened to an empty room, wide enough for him to enter, but she was nowhere to be seen. He stepped inside to find her hiding behind the door. He met her eyes as she shut it behind him.

There she was. Just as he remembered her.

Martina's hair hung in ringlets over her shoulders, darker now, and time had settled gracefully at the corners of her eyes. Yet her face was soft, her smile warm. She stood several inches shorter than him, her figure hugged at every inch by a silk dress that cascaded down from her hips in purple pleats. She'd taken as much care as he had, the dress pressing her breasts to a soft mound at the edge of the fabric.

He'd remembered the color exactly.

Despite the regality of her posture, he knew what was expected of him. He scooped an arm around her waist and pulled her against him to kiss her cheek.

"Happy Birthday, sweetheart."

She beamed at him. He ran his hands down her back, trying to hide his nerves with steady hands.

"You remembered!"

"Of course, I did. You're the…"

He stopped himself before the words 'Lady of the house' could pass his lips. Though she'd never minded the term, he'd come to consider it in poor taste when with her. She wasn't like other women. This woman wasn't lonely, nor hard pressed to find a man. She was passionate, she was fun, and she took a man as a birthday present to herself at every spring celebration.

"When I find a gentleman who can do what they do and make me laugh, I'll marry him. Until then, I'll take lovers as I see fit, thank you very much," she'd said after their second meeting. Perhaps that's why he enjoyed her as much as he did, and why his stomach was in knots.

She pressed her hand to the lapel of his jacket and sighed. "Dear me, you look good enough to eat."

He drew close to her lips, ready to break the barrier that existed between them, between any two people who have similar intentions. She laughed and pulled out of his grasp, shyly.

A smile burned his cheeks.

She walked across the suite in her bare feet to a white counter, and retrieved a drink she'd been nursing. She mimed to him that he was free to partake as she sipped clumsily. Unlike him, she wasn't concerned with hiding her nerves.

"So, what would you like to do tonight, beautiful?"

She grinned and set her drink back down.

"I could happily spend the evening listening to you call

me that. Repeatedly."

"It's your birthday, whatever you like," he said before adding with a smirk, "beautiful."

She fidgeted for a moment, visibly searching for the courage to say something. Finally, she found it, and planted her hands on her hips.

"It seems like such a waste not to take you downstairs and flaunt you as my prize for the evening – good grief, you are beautiful - but I think I really just want you to - ehm..."

Her tone was confident, but she faltered. He knew once she was comfortable she'd have no problem saying exactly what she wanted.

"Want me to what?"

She glanced at the clock. "It's seven now. When do I have you til?"

"Whenever you like."

"Oh, cut the polite nonsense. When are you due back to your room?"

"Ten o'clock."

She pursed her lips. "Hmm. Yes, I think I want to stay in. I have a year's worth to catch up on, if you know understand my meaning."

He smiled despite the butterflies in his stomach. The year before she'd made a man perform a scene from a play with her, and the year before that she'd made a man dance with her for hours before retiring, and just about every year she'd taken pride in her birthday dinner. Despite looking forward to their bedroom activities all night, he now longed for those hours of preparation, of flirtation to quell the nerves that a man like him shouldn't have.

She truly was formidable, and he'd wanted to be chosen by her like this for some time.

He swallowed and stepped toward her. "Well, what kind of night is it, then?

She raised an eyebrow. "What do you mean?"

"Are you in a 'wanton trollop' kind of mood, or a 'sweet innocent' kind of mood?"

She visibly shivered before she spoke. "Can it be both?"

She gave a mischievous smile and covered her mouth.

He nodded. "Of course."

He took another step.

"Stop," she said, her hand out before her. He did as she asked. She cocked one hip to the side and took a breath. "Tell me what you want to do to me."

His mouth fell open and he stared. This was new.

"You wouldn't rather I show you?"

"Oh, believe me, you'll show me. I'd rather like to hear you say it first."

He could hear the confidence building in her voice and he liked it.

"I want to tear that dress off of you and -"

"Don't you dare tear this dress, it's my favorite color."

He laughed. "I know it is and it's beautiful, but I'd much rather see it on the floor -"

"I would kill you if you tore this dress."

"That's good to know -"

"In the street. Murder you for all to see."

"Do you want to know what I want to do to you or would you rather just kill me now?"

She smiled and came to him, surprising him as she took hold of the buttons of his jacket, gently unbuttoning him and running her hands across his stomach to his sides.

He leaned in to embrace her.

She stopped him.

"No, you keep your hands to yourself," she said, pressing her cheek to his jaw. Her hands played across his chest, her fingers slipping under the fabric of the shirt. She ran the tip of her nose along his jaw, inhaling deeply. He groaned.

"Not sure if I can."

She pulled away just enough to meet his gaze and gave him a flirtatiously stern look. "You better. Keep your hands to yourself and tell me exactly what you want to do to me."

She took hold of his cravat and loosened it before sliding his jacket down off his shoulders. Before he could find words, she pressed herself to his neck and began kissing him as she unbuttoned his shirt.

"I want to get you out of that dress – in a manner that is respectful to the dress' feelings obviously -" he felt her teeth graze his shoulder, a playful bite as punishment for his wise comment. He let his hands fall at her hips and held them steady despite the rising need to explore her. "- then I want to put my mouth all over those gorgeous breasts of yours."

She unbuttoned his shirt, pulling the shirt tails free of his trousers and was now pulling it down his bare arms with a hint more desperation. When the shirt was halfway down his arms, she pulled it taut, pinning his elbows to his sides.

"How gorgeous, exactly?"

"The most gorgeous and perfect pair I've ever encountered."

"Correct answer."

He smiled. "I thought it might be."

She let the shirt fall to the floor before pulling his undershirt up. Her movements grew more forceful, more intent with each passing second. He felt the satin of her dress graze over his stomach as she kissed his chest. He wanted to feel her tongue on him, wanted to kiss her, but he would let her have her way. The anticipation had long drawn a reaction. He felt almost shy at the thought of her discovering how hard he was. He felt the heat of her mouth as she let her tongue travel across his chest to his nipple. His breath caught in his throat and he let himself grab hold of her hair. She rose to her full height and met his gaze, letting her open mouth draw close to his. Yet she didn't kiss him. Her lips grazed his, and she flicked her tongue against his upper lip, but still she did not kiss him. His grip tightened in her hair and he wrapped his arm around her waist, running his hand up to find the ties of her dress. A moment later, they were loose and her dress fell open. He ran his hand under the loose hem of her chemise and the bare skin of her back.

"Then what?" She barely breathed her words into his

mouth and smiled.

He groaned. "I'm going to punish you for teasing me."

She giggled and squirmed against him. "I'm not teasing you. I'm absolutely going to let you have your way with me."

He smirked, took her by the hair and slid his tongue into her open mouth. Her whole body responded to him as she kissed him back, a soft whimper sounding in her throat. He walked her backward toward the bed and let her fall onto it, smiling up at him. His cock pressed hard against the fabric of his trousers, he felt relief to be free of them. She slid out of the straps of her dress and pushed it down over her hips, kicking it away from the bed. He looked down at the dress, frowning.

"I think you may have offended it, love."

"Shut up and ravish me."

Those words drew a wicked chuckle and he lowered himself down onto her, letting her feel how hard she made him. He held himself there, moving against her as her legs fell apart. Again, she whimpered and he stifled her cries with his lips.

She clutched him, dragging her nails down his back. He knew if he moved in the right rhythm there, she would succumb. Still he knew other ways that were far more enticing. He stripped her of her chemise, but she pulled him onto her before he could properly appreciate her breasts. He let her tongue play at his open lips until pressing his mouth to hers and driving his tongue inside. She convulsed at the sensation, her hands reaching for his backside where she grabbed him and pulled him against her firmly.

He groaned.

He met her eyes and smiled before slipping down to her breasts, clamping his mouth over her nipple. She ran her fingers through his hair and stifled a cry with her other hand. He flicked his tongue against the hardening flesh before sucking gently. She loved this. He languidly shifted to her other breast, letting her squirm under him, her ankle running up the length of his thigh. She hooked her feet behind him and gave a tug, letting him know exactly what she wanted. He lifted himself up to stand at the foot of the bed, looking down at her as he removed the last of his clothing and let them fall to the floor.

She growled appreciatively.

He rose to his full height and was startled by her sudden movement as she pushed herself to the edge of the bed and in one graceful movement, took him in her mouth.

His breath caught as he watched his flesh disappear beyond those soft pink lips. Her eyes were closed to him, as though the act itself were causing her ecstasy. He was too big to disappear completely, but the warmth of her mouth sent shudders through him. He took hold of her hair, wanting to get lost in the sensation, but knowing better than to do so.

"Sweetheart," he started, but the words broke off as she slid her tongue over him to the sensitive skin of his balls, lapping at them as she took hold of him with a firm yet gentle hand, running her fingers over the ridge at the head of his cock. She groaned softly as she sucked at him, finally meeting his gaze. She took a breath and blew gently against his wet skin. He gave a broken exhale and smiled. He felt the sense that he should stop her – it was her birthday after all, it was her time. He was supposed to be pleasing her, not the other way around. Yet as these thoughts drifted through, she closed her lips around the head of his cock and sucked gently. He sighed and let his head fall back. He felt her tongue flitting against him inside her mouth as she moved to take him deeper. He gently pulled her, shuddering as he felt his cock nudge the back of her throat.

Martina released him, taking a deep breath.

Fitzwilliam lowered himself onto her before she could return to her work. He wasted no time, hooking his fingers under the waistband of her petticoats and tugging at them, his intention clear. She shifted on the bed and laughed nervously, her hands covering the dark patch of hair as he pulled the garment free from her ankles. She touched his bare chest and sought his lips, kissing him as he positioned himself over her. She lifted herself to keep his lips to hers as though breaking from him would be painful.

He kissed her firmly enough to press her down into the pillow, letting her hold him there a moment. He knew what she was doing, and when he slid his hand down across her stomach, her hands shot down to cover herself. The shy response was endearing. Every time. He smiled.

He pulled away from her, looking down at her bare breasts, the pale skin of her stomach. She covered her mouth with one hand as she giggled up at him, her other hand still shielding her from view.

"What do you think you're doing?" He asked, running his hand over hers and drawing a shiver.

She covered her mouth, but she beamed at him. "Nothing."

With one purposeful movement, he grabbed her by the ankles, lifted her legs upward and pulled them apart. She shrieked and pressed her hands to his stomach as he quickly lowered himself onto her. She could cover herself all she wanted now, he'd made it quite clear that he would do as he pleased.

"There, isn't that better?"

He kissed her throat, languishing in the sensation of her smooth legs as she wrapped them around him. He could feel how she loved the way his mouth felt on her breasts and he could use that to draw her hands away from more intimate places. He let his hand wander down her side, over her hip to her stomach, just inches above the dark hair she'd been hiding from him. His hand moved lower and she squealed, quickly entwining her fingers with his to keep them at bay. He left her breasts, the nipples now hardened peaks, and slipped down across her stomach, kissing her.

She fought, desperate to keep him from doing exactly what he intended. She hooked her hands under his arms and pulled, whimpering in protest, but he moved lower, pressing his lips to the skin just below her navel. Her hands were between him and his prize, so rather than fight, he kissed them. First at the wrist, then the back of her hand, then her first knuckle. With each kiss he drew lower, toward places she couldn't cover.

She pleaded until her final attempt to fight him; she tried to lift her legs above him and close them. He caught them as they rose up and planted them back down onto the mattress.

He gave her a stern look. "Tsk-tsk."

She inhaled as he took hold of her hands and pulled them aside, leaving her warmth exposed to him. She covered her face, her breath shallow and urgent.

He took his time, first kissing her leg mid-thigh, then higher. He kissed the soft tuft of hair just above his mark and watched her body move in response. He let her feel his breath as he drew close, and as she held hers.

He ran his tongue over the pink mound there for the first time and she gasped. She was so wet, and he relished the taste of her. He quickly did it again, watching her response. She gave a tortured sigh and he moved to attack, pressing his open mouth firmly against her, letting his tongue move over her. She moaned, curling up to watch him. He moved his lips, lapped at her firmly, then sucked at her, turning his head from side to side to make her shriek. He groaned as he pressed his mouth to her again. He knew she liked to hear him, liked to hear when he was pleased, and he knew that hearing his pleasure now would send her reeling. And it did - she lifted her legs up off the bed and her fingers found his hair, scratching across his scalp as he devoured her. He felt her moving beneath him, her hips shifting upward in rhythm. He moved with her as it grew more intense, until she began grinding against him. Her moans were constant now with garbled strings of "yes," and "please," and "don't stop, right there," drawing more heightened with each passing moment. He imagined the aristocrats who might be perched just outside the door listening to this regal creature's primal cries, and it made his cock throb.

He took hold of her hips and pressed himself harder against her. She growled, lifting her backside from the mattress. He moved swiftly to take advantage of her arousal, ran his tongue down before she could realize and slid it into her wet sex. She screamed, grabbed him by the hair so roughly he thought she might tear it loose, and pulled him into her. He gripped her and slid his tongue in and out as she cried over and over.

"Oh god, you *bastard!*"

Though she couldn't see, he smiled. He felt her legs shaking as she dropped back down to the mattress. Her muscles had gone weak. She was getting close. He pressed his hands to her thighs and lifted her legs higher before running his fingers along her wet lips. She looked down at him with pleading eyes and he slid his fingers inside. She moaned gratefully, her fingers clasped firmly in his hair. Her movements grew swifter, more desperate and he let his fingers explore deeply. He played his fingers expertly, pushing them into her over and over with such speed that her moans bled together into one long desperate cry. He let his knuckles slam against her roughly as he moved his tongue against her.

She gasped and held her breath and he knew.

He shifted himself upward so he could finish her, her hands clamped onto the back of his head, holding him to her as her whole body tensed. He felt the muscles in her thighs move and suddenly he felt her tighten around his fingers. In waves it came, and he wanted nothing more than to bury his hard cock in that warmth, and feel her come again. He groaned at the sensation, but did not slow. He knew she would give him a sign when it was time to stop. She gasped again and shook under him. Then he felt her grip in his hair loosen, her legs went slack and she fell back onto the pillow with a breathless cry.

That was his sign. The sign a woman is spent.

He kissed her once more, then her thigh, then slid his fingers slowly out of her, waiting to be sure she would see.

When she met his gaze, he sucked her from his fingers.

She gasped.

He was throbbing now to the point of near pain. He ran his hand over his mouth and moved up the length of her body, kissing her white skin as he did. He settled himself above her, one hand stroking what was now his achingly hard sex. She grabbed him and kissed him deeply, then hooked her ankles at his hips once more and tugged. He obliged, moving himself over her until he pressed the head of his cock against her now overly sensitive sex. She shivered as he ran it over the wet mound again and again.

"You like to be teased, don't you?"

She shook her head no, but she was smiling. He lowered himself closer to her lips and spoke low.

"Do you want it?"

She growled again and dug her nails into his back. "Yes."

"Tell me, Mistress. Tell me you want it."

"I want it," she said and moved under him before whining in protest of his tease.

"What do you want?"

She blushed, her voice just a whisper. "Mmm, I want your cock inside me."

He slid the head down and pressed himself until her body yielded to him. She gasped and clutched at him as he slowly slid inside.

He moved slowly, watching her. She shifted beneath him, her hands pulling at his hips for him to move deeper. She was warm and wet, and he fought the urge to move faster, to fuck her. He would wait until she asked.

He let her lead, her hips grinding beneath him and against him. He watched her closed eyes, waiting for his signal. Finally, she scratched her fingernails into his backside. She looked at him, smiling before biting at his lower lip.

"Come on, punish me with that beautiful cock of yours."

He smiled wide and kissed her, pressing himself down onto her. Then with a swift move, he pulled himself up to his knees, grabbed her at the hips and tugged her toward

146

him. She shrieked, softly.

"Are you quite certain?" He accentuated his question with a sudden thrust, his pelvis slamming into her thighs. "You think you can withstand that?"

She gasped and nodded, all the while keeping his gaze. He thrust again and watched her. Her face contorted, but she did not look away. He thrust faster this time, building a rhythm at a torturous pace. She cried out, but continued to watch his eyes, a wicked smile on her face.

He was fighting to hide his own need. This game was intended to thrill and tease her, but he felt the ache himself. He was ready to take her, but he wanted to draw it out as long as he could. He wondered who he was torturing more.

"I want you to annihilate me," she said.

"Well, when you say so plainly -"

He gripped her tightly and thrust himself into her, then without pause, slipped out and thrust again. She gave a shocked cry and turned her eyes to where their bodies now met, watching him disappear into her. She pressed her hand to his stomach gently, a sign he'd driven deep, but he did not waver. He thrust again, the sound of their bodies slamming into one another in quick rhythm. She watched, touching him as he built up speed. Her gasps quickly grew to full moans.

He slipped in and out with ease, his generous cock driving as deep as it could. He bent to her breast, clamping his mouth over her nipple. She writhed beneath him, grinding against him, meeting his thrusts with equal intention. The sensation was growing irresistible. He felt her legs around him, her pussy like velvet as he thrust inside her. He felt the pressure building. He had to settle himself in the sensation, or he might lose control. Her legs began to shake at his sides and he slipped his hand down to her quivering sex. She shivered as his fingers began to play against her.

She curled herself up into him and grabbed his shoulders. "Oh God, don't stop!"

He set his elbows into the mattress and moved quickly,

pressing himself into her as she slowed beneath him. Her mouth opened in silent protest and her head fell back. She was close. He steadied himself there, driving down into her, watching her.

Yet as she grew close, his own body sought release. He felt the heat in his sex rising against the heat of hers – the pressure building with every thrust. He looked down at her and felt her legs and her sex tighten around him as she gasped, digging her nails into his shoulders.

If he stopped now, she would kill him. Literally, she would kill him. He couldn't stop, under any circumstances. He searched his mind for anything that might delay it – hunting, riding, he even tried to mentally compile an accounting list of household expenses, but it was no use, her whispers of need couldn't be drowned out with mundane thoughts. With each thrust, the sensation grew more intense, more difficult to withstand, but she was not yet spent. He did not stop, his breathing growing sharper with effort.

She lifted herself, holding tightly to him, breathing the word, 'Please.'

He sped up despite the consequence.

Heat pulsed through his cock with each thrust, rising - hotter, higher. She convulsed beneath him and exhaled. He kept his rhythm, hoping to let her ride the sensation as long as he could. He stifled a cry as he came in her warm, wet sex, filling her with his seed.

He fought to keep his rhythm as she relaxed, running her fingertips down his sides. He slowed, gratefully, the sensation growing too intense to continue. He slumped onto her, his face buried in the crook of her neck.

"You layabout," she said.

He chuckled. "I tried, darling. I couldn't help it."

"Psh! What did I ever see in you?"

He laughed again, rolling onto the mattress beside her. She was smiling, her face flushed. He kissed her and told her she was beautiful.

She accused him of trying to change the subject.

"Give me a moment and I'm all yours."

"You better be," she said and climbed on top of him, her warm sex now pressed onto his. She beamed at him before bending to kiss him. He ran his hands over her thighs, rubbing her backside. She wriggled on top of him, letting him feel her wetness. As she shifted there, taking hold of his hands and pinning them to the mattress above his head, she growled softly. His sex was already responding to her.

"That was a rather short moment, hmm?"

\*\*\*

He sat up on the edge of the bed, scanning the floor for his clothes, but feeling little inspiration to collect them. He was tired and warm and more than willing to curl into that bed and sleep with her, but the time was up. He had to leave.

"You're the best birthday present I've ever given myself."

Fitzwilliam chuckled. "I'm glad you think so."

She shifted to him on the edge of the bed, pressing her bare breasts to his back as she embraced him. This did not help fuel his desire to leave. They'd ended up making love several times in their three hours, including one last time in the bath as a close to the evening. She smelled of soap and rosewater, though the scent of their activities still lingered in the room.

"I'm actually considering adding another celebration. Once a year isn't nearly enough."

"Oh really?"

"Yes. What about Valentine's Day?"

He took her hand and kissed it. "I'm spoken for on Valentine's Day."

She moved to meet his gaze. What little makeup she wore had shifted, leaving her eyes smoky, but bright. She was smiling.

"Well, maybe I should just let you have me on your birthday."

He laughed. "Is that so, thinking of coming to Pemberley?"

"No, but I might make an exception for you."

He raised his eyebrows and scratched his chin, appraising her.

"Though, wouldn't that be a lovely notion. Pemberley at night," she said, grinning. "I'll be an expensive houseguest, though. Would take quite extravagant measures to draw me away from Kenilworth."

"I bet you're worth every penny."

They both glanced at the clock ticking on a corner table - 9:50. She whined and kissed him before slumping back down onto the mattress. He stood up and bent to retrieve his trousers at the foot of the bed. She gave a few appreciative catcalls. He began getting dressed, and by the time he was lifting his jacket from the chair in the corner, the urge to leave was as weak as it had been when he lay beside her.

Still, the time had come.

She stood and crossed the room, collecting her own dress from the floor. He put his jacket on and straightened his tucked his cravat into his collar.

"Will you do me a favor before you go?"

He turned to find her standing with her back to him, her dress ties open down her back. He let his fingers graze her skin as he pulled the laces up the back of her dress. He couldn't help but note that she wasn't wearing her chemise underneath.

She turned, threw her arms around his neck and kissed him deeply, her fingers firmly gripping his hair. He held her around the waist, remembering the initial touch of that evening, a touch that had occurred where they now stood. She released him and he again glanced at the clock.

10:01

"I had a wonderful time," she said, walking him to the door.

"Always a pleasure."

He kissed her cheek and squeezed her one more time, inhaling the smell of her before walking out into the lavish hallway. The latch of the door clicked behind him.

He stood in the empty hallway for a long moment. He walked a few feet down the hall and waited.

He tapped his fingertips on the table. He let another long minute pass.

Finally, he walked back to the last door on the left and raised his hand to knock on the door. It opened before he could.

Elizabeth opened the door and smiled at him. He looked at his wife, her hair up in pins again to hide its wild nature. Her wedding ring was back on her finger.

She burst out of the door and closed it behind her, kissing him as she moved past. "Dear God, I had a great night! How was yours?"

"I found it rather pleasing."

She squeezed his hand and plowed past him down the hallway, her hips swaying with each step as she went. He followed.

"Sorry, but I'm starving! Tell me dinner is still going on downstairs?"

"It is," he said. "Food is served throughout the evening to – in case guests need to refuel."

Lizzy gave him a mischievous grin.

They reached the stairs and she took his arm to let him lead her downstairs. He took hold of her hand and pulled her over, her ring cool against his skin. He kissed her neck. She smiled at him and pressed her nose to his before kissing him. The chime of glasses clinking somewhere downstairs reminded them they weren't alone. She released him, grabbing his arm and pulling toward the steps.

He stayed in the hallway a moment. "I'm contemplating having a ball for my birthday this year."

He looked up to find her smirking at him. The look was wicked.

"I can't wait," she said.

She stepped toward him, grabbing his sleeves as she stood on her tiptoes to kiss him. He wrapped his arms around her waist, half wanting to whisk her right back to their room.

"Tell me, dears. Will you be joining us downstairs at all this evening?"

The voice startled them apart, and Fitzwilliam turned his gaze down the grand stairs to find Lady Carrington, a middle-aged woman of gray hair and stern blue eyes watching them from below. He stumbled over his words a moment.

"Of course, Madam. We are joining you just now."

She smiled and held out her hand.

A young man with a thick shock of blonde hair slid up to her side, offering the crook of his arm. Lady Carrington took it and shot them both a wicked smile to match Lizzy's then disappeared into the throng of people below.

The Darcy's made their way down the steps and joined the wild foray.

# CHAPTER THIRTEEN

## *The Wanton Mr. Wickham*

The ball was as sumptuous and regal as any she'd ever been to, and Lizzy couldn't help but wonder how many other such events she'd attended with absolutely no knowledge of the tawdry affairs playing out in the rooms above.

Fitzwilliam took her hand and led her out onto the dance floor. He was a head taller than the rest of the room, and he held his shoulders so straight, he looked like he might have a broomstick up his backside – as her mother would say.

Still, Fitzwilliam could dance, one of the things Lizzy always adored about him. They were moving across the floor in a Scotch Reel when Lizzy noticed she wasn't the only one gazing up at her impressive husband. Several ladies were watching him as he turned her on the floor – and as Lizzy had to admit, a few men had the same flirtatious look in their eyes as they watched him.

Lizzy fought to hide her smile.

*He's mine*, she thought. *And you cannot have him.*

The music lulled a moment, then as the band began to pick back up, a figure appeared at Darcy's shoulder.

"May I cut in?"

Etiquette would state that her husband allow this new partner an opportunity to give her a turn around the room, but as Lizzy looked up at the face of her new partner, she felt Darcy's grip tighten on her hand.

"I dare say not," Fitzwilliam said, making a point of controlling his volume.

Mr. Wickham's eyes went wide with feigned shock and offense. "Brother, you wound me."

"Be grateful I *don't* wound you."

Lizzy took Mr. Wickham's hand, shooting Fitzwilliam a loving glance. She didn't want Darcy to draw attention to himself as rude or draw the disapproval of their host, Lady Carrington. "It's fine, darling. It will be a short reel."

Darcy's lips pressed together until they were near white, but he graciously stood aside to let the two of them dance.

"My dear Lizzy, how lovely you look this evening."

Liz rolled her eyes. "I did not agree to dance with you for your company, Mr. Wickham. I simply wish to save my husband the embarrassment."

"Ah, come now. We both know Fitzy can take care of himself."

With that, Wickham shot a sideways glance back toward Darcy, a touch of feigned flirtation in the glance. Darcy huffed quietly, turning to take a glass of wine from a passing tray.

"Yes, yes we do," Lizzy said, and she let her words caring a foreboding tone.

Wickham wrapped his arm around her waist and yanked her closer. "Tell me, Mrs. Darcy, why haven't you invited me back to your bed?"

Lizzy stiffened, both shocked and angered that Wickham would mention the night the three of them enjoyed her bed together all those months before. "You scoundrel."

"Come now. I know you loved it."

"Whatever enjoyment I took from the experience is in the past, George," she said, making a point of using his first name.

He sighed. "Well, I think of it fondly."

Lizzy fought to keep her expression calm as Wickham's hand moved across her lower back. It was no more intimate than any random dance partner, but Wickham's comments brought all those memories flooding back – memories of Darcy and Wickham ravishing her in the dark like some common vagrants that broke into Pemberley to defile the mistress of the house.

Her sex began to ache with the thoughts. She'd mentioned to Fitzwilliam how much she loved the way it felt, but made a point of railing against the idea of Mr. Wickham being their third again.

"He was the logical choice for the purpose, Elizabeth. He's as wanton as any woman of ill repute, and however poorly he behaved toward your sister, I knew he'd deliver what you wanted, and that he'd not harm you. That was my greatest concern," Fitzwilliam had said. Whatever misgivings Darcy had toward Wickham, he knew him to be a kind lover.

Wickham's feet suddenly slowed, and Lizzy stopped with an almost stumble, only saved the embarrassment by Wickham's quick thinking.

If nothing else, she was grateful to him for that.

The sound of a silver spoon clinking against a glass drew everyone's attention to the stairs where Lady Carrington stood on the fourth step, gazing down at her gathered guests. She did not speak, choosing to remain silent behind her ornate black mask and high collar.

Her young footman did the speaking on her behalf.

"Ladies and Gentlemen, the Lady has an exciting announcement. A challenge for those so inclined. To enter the challenge, you must have a willing partner."

There was an excited tittering sound throughout the room. Elizabeth shot a glance over to Darcy. He met her gaze with a stern look of reproach.

Darcy wasn't one for games.

Still, Lizzy knew he'd do anything for her – even play a game.

She gave him an excited nod and he visibly sighed.

"All those who wish to take part, find your partner and

please join us, upstairs in the Lady's drawing room."

Wickham quickly released his hold on her and smiled, raising his eyebrows as he left her on the dance floor. Elizabeth turned to make her way through the milling crowd to her husband.

"Let's go," she said, hooking her arm at his elbow.

"Must we? I'm not in the mood for parlor games."

"Oh, come on, Mr. Darcy. Aren't you a little curious?"

"Not in the least."

She couldn't help but laugh. This was the side of Fitzwilliam that she'd first encountered all those ages ago – the proud, haughty version of him. She'd met the other versions of him over time – the saint, the clown, even the lustful beast. She knew that no matter how disinterested he was, he would feign such if she truly wished him to.

She tugged at his arm, and he exhaled with a barely audible groan, then led her up the stairs with several other curious couples.

The drawing room to Lady Carrington's chambers was filled with couples, each of them wearing their masquerade masks and clutching each other in curious excitement. There was a strange energy to the people around them, and as Lizzy waited to hear the challenge from Lady Carrington's footmen, she caught sight of several couples' hands reaching for each other in brazen acts of lustfulness, right there in the middle of the crowded room.

It shocked and excited her.

"Good. I'm glad to see so many willing participants," the Lady said. "Tonight, our challenge will be quite exciting, as each room will offer a different task for you to perform."

Darcy shot me a glare. "Must we do this? I'm not a work mule."

"Shhh!" Lizzy hissed. She wanted to hear what was in store. It seemed quite clear that the other couples knew what manner of challenge this would be, and if it made them so brazen with their intimacy, Lizzy was determined to be a part of it.

156

"There will be five separate rooms, each with a different challenge. Once you've performed the task in your first room, you will move on to the next. The couple – or person to successfully complete two tasks will move on to tomorrow evening's challenges."

Lizzy gave a giddy hop. What on earth would they be required to do?

With that, the Lady Carrington disappeared into her chambers, leaving her footman to take up the helm. "Ladies and gentlemen, if you would please move into the corridor."

The crowd did as they were told, the sound of music and dancing still echoing up the stairs from below. Lizzy clutched Darcy's elbow, patting him excitedly as they were led to another room. The footman directed up to three couples into each of the separate rooms along that hallway, informing each of them to await their challenge.

Lizzy entered their room - a library - with Darcy frowning at her side. A moment later, two other couples were brought into the space. Darcy visibly stiffened.

One of the two couples was Mr. Wickham and the widowed Mrs. Jenkins. Mrs. Jenkins was not much older than Lizzy and known for her carousing behavior in such circles since her husband's death. He'd left her a considerable fortune, making her quite content to remain unattached.

Elizabeth respected her, immensely.

"Well, Darcy. I didn't imagine you to be such a sport," Wickham said, but before Darcy could respond, the footman returned.

"Welcome to your first challenge."

Mrs. Jenkins gave a giddy wiggle, something Lizzy managed to keep inside.

"Gentlemen, this first challenge is for you. Ladies, if you would kindly take a seat on the edge of the table."

Elizabeth shot a glance toward Mrs. Jenkins and the second woman. Mrs. Jenkins had curly blonde hair, pinned up around her face in perfect ringlets, and her blue eyes were flirtatious and warm. The glance almost unnerved Lizzy.

*Was she flirting with me?* Lizzy thought.

All three women took their seats on the table with some trouble. Despite the blatant sexual nature of the evening, the Lizzy and the third woman tried to summit the table without showing their ankles. It was nearly impossible.

Mrs. Jenkins, on the other hand, threw her skirts aside and hopped right up.

"Well done, ladies. Now gentlemen, the Lady's challenge for the three of you is this – the first man to succeed in pleasuring his partner wins."

Darcy's eyes went wide with shock, but Wickham shot Mrs. Jenkins a naughty eyebrow wiggle.

"Now, the stipulation is this – you must use your mouths and hands, only."

Mrs. Jenkins gave a squeal of delight as Lizzy's face turned beet red. Darcy was glaring at her as Mr. Wickham quickly stripped off his red coat and took up a chair, pulling it to the edge of the table.

Lizzy watched Darcy come toward her, glaring at her as though he would have words were they alone, yet as Lizzy waited for him to straighten his spine and flatly refuse to perform for some footman's entertainment, Fitzwilliam took up a chair and pulled it over to the table.

*Oh my god*, she thought, and her sex ached with sudden overwhelming need.

"Come on, Titus. Don't be so -"

The woman to Lizzy's left frowned as her stout husband waved a hand toward her, refusing. The woman's head dropped and Lizzy felt pained on her behalf. The thought of being in a marriage that didn't fulfill you wholly was painful. As Fitzwilliam and Wickham took up their posts in preparation for the challenge, Lizzy leaned toward the third woman.

"I've no doubt you could find a better partner for the games downstairs."

The woman's eyes went wide, and she smiled.

"Yes, Madam. If you would like to take part and your current partner is unwilling, by all means, we have several volunteers at the ready."

"Really?" She said, and her excitement brought her voice up a whole octave.

"Of course," the footman said. "Come. I will introduce you to the gentlemen. Once you've settled on a new teammate, you can take part in the next round of the challenge."

The woman hopped up from the table with a new spring in her step and marched out of the room with the footman. Her stubborn husband scurried after her, his pompous demeanor crumbling before their eyes as he saw his wife happily skipping off to pretend he didn't exist.

*Serves him right*, she thought.

The footman returned a moment later, turning to glance at the nearby clock. "Well then, shall we begin?"

Wickham gave Mrs. Jenkins a beaming grin, quickly untying the waistband of her petticoats and pulling them down the length of her legs.

Lizzy was no longer wearing petticoats, having spent the early portion of the evening making love with her husband in their room. Still, Darcy lifted up her skirts, baring her thighs to cool air of the library.

"Now, remember gentlemen. You are to use your mouth and hands, only. The first to succeed, wins."

Wickham suddenly shot Darcy a sideways glance. "May the best man win, old chap."

"And go."

Wickham slammed his face between Mrs. Jenkins legs, leaving her to squeal in surprised response. The squeal quickly shifted to a moan.

Darcy shot Lizzy an angry glare, then grabbed hold of her hips, yanking her to the edge of the table before bringing his hot open mouth to her sex. Lizzy sighed as she felt the familiar warmth of his tongue slide between her wet lips and dart against her with practiced precision.

159

She gasped, reaching down to run her fingers through his dark hair.

Lizzy's head fell back, feeling his hot mouth moving against her. The sensation was so strange there in the grand space of the library, the cold surface of the table beneath her, cold against her bare backside. And above all else, another woman lying beside her, sighing and moaning as Mr. Wickham worked his own magic on her sex.

A moment later, Mrs. Jenkins' moans grew louder. Clearly, Mr. Wickham was doing something right.

As though in response, Darcy's fingers slid inside Lizzy, and she tensed, whimpering in surprise as he thrust into her. She was so wet, he slipped in up to his knuckles without pause, and he quickly begin drilling them into her, all while his tongue darted against her.

Lizzy gasped, unable to make a sound as he moved in her.

Suddenly, Mrs. Jenkins shrieked and Lizzy looked in time to see her grab hold of the edge of the table as Mr. Wickham's face moved between her legs – he was using his tongue to penetrate her.

"Dear God, George! Where did you learn that?" Mrs. Jenkins screamed, her head falling back.

The warmth of Darcy's mouth was gone a moment, and Lizzy looked to see him bring his fingers to his lips. A second later, his slick fingers were sliding down between her buttocks, leaving her ass slick. Before she could protest, Darcy's fingers slid back inside her sex, a third finger now sliding into her ass.

Lizzy gasped. "Oh god, yes!"

Despite his mood, Fitzwilliam smiled up at her before slamming his open mouth to her sex again, darting his tongue from side to side as he fingered her with such speed and tenacity that she feared she'd be shot off the table from the force of it. Lizzy grabbed onto his hair, pulling his mouth down onto her as her hips ground up into his face.

"Yes, my love! Yes! Just like that!"

As though in response, Mrs. Jenkins screamed anew as

160

Wickham tripled his efforts. It was as though the two men were at war with one another, their weapons of choice being the screams of their partners.

Lizzy curled into herself, watching her husband's stern brow as he devoured her with complete focus. She was close, the heat of release was rampant and only growing stronger with each passing second.

She was so close. Right there. "Yes! Please, yes!"

"Gentlemen!" The footman called, his tone one of announcement and authority. Both men rose from their work, their lips glistening. "As per the Lady's challenge, you are now required to switch."

"What?!" Fitzwilliam said, astounded and quite clearly offended. He rose from his seat to face the footman, running his hand over his mouth before he spoke. "What do you mean?"

"Switch partners."

Mrs. Jenkins and Wickham met each other's gaze and grinned. Lizzy watched her husband take a step toward the footman as though he wanted to fight him.

"Darling, it's -"

Lizzy screamed, the sudden sensation of a hot mouth on her sex driving her to new heights of need as Mr. Wickham's face dove between her legs. She felt her body convulsing as she tried to fight the sensation with sense. She watched her husband, trying to assure him that this wasn't her idea, but she didn't dare stop it.

It felt too good.

"Are you going to complete the challenge, sir?" The footman asked, fighting a smile as Lizzy grabbed Wickham by the hair, pulling him with every intention of causing pain. He growled against her, his fingers sliding inside.

She was helpless to it. She was going to come.

"I refuse. You have my apologies, madam," Darcy said, turning to Mrs. Jenkins. "But I cannot tend to you. I am sorry."

Mrs. Jenkins laughed. "That's quite alright, sir. I can take

161

care of myself."

Lizzy turned her eyes away as Mrs. Jenkins hands disappeared between her legs, pleasuring herself as she watched Mr. Wickham devour Lizzy. An instant later, Wickham's second hand moved to Mrs. Jenkins sex, and Lizzy could see his arm moving in rhythm as he fingered both women furiously.

Lizzy's body tensed and seized, her legs shaking over Wickham's head as her body convulsed. She moaned, throwing her head back as lithe, dainty fingers entwined with hers. Lizzy squeezed Mrs. Jenkins hand back as they both wailed in sudden overwhelming release.

Mr. Wickham's efforts slowed, but did not stop, letting both women ride the wave of release for a long moment. When he finally retreated from his work, standing up to wipe his hands on a handkerchief he pulled from his pocket, he took a moment to stare down Fitzwilliam, as though challenging him to some unspoken duel.

Darcy met the glare with a new tenacity that frightened Elizabeth. Had she angered her husband beyond reprieve?

How could she recover from it if she did? Because the crime wasn't that Mr. Wickham had done exactly as the challenge required – the crime was that Lizzy loved it. Every single second of it.

She felt tawdry and alive and free. Two men had just spent the better part of a quarter hour burying their handsome faces between her thighs.

There was a power to that knowledge that felt intoxicating.

"Congratulations, sir. You are the victor."

Wickham shot a wide grin at both ladies. "I couldn't have done it alone," he said.

Mrs. Jenkins laughed, heartily.

"That means the two of you are moving on to the next challenge," the footman said. He then turned to Darcy and Elizabeth. "I am sorry to say the two of you are dis -"

A sudden clanging of a bell startled everyone toward the

nearby wall. The footman moved with such speed, it was startling. He moved toward the wall, leaning into a small compartment over the liquor cabinet. He leaned in, as though the wall itself was whispering to him, then turned back to the waiting couples.

"Excuse me, I am mistaken. It seems the Lady wishes for both couples to advance to the next round."

Darcy shot Elizabeth and confused look, but Elizabeth simply glanced toward the wall, searching for the secret screen through which she was now sure the Lady Carrington was watching them.

"Follow me," the footman said, and both couples did as was commanded. Lizzy walked down the corridor, listening intently to the sounds coming from the closed doors as they passed. There were moans and cries of pleasure, and in some rooms, the accompanying sound of loud smacking – someone getting paddled, it sounded.

The footman stood aside to let them enter a new room. Unlike before, this room had a four-poster bed on the far wall. Lizzy felt a sudden gush of warmth between her legs. She wanted this, badly.

Whatever it was.

"Gentlemen, if you'd be so kind."

With that, the footman summoned two new figures in from the hall. These were not other gentlemen from the party downstairs. These were Lady Carrington's private staff, and each of them had clearly been hired for reasons other than their command of a carriage.

The two footmen were in their twenties, wearing breeches and suspenders and nothing else, their smooth bare chests declaring their purpose quite clearly. Mrs. Jenkins gave a hoot of approval, summoning one of the two men to her with a come-hither gesture.

The two men smiled and approached her.

Darcy stood near the bed, Mr. Wickham at the center of the room. The footman stood by the door, silent. Everyone waited for him to speak.

There was a soft click in the far wall of the room, and Lizzy glanced toward the paintings and pictures hanging there. She was certain their host had taken up post to watch, again.

"This new challenge," the footman started, taking his time for full effect. "- is for you, ladies."

Lizzy swallowed. Mrs. Jenkins giggled, running her fingers alone the chiseled jaw of one of her new friends.

"What is it?" Lizzy asked, taking a cautious step toward the footman. She was determined to reclaim the upper in this challenge, having lost their edge to a far more wanton Mr. Wickham.

"Ladies, you are required to pleasure two men – at once."

Mrs. Jenkins laughed, giddily.

"And the one who finishes first wins?" Lizzy asked, anxious to know the parameters of this new challenge. Was this challenge going to change halfway through again, leaving her unable to compete with the completely unattached Mrs. Jenkins?

"No, not the first. The most imaginative," the footman said, smiling, before shooting a glance toward the far wall.

The Lady was definitely watching.

Lizzy swallowed, turning back to face her clearly flustered husband. Would he be willing to take part or was he too furious to ever consider touching her again?

It was clear Mrs. Jenkins interests were fully ensconced in the two new men as she dropped to her knees there on the floor between them, untying their breeches to release their cocks from within. Both men were hard and ready – and both of considerable size. Mrs. Jenkins was devouring them heartily a moment later, her wicked laughter growing quiet with the work.

Lizzy grew nervous. She wanted to take part – wanted to know what lay waiting at the end of this challenge, but she couldn't very well compete without her husband – and Mr. Wickham.

She took a deep breath, ready to speak and accept

whatever response her husband might offer.

"What do you say, George?"

Lizzy startled, watching Fitzwilliam turn to his old friend.

"Will you help me punish my willful wife?"

Mr. Wickham's grin was beaming as her gave a quick nod, then turned on Lizzy, moving toward her.

"God, I thought you'd never ask."

Lizzy fought the urge to scream and giggle at the same time. She was terrified and desperate to feel them both – the way she had before. She shot a glance toward Mrs. Jenkins, who now held both men's cocks in her hands, taking turns sucking each of them deeply. The men were watching her intently when their heads weren't falling back in ecstasy.

Fitzwilliam slumped back onto the bed as Wickham took Lizzy toward the bed. He was quickly behind her, his hands working on the ties of her dress. She felt his body moving up behind her, letting her feel his hardness pressed to her backside as he pushed her onto the bed. Lizzy caught herself, planting a hand on both sides of her husband. Then she quickly moved to untie his breeches.

Darcy moved to help her, but she swatted his hands away.

"No, the challenge is that I please you. Don't help."

Despite the frustration of the evening, Fitzwilliam smiled wide at her. The smile took a wicked turn as his cock sprung from beneath the fabric of his trousers.

Lizzy moved quickly, taking him in her mouth as Wickham's hand slid up between her legs. She reached back to grab hold of him, stroking and caressing the front of his trousers as his cock grew throbbing and rigid beneath.

*Please both*, she thought. *To meet the challenge, please both.*

She knew exactly how she intended to do that, but it had been so long since the last time she'd been taken like that, she was cautious, to say the least. Still, she was sure that would be a challenge winning sexual exploit.

The ties of her dress were free, and Lizzy pulled the garment down, leaving her in her stays and nothing else. She climbed atop the bed, straddling over her husband and slid

165

down onto his cock without preamble.

Darcy gasped, clearly shocked by the lustful attack of his newly dominant wife. Despite his usual preference for control, he seemed to be enjoying this thoroughly.

Lizzy moved slowly at first, rising up and down over him as he gripped her by the hips.

"Get up here," Lizzy said, shooting an impatient look at Mr. Wickham.

He instantly did as he was told, coming to kneel on the bed. She grabbed hold of his cock and gave a gentle, yet forceful pull, leading him to where she wanted him to be. He rose to his feet on the bed beside her, and Lizzy took Mr. Wickham's generous cock in her mouth. She held one hand on Darcy's stomach to brace herself, the other was gripping Wickham, sliding up and down the shaft as her saliva left him slick with each passing second. She doubled her pace, bouncing on Darcy and trying to maintain her hold of Wickham. It was growing more and more difficult.

Frustration won, and Lizzy released her hold on Wickham, lifted herself from atop her husband, and turned herself around on the bed before straddling Darcy again.

"Oh, I think I might enjoy this view," he said as she slid back down onto his cock, her whole body now turned away from him.

Fitzwilliam gripped her hips and thrust up into her, letting her take hold of Mr. Wickham with both hands. As Darcy plunged up into her, she whimpered, fighting to keep her focus as Darcy plundered her insides from below.

Mrs. Jenkins hooted suddenly from across the room. Apparently, she'd caught sight of what Lizzy was doing and wholly approved. The thought of being watched – of causing other men and women lustful thoughts was enough to send her over the edge alone, but she had to focus.

It was not about her, this time.

Lizzy sucked at Mr. Wickham with abandon, taking him as deeply as she could as he groaned and whispered what a good girl she was. All the while, Darcy was plunging up into her, the force of which made it clear he was happy to take out his frustrations on her body.

It felt wonderful.

Suddenly, view of Mrs. Jenkins distracted Lizzy from her work. Her gentlemen had moved to the floor, and she was now pleasing them in a similar manner to Lizzy.

She felt a moment's panic despite her constant cries of need.

*It's not about speed,* she thought. *It's not who pleases them first, it's who pleases them best.*

It was time. She had to demand what she wanted now. If there was even a chance of Mrs. Jenkins having the same notion and acting on it first, Lizzy would look like she was simply following her lead.

And Mrs. Jenkins was wanton enough to come up with the idea herself, Lizzy was she.

"Take me," Lizzy whispered. "The way you did before."

"But of course, madam," Mr. Wickham said, dropping to his knees on the bed before.

"No."

They both startled, turning to look at Darcy as he suddenly stopped thrusting into her.

He lifted her off his cock and pulled her around. "George, you're the back-door man this time."

"Really?" Wickham said, and it was with relish as much as surprise.

"Wait," Lizzy said, suddenly nervous. Darcy had taken her that way before, and she'd learned to trust his gentleness enough to let him have her that way often. Wickham, she feared, might not know how to do it as gently – might not make it feel as good as her husband could.

"It's alright, love. He knows what to do," Darcy said, pulling her onto him again.

Lizzy gasped as Darcy pushed his cock up inside her, filling her to the point of almost pain. He glared up at her, a wicked smirk playing at the corner of his lips as he pulled her down onto his chest, forcing her to present her ass to

167

the waiting Mr. Wickham.

Darcy brought his strong arms around her and held her there, pinned to him.

"Come on, Georgie. Show her how it's done."

Darcy pushed himself up into her as Wickham's slick fingers found her ass and began to tease inside. Lizzy flinched at first, frightened of how Wickham's ways might feel. Yet, his fingers were lithe and gentle, slipping into her with expert hands. After a moment of teasing, he plunged two fingers into her, burying them wholly. He pushed with enough force to press her down onto Darcy's throbbing cock, drawing a moan she hadn't expected.

Fitzwilliam grabbed her by the hair, turning her face so he could whisper in her ear. "You want him, don't you? Want him to ravish you with me?"

She whimpered, feeling him pulse into her, as though waiting for the wrong answer so he could fuck her. She nodded.

"I know you do."

Wickham suddenly slid three fingers inside her, then four, his speed of approach growing faster with each second. He filled her ass, letting his fingers stretch her and make her ready for him.

With a sudden burst of movement, he began fingering her ass, spitting onto his hand as he pounded into her knuckles deep.

She cried out, begging him, for what she couldn't decide.

Suddenly, Darcy reached behind her, grinning wickedly as his fingers joined Mr. Wickham's, sliding in just as much as he could to let her feel their thickness.

She opened her mouth to cry out, but no sound came.

She was ready. She wanted to feel them both fucking her.

"Do it! Do it now," she begged, reached back to open herself to him.

"Good lord, you're going to make me come before I even begin," he said. Then a second later, as Darcy lay back onto the mattress, Lizzy felt the smooth slick head of Wickham's

168

cock sliding between her buttocks. She clung to her husband, holding her breath as Wickham teased the head of his cock into her, then retreated. He did it again, a little deeper this time, as Darcy waiting beneath her, poised to attack.

"Oh, your ass is like velvet, Elizabeth. Our Fitzwilliam is a lucky man," Wickham said, and with each word he slowly slid his cock deeper until his balls were pressed to her thighs.

Lizzy's head was back, her mouth open wide as she felt the two men fill her, her body shuddering in the wake of it. Once they were both buried inside, she finally took a breath.

Her husband moved first, thrusting up into her as he watched her face for response. She gasped, clutching him. He took that response as permission and thrust again.

This time, he didn't pause, planting himself into the mattress and pounding up inside her. She winced with each thrust, feeling his cock slam into her inside, but before she could protest, the sudden movement from behind stilled all thoughts.

Wickham took hold of her hips and began to drill up into her ass from behind, humming his approval as he did. His hands moved from her hips to her ass, squeezing her buttocks and opened her to him as he slid deeper and deeper, slamming his cock into her ass.

She braced herself on the mattress, feeling both men thrust in and out of her, their cocks moving in tandem at one moment, then in alternating thrusts at another. She found herself moaning loudly, grinding her hips onto her husband as Wickham fucked her ass. She reached back, entwining her fingers with his as he opened her ass to him.

"Harder, George. Make her take it."

Wickham chuckled and doubled his efforts as Lizzy screamed, collapsing down onto Darcy's chest. Their cocks continued to annihilate her, leaving her helpless in their wake as she fought to simply hold on.

Wickham shifted over her, pressing her down onto Darcy as he fucked her from above. The sensation was overwhelming, and with the friction of her husband's belly beneath her, she felt that familiar heat rising in her sex. She was going to come so hard.

She clutched Fitzwilliam, moaning and begging them not to stop as Wickham let his weight hold her down and his cock fill her willing ass.

Suddenly, there was a beautiful face just before her own, and before Lizzy could speak, Mrs. Jenkins grabbed Lizzy's face in her hands, and kissed her.

The woman's tongue darted into her mouth, teasing her now in such a way that Elizabeth lost all control, she wailed into the woman's mouth, her body bucking and convulsing between the two feverish men.

Darcy and Wickham's grunts had grown desperate and loud with the sudden appearance of Mrs. Jenkins, and it was clear that seeing Lizzy touched that way had done something to them as well.

Wickham pounded deeper, his thrusts growing sporadic and slow. A moment later, Lizzy felt him spill his hot seed in her ass.

Wickham thrust twice more, slowing his movement as Darcy plunged up into her from below, his breath growing hoarse and quick. Mrs. Jenkins grabbed Lizzy by the hair, pulling her upward just enough to grab Lizzy's breast in her hand as she kissed her. Lizzy's body seized anew, and she whimpered in shock and desperation. She was coming again, twice as hard.

She clutched her husband, pulling at him as Mrs. Jenkins kissed her. Darcy seemed to read the message and fought to continue thrusting, despite his own seed spilling deep inside her.

Mrs. Jenkins moved quickly, planting her mouth over Lizzy's breast, sucking at her nipple with an expert tongue. Lizzy threw her head back and screamed, the force of her release pouring warm over Darcy's cock.

He groaned, gripping her by the hips as he pulled her down onto him twice more, then stopped, his grip going slack.

Mrs. Jenkins released her hold on Lizzy's breast and rose to look Lizzy in the eye. She gave Lizzy one last kiss, then giggled softly, turning to roll back off the bed.

Wickham pulled from inside her, collapsing there on the mattress as Darcy and Lizzy remained as one, his cock throbbing and retreating from inside her, slowly.

Lizzy lay there with her eyes closed for a long moment, listening to their rapid breathing slow with each passing moment. Finally, after what seemed like ages, a quiet click reminded her of where she was. She turned to look at the far wall, still unsure of where the Lady Carrington could be watching from.

The footman appeared in her view, leaning into one of the paintings as though it might tell him a secret. A moment later, he turned back to the room, and Lizzy caught view of him adjusting himself under the fabric of his trousers.

Clearly, their display had affected even him. She wondered if the Lady would give him release as reward for his work this evening.

"Congratulations. You've all successfully passed this portion of the challenge."

Lizzy heard Mrs. Jenkins giggle and hop up and down somewhere in the room.

"The Lady bids you all a fine and restful evening, and suggests you have a hearty breakfast in the morning. The next challenge will require an equal amount of energy from the four of you."

With that, the soft click sounded again, announcing the Lady Carrington was no longer partaking in their display.

Wickham rose from the bed, crossing the room to Mrs. Jenkins for a newly stirred flirtation.

"I will see the two of you tomorrow, then?" Wickham said, offering a tip of an imaginary hat before scooping an arm around Mrs. Jenkins' waist and marching out of the room with her.

Fitzwilliam helped Lizzy dress, the footmen following

Mrs. Jenkins and Wickham out into the house.

For a moment, this aftermath felt almost anti-climactic. What was the grand prize, she wondered? But then she tried to stand, and her legs gave way beneath her.

Yes, there was nothing anti-climactic about her evening.

She thought of Mrs. Jenkins appearing at her side, of the way she tasted like Cognac and smelled of lavender. Somehow, despite having never viewed a woman in such a way, Lizzy wondered whether Mrs. Jenkins was as fond of women as she was of men – and what being with a woman would feel like.

"Are you recovered, darling?"

Lizzy nodded, feeling the ties of her dress tighten as Darcy looped them into a bow at her back. "I am."

"Good. Shall we to bed, then?"

Lizzy nodded, letting Darcy put an arm around her to help her walk across the room.

They made their way out into the hallway, the neighboring rooms still echoing with the sounds of pleasure and lust and punishment. Lizzy smiled. Were she any less exhausted, she might want to explore the adventures in other rooms.

Darcy opened their bedroom door for her, waiting for her to enter. She stepped inside, instantly turning her back to him again for him to release her from her dress for bed.

He did so without being asked.

Lizzy leaned her weight back onto him, the exhaustion creeping over her like a storm cloud. "Fitzwilliam."

"Yes, Elizabeth?"

She took a breath, her eyes closing as she felt the solid warmth of his body behind her. "Why did you let Wickham have me that way?"

Her dress fell from her shoulders to the floor at her feet. She shuddered against the cold air. Before she could move, she yelped as Darcy scooped her up in his arms and carried her to the bed. He let her pull the blankets back before setting her down. Then he lowered himself over her there, bringing his nose close to hers.

"Well, I had a realization after last time that if we were to suddenly be blessed with a child -"

She inhaled, sharply.

"- I would always wonder if the babe was mine, or Wickham's."

Lizzy grabbed his face in her hands and pulled him to her, kissing him.

He let his weight fall on her.

"Then I understand," she said.

She took hold of his hand, pulling him into the bed as she turned onto her side. He obliged, crawling under the covers beside her. She drew his arm around her middle, shimmying her backside into him as she closed her eyes.

She smiled, letting the exhaustion take hold.

"I can't wait for tomorrow," she said. Then she was sound asleep.

# CHAPTER FOURTEEN

## *An Unlikely Quartet*

---

The afternoon had gone as was to be expected. Walks on the grounds, luncheon with fellow guests of the Lady Carrington, even a little tawdry conversation found its way into the day's activities.

Elizabeth overheard a couple of the younger women gossiping about their exploits the previous night. They'd spent the evening on the East wing, and much as Lydia professed, many a young, single woman had found themselves a generous benefactor in the upstairs of the East Wing during the Lady Carrington's Springtime Celebration.

Elizabeth wondered if Lydia had done so, as well.

She didn't dare attempt to find her sister to inquire.

She was rather content in the knowledge that her sisters Lydia and Mary were safely tucked away in their rooms on the East wing of the house. The east wing was for single ladies and couples who, as rumor had it, spent their evening room hopping – wives and husbands alike sneaking off to enjoy the night with their mistresses and lovers.

She didn't dare wonder how Mary was fairing.

Fitzwilliam was rather grim throughout the afternoon, putting on pleasantries when he was directly addressed, but otherwise, he was rather difficult to tolerate for Lizzy.

Still, when the evening feast was over and it was time to retire upstairs, Mr. Darcy marched ahead of Elizabeth like a man with purpose.

"Join me in the upper parlor for your challenge," the Lady Carrington requested.

Lizzy was beside herself with excitement. Her body had been tingly and warm throughout their walks on the grounds, and though Fitzwilliam was keen to remain grumpy and disinterested, he'd rather enjoyed it when Lizzy attacked him behind the boathouse, demanding he allow her to please him with her mouth.

The dower glare faded then, certainly. Of course, it settled right back in place thereafter.

*Stubborn mule*, she thought.

Elizabeth and Fitzwilliam made their way down the hall to the Lady's parlor at precisely eight. Elizabeth didn't dare miss any of the activities.

The room was as palatial as any other portion of the house, with settees of silk brocade fabric and club chairs to match. She glanced to the small screen in the wall, wondering if the Lady Carrington might already be watching them.

"I see the Darcy's are rather punctual, aren't they?"

Elizabeth turned to find, Mrs. Jenkins, the woman from the night before entering, George Wickham close on her heels.

"But of course," Wickham replied. "Fitzwilliam likes to be first in almost everything."

Fitzwilliam rolled his eyes, but quickly straightened as the Lady Carrington entered the room, a new, handsome gentleman on her arm.

"Good evening to you all," she said, some of the only words Elizabeth had ever heard directly from her lips.

The gray-haired woman nodded to the group, then turned with a whoosh of her skirts back into the hallway. Her groom remained with them, smiling a wicked grin that made Elizabeth's heart race.

It was about to begin.

"The Lady rather enjoyed your exploits last evening. She has decided that she would rather like to see something similar tonight -"

Elizabeth felt a shudder run down her spine as Mr. Wickham shot her a sideways glance, the corners of his mouth creeping upward.

"- however. She has requested that the three of you, as it was last night, become the four of you."

"Pardon?" Fitzwilliam said, his voice low and almost foreboding.

"Your challenge this evening is to enjoy each other – all of you. Ladies, you are charged with the pleasure of these two men. Gentlemen, the ladies pleasure is your responsibility as well. The contents of the trunk are at your disposal. You may engage them in any way you see fit – in tandem or otherwise, but you must all be either receiving pleasure or giving it, at all times. The more imaginative, the better. I will lead you to your room?"

Elizabeth swallowed, glancing to Mrs. Jenkins. She was grinning with a cocked eyebrow.

Wickham gave the trunk a kick, but didn't open it. "Let's save that surprise for once we're underway, shall we?"

Elizabeth averted her eyes, a shiver running down between her legs as she stepped out into the hallway to follow the groom. Fitzwilliam was beside her, his back stiff and his shoulders squared. If she didn't know any better, she might think he was angry, or averse to the events that were about to take place, but as soon as they entered the massive bedroom, Fitzwilliam was tearing his jacket down the length of his arms and pulling the cravat from his throat.

He would be wasting no time tonight, it seemed.

Elizabeth stood aside as the groom bowed by the doorway, then took his leave. Before she could contemplate what was expected of them, she caught sight of Mr. Wickham tugging at his own collar, giving her a meaningful look. She turned away. She didn't even dare begin to undress. She'd done this now more than once, and as the sound of a screen shifting to the sound announced the Lady Carrington watching on with expectation, she knew it was time to throw caution to the wind and explore her basest needs and desires.

Still, something about the way Mrs. Jenkins looked at her made her stomach flit into her throat.

Did she want to be touched by the beautiful and fearless Mrs. Jenkins. Could she possibly enjoy a woman the way she so enjoyed her husband?

And what would he think of her if she could?

"After you, Mrs. Jenkins," Mr. Wickham said, now stripped down to his drawers. She was in little more than a chemise now.

Mrs. Jenkins smiled. "Please, do call me Clara."

Elizabeth stood at the corner of the room, still fully clothed as Fitzwilliam turned to her with a cocked brow. "Are you not taking part? You are, after all, the whole reason we're here."

He held a hand out to her, and that glower he'd harbored all day seemed to evaporate.

Elizabeth felt a tension in her chest melt. He hadn't been angry or displeased with their evening's plans, he simply didn't want to interact with any of Lady Carrington's other guests.

She remembered the dower look he'd harbored the very night they met and couldn't help but smile to remember. Then, with her heart racing like mad, she took his hand and let him lead her toward the bed where Mrs. Jenkins and George Wickham were already in a tangled mess of limbs, kissing each other with contented hums and giggles of excitement as he slipped his hand up under her chemise.

Lizzy froze by the side of the bed, watching the two of them there. Fitzwilliam came to stand behind her, his hands sliding up beneath her skirts to caress her thighs. She wanted to give in to the sensation, but her nerves were unrelenting. She'd read the scenes in Fanny's book of women enjoying each other, and though it seemed foreign and torrid, somehow she'd found herself just as aroused in the reading of those scenes as she had many others.

"Come on, darling. I won't bite – you."

She gave George a look, then sank her teeth into his shoulder. He grinned, grabbing her and pinning her down onto the mattress.

Elizabeth felt the buttons of her dress coming loose at her back, and she could feel Fitzwilliam's fingers sliding down the length of her spine. It felt soothing and familiar, but the laughter of the second woman was so foreign and strange.

"Lady and gentleman, I do believe I am going to need your aide, here," Fitzwilliam said, drawing the attention of both Wickham and Clara.

They grinned up at her, moving across the bed to come closer.

Elizabeth yelped, softly, and froze. George took hold of her face and kissed her neck as Clara took the ends of her sleeves and pulled her dress down the front of her, leaving her in little more than corset and shift. Darcy was making quick work of the ties at her back, and before Elizabeth could speak, Clara's hands cupped her under the breasts, squeezing her gently as Wickham watched.

"Oh, I'm going to enjoy this," he said, slumping back on the bed as though the two women had been provided for his entertainment.

A second later, the corset was free, and Fitzwilliam pulled it aside, tossing it onto to floor. Without another word, Lizzy felt his hands on her, forcing her shoulders down toward the mattress.

"Come on, then, George. Service the lady."

George sat up on the bed. "But I was so enjoying the view."

Without a word, George grabbed Clara about the waist and pulled her toward him. "It seems Elizabeth is a bit shy, this evening, Fitzy."

"Yes. I've observed."

178

George pulled Clara back onto his lap, pulling her to lay against his chest as he sprawled out before Elizabeth. "There you are, Clara. Ride me like a good girl, would you?"

She smiled, throwing one of her legs over Mr. Wickham as she turned to face Lizzy. Darcy was behind her now, the head of his cock pressing against her thigh as his hands slid up between her legs. She glanced over her shoulder toward the screen, scolding herself for her shyness.

Darcy grabbed her by the hair, pulling her to her full height again as Clara and Wickham moved closer to the edge of the bed. Clara's eyes closed and she sighed as she lowered herself down onto Wickham. Elizabeth gasped, realizing she was now watching Clara ride Wickham's cock.

She felt a surge of warmth between her legs and was overwhelmed with need.

Fitzwilliam cooed to her as his fingers slid up between her legs, finding the wetness there with a groan of relish. "She may be shy, but her body certainly isn't."

George made some comment from beneath Clara, but Elizabeth couldn't make it out as Clara reached for her, grabbing her by the hair and pulled her forward. Before Elizabeth could prepare, Clara's mouth was on hers, kissing her deeply.

Elizabeth whimpered in surprise, but she didn't pull away. Clara's lips were soft and smooth, and her tongue was more focused than Darcy's, flitting against hers and teasing her upper lip.

Darcy moved up behind her then, pressing the head of his cock between her thighs. She felt him bending her forward into Clara. An instant later, the head of Fitzwilliam's cock slid inside her, unrelenting against the wetness of her arousal. He drove wholly inside, buried to the hilt as his hips pushed her forward into Clara.

Suddenly, there was a loud tearing sound, and Elizabeth's arms jerked back as Darcy tore open her shift, baring her breasts to the cool air. Clara laughed as she fell backward onto Wickham's chest, Elizabeth now pushed over her, planting her hands into the mattress to hold herself up.

Clara grabbed her arm and pulled it from beneath her, knocking Elizabeth off balance. She fell, her bare breasts pressed to Clara's as both men held them pinned against each other.

The touch of this woman's bare skin against hers felt strange, but delicious, and before Elizabeth could show her appreciation, Clara kissed her again, and slid her hand down between Elizabeth's legs.

Lizzy screamed, but Clara had her fingers wrenched into Lizzy's hair, and she held her there, kissing her deeply as her fingers played between Lizzy's legs. Unlike the men, whose rough touch could sometimes be too much, Clara's fingers moved with precision, pressing against Lizzy and moving from side to side with intense speed.

Lizzy's mouth opened and she wailed as the sensation grew in intensity, her body responding to her husband's pounding cock and this beautiful woman's fingers.

Clara slowed her movement, letting her fingers move with Darcy's rhythm. Lizzy held her breath, her head held back by Clara's other hand still holding her hair. A faint glistening of sweat was gathering at Clara's collarbone and throat as she strained to hold herself upright despite both Lizzy and Wickham's bodies moving against her.

Darcy shoved his hips into Elizabeth, pressing both her and Clara down. Then he thrust hard, deliberately slamming his body into hers, pushing her down onto Clara so that the four of them formed one undulating shape of skin and sighs.

Elizabeth could feel Clara's body beneath her, feel her thigh pressed between Clara's legs, grinding against her as Wickham's legs strived beneath. Clara gasped, still moving her fingers between Elizabeth's legs despite her hand's movement being stifled by the weight of her body.

"Fitz! I've an idea," Wickham said.

Darcy groaned, but moved behind her, pulling her away from the bed and leaving Clara's body bared, her legs splayed wide apart as he pulled Lizzy away. She gasped as Wickham gave two more thrusts, watching as his rigid and flushed cock disappeared into Clara's sex, moving inside her for Lizzy to watch.

The image burned into her mind and she ached for release.

Wickham moved Clara to the end of the bed, and without a word, gestured to Fitzwilliam. It was at moments like this that Lizzy felt painfully inexperienced, and almost jealous of the wildness her husband once engaged in with other women.

Still, there was no time to contemplate this at length, because Fitzwilliam was quickly moving her toward the bed. He lay back on the mattress, his shoulders propped up by the pillows as he pulled her by the hips onto the bed. She tried to climb atop him, but he gripped her roughly, turning her around to face Wickham and Clara at the end of the bed. He grabbed her, pulling her onto him, making her straddle his hips as he pulled the shift up over her head. Lizzy was as naked as Clara now, and she felt utterly exposed.

That feeling was tripled as Darcy slid up into her, wrapped his arms around her waist and pulled her back onto his chest.

"You're going to love this, you tawdry thing, you," he said, whispering into her ear.

With another swift move of his legs, he kicked her feet out before them, grabbing her legs and holding them wide open over her.

As Fitzwilliam moved her into this glaringly open position, Wickham took up his post behind Clara, pounding her from behind as her hair fell in loose tendrils across her face. She was grinning, wickedly, pushing herself back into him with each thrust.

"Lizzy's new to this, Clara dear. Can you show her exactly what we were thinking?" Wickham asked, stilling his thrusts for a moment as Clara flipped her hair out of her face.

"Oh, I thought you'd never ask," she said, and with a wild

look in her eyes, she lunged away from Wickham and devoured Lizzy's sex, her hot open mouth moving against Lizzy like some wild animal.

Lizzy screamed, trying to move away from this overwhelming sensation as Fitzwilliam's cock slid up into her over and over again. He grabbed her arms, pulling her down onto his chest as he forced her to lift her legs higher. Clara's soft hands found the inside of Lizzy's thighs and pinned them open to her as her mouth moved against Lizzy, her tongue darting from side to side, playing Lizzy's most sensitive parts with the precision that only came from a woman who knew how to please how own body.

Darcy groaned, holding Lizzy in such a way that he could watch what was happening himself. He reached down, curling his fingers in Clara's hair and pressed her head down into Lizzy's sex.

"That's right, Clara. Show her what we do to timid little things like her."

Lizzy screamed as Darcy's thrusts doubled in force.

Suddenly, Wickham moved up behind Clara again, and as he reached down to his cock, Lizzy could feel Clara moaning against her sex. An instant later, Wickham was thrusting into Clara from behind, shoving her into Lizzy with each movement of his hips.

Lizzy cried out, helpless to the sensation, but unable to take her eyes off of Clara's face, watching the wild woman's movements. She looked as though relished every second of it, and Lizzy felt her sex growing hotter and hotter with each passing instant.

Suddenly, Wickham and Darcy both reached for her, pressing her head down against Lizzy as Wickham thrust home with furious force. They were both working to male Clara's pressure ever stronger, and soon the sensation of any part of Clara's mouth was grinding against Lizzy's sex in the rhythm of their thrusts, over and over again, unrelenting and hot and feverish.

Lizzy's head fell back as her own fingers found their way

into Clara's hair, and in a soundless scream, Lizzy's body shuddered there, helpless against the sensation.

She could feel Clara laughing softly between her legs.

"That's a good girl," Darcy whispered. "I think she deserves a reward for that, don't you two?"

Wickham relented, and Clara rose to her knees, wiping her mouth and brushing her hair out of her face as she caught her breath. Darcy moved beneath Lizzy, letting her fall onto the mattress as he stood up. Before she could even take a breath, Clara was on her, her lips pressed to Lizzy's kissing her deeply as her fingers found her sex and moved furiously, drawing a wild scream from deep in Lizzy's throat as the pique of sensation doubled, tripled, then flooded through Lizzy's belly, drawing an unending wail as Clara's fingers didn't cease their movement.

"Please! No more," Lizzy begged, breathless as her body melted against Clara's.

Clara smiled wide, the wickedest smile Lizzy had ever seen, and it made her sex flush all over again.

"That's how it's done, lads. Two of you could use a lesson," Clara said, licking her fingers for them to see.

Lizzy fought to catch her breath, her body throbbing from head to toe. She'd felt release before, but nothing like that – nothing even close to that.

She met Clara's gaze for an instant and had to avert her eyes for fear she might betray her lust.

Clara smiled. "Don't worry, love. I'll let your dear Fitzy know how it's done."

"Well, well, well. Look what we have here," Mr. Wickham said from halfway across the room. He was standing over the trunk, its lid open to display what was inside. Lizzy was unable to catch sight of anything, but Clara quickly moved across the bed, rushing across the room to join Wickham at the trunk.

Darcy was standing by the side of the bed, watching Lizzy. He had a dark look in his eyes, but he was smiling. It was clear he'd liked seeing her at the mercy of Clara.

Lizzy was sure he simply like seeing her at mercy.

"Oh, Elizabeth. Oh, we're going to enjoy this," Clara said.

Lizzy sat up on the bed as Wickham and Clara moved back toward the bed. She caught sight of something huge and black, but Darcy grabbed her ankles and pulled her toward the edge of the bed before she could catch sight.

In an instant, Wickham was at the other edge of the bed, grabbing hold of her wrists. She was now splayed across the mattress, her bare body helpless to her three partners.

Clara appeared beside Darcy holding a long, thick shape made of smooth black leather. Lizzy squealed as Clara spit oil onto one end of the massive snake-like this.

She grinned down at Lizzy as she climbed onto the bed beside her. "I cannot wait to see how much you enjoy this."

Then, Clara held to long shape before Lizzy so she could see her fate. It was a massive double-edged phallus, bending at its center in a smooth curve as the leather buckled and groaned against the effort.

Clara moved down to Lizzy's hip as Darcy held her legs apart.

Lizzy screamed, throwing her head back as she closed her eyes, she was so desperately aroused, but the excitement was coupled with shame and embarrassment. How could she let her husband see her so affected and so touched?

The head of the black phallus was slick and smooth as Clara slid it against Lizzy's sex. She squealed, jerking against her husband's grip, pulling at Wickham's hold on her wrists.

"Come now, darling. Be a good girl. You are being watched, after all."

Darcy's voice came with such sickly-sweet relish that it sent a shudder down her spine. He was enjoying this. He was basking in the sight of her being displayed and handled by this other woman, and he loved it.

The phallus slid inside her, filling her wholly as Clara pushed it deeper, pushing it in and out slowly as she drove it as far as her body could take it. Once it was as deep as it could go, Clara gripped the object and made quick work of thrusting it in and out of her as she screamed.

Wickham released his hold on one of her wrists and began stroking himself. "Good god, Fitz. I'm not sure I can take much more of this. What a wife you have there."

Fitzwilliam grinned. "Don't worry. We'll show her just how far this goes."

Clara stopped thrusting the phallus into her, and quickly moved over Lizzy as Wickham grabbed Lizzy's ankles and pulled them upward, leaving her ass high in the air. Without word, Clara straddled over Lizzy's raised legs, pinning them down against Lizzy's stomach as she turned the other end of the long phallus upward. Then as Lizzy watched on in shock and need, Clara slid the other cock headed end of the double-edged phallus up into her sex, then lowered her body down onto Lizzy until the other end was wholly buried up inside her and their sexes pressed against one another, drilling the hard, leather-bound cocks deeper into each of them.

"Oh, god," Clara cried. "This is going to be endlessly fun."

Then, Clara wriggled herself down onto Lizzy, taking hold of Lizzy's ankles, pushing them forward, and without further preamble, proceeded to bounce up and down on Lizzy.

Lizzy screamed, the leather cock buried as deep as it would do inside her sex, but with each bounce, Clara's sex slid up her end of the phallus, letting Lizzy see where her body swallowed it up, then she dropped back down, not only taking her full end inside herself, but slamming the other one deeper into Lizzy.

Wickham appeared at her shoulders, his knees parted just over her as he grabbed her ankles and pulled her legs further upward, giving Clara better ground to bounce up and down, pounding her own sex down into Lizzy's and the cocks deeper and deeper.

Lizzy could barely breathe. The sensation was enough to end her, but furthermore, the visual of Clara's freely lustful display, the sight of the phallus buried inside her over and over as Wickham knelt over her, watching with his cock in his hands.

Clara continued to ride the phallus, pounding it into Lizzy's sex until she could barely breathe.

"Serve your bloody purpose, Georgie."

Lizzy turned to find Darcy coming around the bed just as Wickham laughed at his friend's demand.

"Don't mind if I do," he said. Then with that, Wickham dropped onto the mattress, his face coming close to where Lizzy and Clara's bodies met. Lizzy shrieked as Clara leaned back from her post, propping herself back on her hands as she leaned away from Lizzy, baring their most sensitive parts to Wickham searching mouth.

Lizzy gasped as Clara, holding her hips up from the bed, rocked her body into Lizzy's with a constant rhythm as Mr. Wickham's mouth found Lizzy's sex. His tongue moved against her, sucking and lapping at her as the phallus drilled deeper. Then he turned his head and bestowed the same lavish treatment on Clara. She moaned, gripping him by the hair as she thrust her hips onto his face, tugging his hair hard as she ground her sex onto his mouth, moving the phallus in Lizzy with every twitch and shake.

Lizzy reached up toward her husband, curling her fingers against the skin of his bare thigh. He took hold of her hand and moved it, wrapping her fingers around his rigid cock which now hovered, throbbing, just inches from her lips.

She gasped, stroking him as Wickham's mouth returned to her sex. She hummed her appreciation, opening her mouth to invite her husband.

Yet, he didn't move closer to her. He simply held his hand over hers, making her stroke him in tandem with Clara's slower thrusts.

"You love this, don't you, darling?"

The words were whispered for her, but she knew their partners could hear. She gasped as Mr. Wickham lapped at her with new speed and nodded her head.

186

Fitzwilliam smiled down at her, an eyebrow cocked. "I knew you would," he said, as though he'd planned this event.

Lizzy's mind reeled a moment. That afternoon, the short exchange between Darcy and Mrs. Jenkins. Had he planned this?

"Come now. Time to finish what we've started," he said, coming to kneel on the bed beside the trio. Clara slipped off the phallus, leaving one end still inside Lizzy. Wickham rose to his knees, wiping a hand over his mouth before moving aside for Fitzwilliam to lay back on the pillows. He held a hand out to Lizzy, and she reached down to retrieve the phallus that was still deep inside her. Before she could pull it from its place, Clara and Wickham both reached for her hands, stilling her from removing it. They then raised their brows, silently informing her that she was expected to move with it still inside her. She did her best.

Clearly, they weren't done with the tool.

Lizzy was silently gleeful at the notion.

She let Fitzwilliam draw her to the head of the bed, then without a word of warning, he turned her, moving her to straddle him as she faced the incoming Wickham and Clara.

"What are you doing?" She asked, her voice barely a whisper as she felt his hands moving beneath her. His fingers slid down between her buttocks, and without another word, slid inside her with slow, deliberate precision.

She hissed, moving as though to pull away, but he held her there over him, sliding his fingers in and out of her as he stroked his cock with oil.

She knew exactly what was coming now.

"Slide down on me, love. Do it, now."

Lizzy craned to look over her shoulder at her husband as Clara's soft sighs filled the air – she was receiving the same treatment from Wickham.

She felt his cock centered against her ass, felt him surge beneath her until he was inching inside. Before she could move to take him deeper, another sensation startled her attention forward — a warm slither of a tongue dancing against her sex.

She gasped to find Clara before her on all fours again, Wickham moving in behind her as she lapped at Lizzy again.

Lizzy's head fell back and she sighed, slowly lowering her ass onto Darcy's rigid cock.

He groaned his approval. "Dear god, I am a lucky man," he whispered, kissing her ear as she leaned back onto him.

Darcy thrust up into her with slow deliberation, letting her grow accustomed to his size now buried inside her, all while Clara devoured her with an eager mouth as Wickham slowly took her from behind. When Clara slid her fingers inside Lizzy's sex, she felt her whole body convulsed. She would soon have a full body release like nothing she'd ever felt before if they continued.

Yet, Clara's mouth and fingers soon moved away from her, and Lizzy couldn't help but seek a reason.

The reason became quite clear as Clara moved closer to her, rising over her sex to take the other end of the phallus into her again.

Lizzy watched breathlessly as Clara lowered herself onto the glistening black cock until her sex was again pressed to Lizzy's.

Then without pause, Wickham moved up behind Clara again, and as the woman's beautiful face contorted in discomfort then relish, he slid inside her ass as well.

Before Lizzy could brave a word, Wickham smiled down at her, then pressed Clara's body forward, pinning the two women together.

The weight of Clara and Wickham over her caused both Darcy's cock and the phallus to drill ever deeper inside her. She cried out in near pain, but gripped the blankets beneath them to hold herself there.

Wickham withdrew, then an instant later thrust into Clara again, driving the phallus as deep as it would go into Lizzy's quivering sex.

She cried out again, a sigh of need she'd never imagined.

The sensation of Clara's body grinding against hers, the fullness of both Darcy's cock and the phallus striving inside her, her husband's body writhing beneath her as his breathing grew more hoarse and labored. Soon, he was growling into the bare skin of her shoulder, threatening to bite as the four of them moved against one another, as though becoming one massive lustful thing.

Clara's body stroked against Lizzy's in such a way that she knew her release was coming – and fast. Lizzy gripped her husband's hand at her hip and craned to look down at the place where her and Clara's bodies ground together, the wetness of them both leaving the black phallus glistening between them before it disappeared again.

Lizzy threw her head back, letting her weight fall on Darcy as Clara's fell on hers, then the two men jerked and moved on either side of them, slamming them into each other as they drilled themselves deeper and deeper.

Clara's arms reached past Lizzy, taking hold of the headboard as she pulled herself down onto Lizzy, their bodies mashed together and writhing in search of release.

Lizzy reached for Clara's backside, pulling her down into her sex, heightening every sensation. Lizzy's body quivered, then shook, and her head fell back in a sudden desperate wail. Clara's own voice rose, and before Lizzy's body was done shuddering, Wickham convulsed behind Clara, shoving himself into them both as his shoulders hunched.

He gasped, held his breath, then jerked again just as Darcy did the same beneath her. The men had found release as well, shuddering violently against them.

Lizzy took a deep breath, collapsing onto Darcy as Clara and Wickham's weight pressed down onto her. The four of them sought to still their panting, Wickham being the first to pull away from the cluster. He slumped across the foot of the bed, his naked body flushed and sweaty. Clara followed suit, kissing Lizzy's throat before leaning back until the phallus slid out of them both. She leaned back on the mattress, leaving the massive black snake strewn across the bed between them.

Wickham was already standing when Fitzwilliam finally withdrew from inside her, his breath catching in a quiet gasp. Yet, he didn't attempt to move or disturb her. He simply wrapped his arms around her middle and held her there against him.

"I dare say, this was by far my favorite group for such sport," Clara said, scooting to the edge of the bed and onto her feet. She marched across the room to a closet and swung open the doors. A moment later, she was wrapped in a beautiful satin robe.

Almost as though the contents of this closet were hers.

Clara spun around, wrapping the tie around her waist and knotting it. She leaned into Mr. Wickham as he pulled his britches up about his waist and gave him a quick peck on the cheek.

Then she sashayed back to the side of the bed and offered the same gesture to Fitzwilliam's cheek.

Then, Clara Jenkins, her untied hair now flowing in a cascade of auburn waves, leaned over Lizzy and kissed her deeply on the mouth.

Lizzy's sex ached anew.

"Do find me for breakfast in the morning before you take your leave. I will discuss the details of my visit to Pemberley."

Lizzy sat up, but it was Fitzwilliam who spoke in surprise for them both. "You are visiting us?"

Clara turned and grinned. "Of course. That was the prize, was it not?" Clara turned toward the screen in the wall and gave a wave. "It's all done, Mrs. Jenkins. I'd love it if you'd prepare me a bath before bed tonight, darling."

With that, the screen slid shut and went dark.

Lizzy moved closer to the edge of the bed. "Wait. If she's Mrs. Jenkins, then -"

Clara turned and smiled, then gave a graceful curtsy. "I am the Lady Clara Eldemere Carrington. And I look forward to being your esteemed guest. Until morning," she said, then with a whooshing flourish of her robes, disappeared out into the hallway, the sound of giddy, lustful laughter carrying down the hall from places unseen.

# CHAPTER FIFTEEN

## *The Not So Dowdy Dowager*

———◆———

Kenilworth House was strangely quiet.

The guests had filtered out over the course of the morning, the sound of carriages waking Elizabeth from her sleep.

Fitzwilliam was beside her, snoring. He'd slept well after their adventures the nights before. She had, as well, but something about the adventure ending left her saddened and disappointed.

She wasn't ready to go home.

Elizabeth slipped out of their chambers, making her way down the quiet hallway. There were no telling sounds of lovemaking behind every door, and many of the rooms now lay open, maids bustling about within to set the rooms back to sorts.

She made her way down the grand staircase to the ballroom, scanning the space for any sign of a familiar face.

A young groom marched past her toward the stairs, stopping for only an instant to give her directions.

"If you'd like, breakfast is being served in the garden this morning."

The notion of food set her stomach to churning. The thought of something savory was almost as orgasmic as her activities the night before. Elizabeth made her way past the stairs and down the hall toward the garden doors. She could make out the shapes of a few ladies and gentlemen huddled at tables, their demeanors all similarly lovey and attentive.

Clearly, the Spring Celebration left people in a rather good mood.

Elizabeth exited through the doors and stopped, feeling the cool morning air on her skin.

"Ah, Mrs. Darcy. Won't you join me, darling?"

Elizabeth turned to find a familiar face sitting at a nearby table.

Mrs. Jenkins – or as she'd discovered the night before, the Lady Carrington was gesturing for her to come over. Elizabeth did so, a sudden twinge of nerves.

Despite her desperate affection for her husband, this woman had stirred unknown desires in her, and she'd enjoyed every second of it.

The thought of having breakfast with her now was almost surreal.

Elizabeth just hoped she wouldn't bring up their foursome over eggs and toast.

"Good morning, you lovely thing. The tea is fresh," she said as Elizabeth took her seat.

"Thank you, Lady Carrington."

"Oh, enough of that. Clara, darling. Call me Clara."

Elizabeth smiled, settling in as a groom appeared beside them, lifting up the pot of tea to offer her a cup. She smiled and accepted.

"I'm glad to see you and your dear Fitzwilliam are still with us. Will you be staying the night again, then?"

"No, sadly. We'll be leaving in the afternoon, but I wanted to say thank you -"

"Oh, enough of that. Have you enjoyed yourself, darling? Was it as you hoped it would be?"

Elizabeth smiled. This felt like such a direct and intimate question. Still, she'd known this woman biblically. There was little in the ways of intimacy that they hadn't already shared.

"Yes," she said finally.

Elizabeth stared at Lady Carrington for a moment. She was older, but by no means an old maid, and her dark blonde hair cascaded down this morning in smooth waves. She hadn't pinned her hair up before making her way to breakfast. Nor had she dressed.

She was clad in little more than dressing gown and robe.

Elizabeth was almost jealous. The notion of being so confident and carefree – it was appealing.

Clara met Elizabeth gaze and smiled. She'd caught her staring.

Elizabeth blushed.

"On another matter – your sister."

Elizabeth stiffened. She hadn't seen Lydia anywhere at Kenilworth, and she was quite grateful for that fact. Mary had been at dinner each night, but she retired to a completely separate part of the house. As far as Elizabeth was concerned, Mary was on the other side of the world each night.

At least, that's what she'd told herself.

"Mary?"

"Yes," she said, and the tone was like that of a cat sauntering up to a saucer of milk. "She's a peculiar thing, isn't she?"

Elizabeth swallowed. "I'm not sure. She can be."

"She likes women, yes?"

Tea nearly splattered across the table as Elizabeth fought not to choke.

Lady Carrington just laughed. "Darling, really?"

Elizabeth took a couple deep breaths, fighting to stop her coughing fit.

"I'll take that as a yes. Good. I'd hoped so."

"You'd hoped so?"

"Yes. I'm rather fond of women, myself, dear."

She winked at Elizabeth, and Elizabeth couldn't help but blush.

"Men are good for a bit of fun from time to time, but Mr. Carrington knew my preference even before we married. Lovely man. So kind to leave me all of this," she said, gesturing around her as she chewed a piece sausage.

"Goodness," Elizabeth said, instantly regretting her involuntary shock.

"Yes, goodness, indeed. I've requested that your sister stay on for the week. She strikes me as a rather intriguing creature."

"Does she?"

Clara Carrington smiled at her. "She does. I'm looking forward to having the time to get to know her better – without all the distraction, of course."

She reached across the table and touched Elizabeth's hand at this.

Elizabeth's face burned.

"Good morning, ladies."

Elizabeth startled, turning to find Fitzwilliam walking up to join them just as another couple sauntered off across the grounds to meet their carriage.

"There he is. Darling, I must thank you for bringing such a star to my home. And of course, on your taste in women."

"Yes, I'm rather impressed with myself," he said, without pause.

Elizabeth's mouth fell open to see him so playful. Did he know of Lady Carrington's proclivities?

Beyond their own shared ones, that is.

"Tell me, how many will you two be inviting to Pemberley for this affair?"

"Pardon?" The Darcys said in unison.

"Well, you did win my little competition. Surely, Mr. Wickham doesn't have the space to invite our brood, now does he?"

"Invite to Pemberley?" Elizabeth said.

"If you have a suggested invite list, we will happily take your suggestions."

Elizabeth turned to her husband, shocked at his demeanor. Was he really agreeing to having an event at Pemberley the likes of this? Would she truly be holding court at such an affair?

The thought startled her with just how thrilling it felt.

"That sounds perfect. I can have Thomas write something

195

up for you. Suggestions, of course, but it will give you an idea. There are certain figures you simply must have. No gathering will be complete without Dr. Barnes and his trusty ropes, or Madame Le Pen and her paddles. Tell me, have you visited any of the clubs? I can procure you both an invitation if you're curious."

Elizabeth opened her mouth, but no words came.

"That would be lovely, thank you," Fitzwilliam said, taking a scone from the tray and buttering it, quickly. He then ate it in two bites and stood up from the table, sipping the last of Elizabeth's tea as he did. "I'm afraid we must prepare for our departure, m'lady. We do thank you for the invitation, as always."

Lady Carrington rose from her seat, offering Fitzwilliam a kiss on the cheek. She then leaned over the table to Elizabeth, offering the same.

Elizabeth couldn't help the butterflies in her stomach. She wondered how long it would take to forget that feeling when Clara Carrington was near.

Or how long it would take the memory of what they'd done from setting her whole body alight.

"I look forward to receiving your invitation, Mrs. Darcy," she said, smiling as Fitzwilliam pulled Elizabeth's chair out for her.

She rose from the table and turned back for the house, fighting the sudden giddiness she felt.

# CHAPTER SIXTEEN

## *Our Esteemed Guest*

"Come now, there must be another table we could utilize, Fitzwilliam."

Elizabeth was in a tizzy.

In the weeks since the Spring Ball at Kenilworth, she'd been in a constant fervor of preparation. Invitations sent, the invite list culled and adjusted over and over until it was absolutely perfect.

Fitzwilliam had suggested the turn of the season. Their invite list was culled and adjusted to include those they felt would garner the most social benefit, if not entertainment benefit.

This Dr. Barnes and his ropes intrigued Elizabeth to no end.

Still, she was trying to get a decision from Fitzwilliam on whether or not they'd be inviting Madame Le Pen.

Paddles were intriguing as well, she thought.

Still, now that the evening of their Beltane Ball was upon them, she was desperate for a second opinion on every choice she'd made.

Her husband was being of little help. He'd been content with every suggestion and notion she had.

"As you wish" and "If it pleases you" were all he seemed to have to say.

It was infuriating, but not unlike him.

"What I wouldn't give to have Molly and Deirdre here, right now," she said, muttering to herself as she bustled around the dining room. The house was alive with groomsmen – workers Lady Carrington had suggested in her lists. These were not the average grooms. They weren't house servants for hire. These were the young prizes of various aristocratic and well-to-do families, and they came at her behest. Clearly, they'd found reward in being at her beck and call.

Elizabeth could only imagine what their rewards were. She was sure access to infinite willing and wealthy ladies had something to do with it.

That and the lust young men were prone to.

"We sent them away, as you suggested. They're enjoying the time off with their families. Please, don't tell me I'm paying them to do nothing without reason."

"No, no! They need to be far from here. I don't want Deirdre or Molly knowing what goes on here, this evening. I can't even imagine what Deirdre might think, let only poor Molly."

"Yes, well. I'm certain we can survive without them."

"Madam," a groom called from the front hall. "Your first guests have arrived."

Elizabeth's heart shot into her throat, and she rushed toward the front hall to greet them. She could only imagine who might be on the other side of the door.

The smile on Mary's face was bright enough to outshine the sun, and Elizabeth couldn't help but smile back.

"Lady Carrington! Goodness, we weren't expecting you until this evening," Elizabeth said, stepping aside as the two women walked into the hall. The lady whooshed into the room with the swish of her skirts, her riding coat just as full and flourished as the dress beneath.

"What nonsense, of course I would come early. I can imagine you want another set of eyes before the guests arrive?"

Elizabeth's whole body sagged in relief. "Oh, yes. I'm doing my best, but Fitzwilliam is no help at all, and I'm certain I'm forgetting something."

"Mary, darling," she said, turning to the woman she had taken to referring to as her ward. "Do have this lovely gentleman help you choose a room upstairs. I will help your lovely sister settle the rest of her affairs."

Mrs. Jenkins, the older maid that posed as the Lady Carrington at the Spring Ball marched through the hall with the ladies' luggage, following the groom and Mary up the stairs with a stern look.

Elizabeth left Fitzwilliam to greet any further guests as they arrived and followed Clara Carrington around the ballroom and halls, taking great joy in every positive word and supportive nod. Pemberley was by no means the size of Kenilworth, but what it didn't have in space it more than made up for in grandeur.

The lady directed her to offer the darker gentlemen's library to Madame Le Pen, and the floral and bright ladies' parlor to Dr. Barnes.

"The gentlemen who visit the Madame may enjoy being in the masculine space when they're having their balls crushed under her boot."

Elizabeth yelped at this, but Lady Carrington just smiled. "Pardon my language, darling," she said, continuing before Elizabeth could speak. "You have a lovely home, Mrs. Darcy. I'm rather looking forward to spending some time here."

"I'm so glad -"

"Clara! Come up and see our rooms. I think you'll be most pleased."

The lady shot Elizabeth a sideways glance and smiled. "Oh, I'm sure I will," she said, then she made her way down the hall with Mary's arm tucked tightly under her own.

The giddy gait to Mary's steps softened Elizabeth's nerves.

If nothing else, she'd given Mary an opportunity to be free.

She'd never seen Mary so happy.

The house continued to bustle around her, but given the Lady's seal of approval, she felt safe in taking a moment for herself. She found herself wandering along the back hallway of the house, a now unused set of apartments with doors that let out to the garden. Though, she'd asked Fitzwilliam about these rooms, he'd never been forthcoming with their purpose, or who may have once called them home.

Elizabeth slipped into the quiet rooms, the furniture all covered in white sheets to protect from dust. She grazed a hand over the back of a covered chair before turning for the garden windows.

A figure startled her back to the work of the day – a figure she'd last seen in the throes of passion at Kenilworth.

Mr. George Wickham was sitting in one of the white garden chairs, staring out at the grounds. He'd been invited or the festivities, naturally, given his cavalier attitude toward intimacy and bedroom prowess made him a rather popular addition to the event.

And he was the only man she trusted to be Fitzwilliam's second if the desire for a threesome were to strike.

She'd hoped he would come, despite all his contrivances in the past.

Still, it was strange seeing him in Pemberley. Strange indeed.

"Good afternoon, Mr. Wickham."

He started, turning to meet her as she exited the garden doors. "Good afternoon to you, Mrs. Darcy."

The words sounded strange in his mouth, but still, they made her heart sing.

"You look well. I'm glad you could make it."

His eyebrows raised. "Really? Well, it's nice to be invited."

The comment seemed to carry a heaviness to it. She didn't press.

"Feels almost surreal to be here, again. I had often feared I'd never set foot on the grounds again."

Elizabeth looked down at her hands and shook her head.

"My husband has softened in that department – but only for certain purposes."

"Of course," he said, forcing a half laugh. "Anything to please the Master Darcy."

Elizabeth knit her brow. "Now, that's enough. I won't have you speaking ill of him in his own house."

He took a deep breath. "No, of course not. I apologize. It's just – being here seems to be opening old wounds."

"Old wounds?" She said, scoffing openly. What wounds did Mr. Wickham have to speak of?

He shot her a sideways glance, and the look seemed pained, almost. "You know I grew up here, yes?"

She nodded.

"Spent much of my youth here, embraced by a man who said I was as good as his son. I had a brother, a home – a had a wonderful life."

"Yes, I knew that."

"It didn't matter where I came from, Mr. Darcy accepted me into his family, treated me like his own blood. Then, he died – and I lost everything."

Elizabeth stared at him for a long moment, not wanting to break the silence with empty words.

"God forbid, Fitzy let me call it home."

"Hold on," Elizabeth said, determined to defend her husband. "You've no right to complain – running off with little Georgiana like that."

He exhaled in a frustrated laugh. "Yes, too true."

"You've only yourself to blame."

He turned back to face the garden, standing still for a long moment. "I remember hearing that he'd died. I was devastated. Came home to pay my respects, to honor the man I knew as a father. Before I could begin to understand how my life would change, Fitz handed me a banknote and sent me on my way."

Elizabeth felt the muscles in her jaw tense. "Mr. Wickham."

"Imagine, Lizzy. Imagine your father promised you the world, that you'd be taken care of the entirety of your life.

Then, when he passes, you discover there was no consideration for you in any will, and your brother hands you a pittance, and tells you to make due."

"It was by no means a pittance."

Both Elizabeth and Wickham turned for the garden doors to find Fitzwilliam standing there, his brow knit as he glared at them.

Mr. Wickham took a step toward him. "It was, Fitz, and you know it."

"It was more than generous."

"Says the man who was accustomed to this life. Says the man who would continue living this life. There was you, Georgiana, and myself, but the moment father dies, I'm cast aside."

Fitzwilliam sighed in frustration. "You weren't cast aside, you were a bloody soldier."

"I wasn't! I became a soldier because you left me destitute."

Fitzwilliam laughed. "I gave you plenty. You spent it on loose women and gambling, I'm sure."

"Plenty? The man who lives in Pemberley says he gave me plenty. After the life I'd been accustomed to. It was nothing. I thought we were brothers, once, but you left me with nothing."

"Damn it, George. How do you imagine it would've been different if we were brothers? It would've been no different. The first son inherits the fortune, the second joins the military. Were Georgiana a son, tradition would place her in the clergy. There would've been no difference."

"I would've still had a home," Wickham said, and his nostrils flared as he fought to steady his emotion.

Elizabeth felt trapped between the two men, desperate to leave them to this overdue argument. Yet, there was no escape. The house was coming to life inside.

Fitzwilliam took a deep breath, but he didn't speak for a long moment. When he finally did, it was clear Elizabeth wasn't the only one shocked.

"You're not wrong," he said.

Wickham's jaw dropped, and he moved toward her husband

with clenched fists. "You admit it?!"

"Of course, I do."

"You bastard," Wickham said, barely audible. "How can you be so cruel?"

Fitzwilliam set his jaw. "Cruel? You want to speak of cruelty? Shall I summon Georgiana to come tell us of cruelty?"

Wickham let his head fall back, and he ran his hands over his face. "My dear Georgiana. You know nothing of Georgiana and I."

"I know she loved you since she was a child. I knew she hung on your every word and would've done anything for you."

"And I for her."

"Shut your mouth!" Fitzwilliam said, and it was his turn to go for Wickham, stopping just inches from the man. "Don't you speak of her like that."

"She was my sister, Fitz. I never wanted to hurt her or lead her astray."

"And yet you run away with her, just like you did with Lydia."

Wickham glanced at Elizabeth then, as though for her support. "There is no comparison!"

"How so?"

"Because – god damn it!" Wickham turned away for a moment, hollering toward the garden before turning back to meet Fitzwilliam. "Did you know why she ran away with me?"

"Because she was a silly girl easily led astray by a scoundrel like you."

"She came to me after father died. You remember how she was then - so frail. She told me then that she'd thought of hurting herself. That she imagined joining father."

"What?" Fitzwilliam said, his voice taking a strange, nervous tone.

"I told her she mustn't dare. I knew she was fond of me, and I hoped that if I told her not to dare, that perhaps she'd listen. When she went away with me, it was the same."

"Oh, what nonsense!" Fitzwilliam growled.

"It isn't! She begged to come with me when I left that day. Said she couldn't bear to be here alone, anymore. And yes, I admit for an instant I thought to steal her away – to marry her and finally make myself a part of this family. To finally have a claim."

Fitzwilliam glared at him.

"But I didn't do it! I couldn't. No matter how smitten with me she might've been, she was my sister. I'm sorry that she was hurt by that. Lord knows how sorry I am to think I might've ever caused that darling girl pain."

Elizabeth stepped aside as Fitzwilliam moved toward Wickham. For an instant, she feared there would be violence, but he stopped inches from Wickham, and the two men held their ground against each other for a long moment.

The tension sparked for a long moment, and Elizabeth couldn't help but wonder how on earth Fitzwilliam had come to invite Wickham to their bedroom. How he'd trusted the man to do something so intimate, but still harbored such rage in his heart for the man.

Just as Elizabeth was going to intervene, Fitzwilliam turned away.

"Perhaps, you're right. Perhaps, I treated you unfairly."

"Perhaps?!"

"Fine, yes. I did. I let you feel unwelcome here."

Wickham's expression softened, but it was clear he was still in pain. "Why?"

"Because of how he treated you!"

"Who?"

Fitzwilliam exhaled. "Father. I did everything to be worthy of his name. I barely laughed when in company, all to maintain that propriety he claimed to hold so dear. Yet, there you were, acting like a bloody fool, and still he thought you a wonder. It was as though you could do no wrong. I was his blood, and I swear, it felt as though he wished you bore the Darcy name – not me."

Wickham touched his hand to his mouth. "Is that true?"

"It is. I'm not proud of it, but yes. It's true."

The house began to hum with sound – the voices of arriving guests and servants giving tours and taking guests to their rooms. Elizabeth was growing nervous, but she didn't dare leave these men. Not until she was sure they wouldn't tear each other's throats out the moment she walked away.

"If what you say is true – about Georgiana – then you have my apologies," Fitzwilliam said. "But you should've told me her state. I've been with her all this time and didn't know she'd harbored those thoughts."

"And you have mine. I should've told you. I should've trusted you."

"I didn't give you reason to."

The moment lingered until finally the two men turned to each other, Fitzwilliam extending a hand first. They shook, and for the first time, Elizabeth understood why it was Wickham that Fitzwilliam brought to their bed.

It wasn't just because Fitzwilliam knew Elizabeth wouldn't run away with Wickham – it was because somewhere in their past, they'd truly been good friends.

They'd truly shared everything.

"Mr. and Mrs. Darcy. I believe you are both needed inside."

They turned toward the garden doors and met the concerned look of one of the hired grooms. Elizabeth's heart shot into her chest.

"Oh, what is it now?" She asked, marching into the house with Fitzwilliam close on her heels.

Before he could wholly explain the situation, she gathered just enough information to put a speed to her step.

Someone had come uninvited.

Elizabeth marched alongside Fitzwilliam, the two of them walking close enough for their elbows to touch.

"Are you alright, darling?" She asked, hooking her arm with his.

Fitzwilliam made a soft noise deep in his throat. "Honestly, yes. I am."

"I'm glad," she said, and it was true. The tension that Darcy and Wickham shared fueled their bedroom activities when the

205

time came, but the tension outside the bedroom made it impossible for them to get along – and impossible for anyone else to be comfortable around them. The thought of their struggles being settled made Elizabeth hopeful – and not just for more frequent nighttime visits from Wickham.

Despite his propriety and his good breeding, he'd once had more than just Charles Bingley, and the thought of him having such a free-spirited friend seemed both silly and delightful.

It would take time, though. She knew that for certain.

"Here you are, Madam."

"Well, silly girl, what is all this, then?" Mrs. Bennet said, offering her coat to one of the groomsmen.

Elizabeth's whole world imploded.

"We thought we'd stop in for a visit. We're on our way to bring Kitty to visit with a Mr. Farnsworth in the nearby village. I didn't know you were having a soiree. How dare you not invite us, darling?"

"Absolutely not," Fitzwilliam said, opening his arms and herding Mr. and Mrs. Bennet right back out the doors of Pemberley before Kitty could even cross the threshold.

"I beg your pardon," Mrs. Bennet protested. She was back in her carriage and folding her jacket into her lap before Elizabeth could say a word.

Despite the rude gesture, Elizabeth had never loved her husband more.

# EPILOGUE

## *Proudly Insatiable*

---

The ball was a resounding success, and letters began arriving within a week. Everyone had loved their time at the ball, and they all wanted to know when the next would be held.

Mary's letter came a mere two weeks later.

She was bliss itself, and Elizabeth knew why.

Without being able to express the cause of her elation, Elizabeth knew.

Clearly, Lady Carrington and Mary were getting along rather well. As Mary explained, being invited to return to Kenilworth with Lady Carrington was the highlight of her year. Now, Mary had been asked to stay – indefinitely.

Jane and Charles arrived at Pemberley the following week. Though Elizabeth had done her best to explain, Mrs. Bennet was still annoyed with her second eldest daughter, refusing to stop back in after spending some time in the village of Mr. Farnsworth.

Despite her wounded pride, she was responding to Elizabeth's letters, so that was a good sign. Another round of invitations, and she was sure her parents would return.

Especially if Kitty had any say in the matter.

Jane was now a constant whirlwind of giddy secrecy. Though Elizabeth loved her sister, she'd heard enough praise for Charles' bedroom prowess to last a lifetime. And besides, even as Jane was exploring her new husband, she was still not someone Elizabeth would invite to such an affair as the Springtime Celebration at Lady Carrington's, let alone a similar affair at Pemberley. It was getting tedious trying to steal time away to respond to all the lovely *thank you* letters.

As he often did when Charles Bingley was in-house, Fitzwilliam was called away for the morning to go riding.

By midday, he was making his way back up the stairs to their chambers, and Elizabeth was too excited to wait any longer for an answer.

She met him in the hallway just outside their room, and it hit her like a slap to the face. This wasn't the smell of an unclean thing, nor of one of those men she'd encountered while visiting London with Fitzwilliam – the men who just don't seem to have the same relationship with bathing as others.

Darcy had come in from hunting all afternoon with Charles Bingley, and he'd clearly exerted himself well.

This was the smell of a man – of him, his sweat, his work, his long day. Fitzwilliam fidgeted in the doorway of the parlor, bowing as the new maid, Ingrid, hurried by him, taking his hunting jacket. He clearly didn't like being in such a state around others and was swift to take his leave.

"You will excuse me, Jane, but I must freshen up before your lovely sister and I are to leave for London."

Jane sat as upright as she could on the settee, nodding with a bright smile before Darcy disappeared from the room.

He'd hardly glanced in Elizabeth's direction, she noticed.

She didn't take offense. She knew well what played on her husband's mind. Intimate, unseemly thoughts. He always averted his eyes when he was feeling lustful. He hated the thought of anything seeing the way he looked at her.

Fitzwilliam despised for others to know his business.

They were leaving for London to attend what can only be called a ball, but this ball was unlike any she'd ever heard of before.

"It's for aristocrats of a certain taste," he'd said, refusing to go deeper into the conversation. It seemed he wanted their experience to be a surprise to his titillated wife.

Given their behavior in private, she could hardly wait to see what this masquerade would have in store.

Charles made a quick appearance, his state just as disheveled as Darcy's. They'd clearly had a good afternoon.

"Hello, my darling," he said, leaning in to kiss Jane on the cheek. Elizabeth watched them, almost wishing Darcy showed similar affections in company. Still, Elizabeth had it on good authority that Charles Bingley was a tender and gentle lover in private, and her beloved Darcy was a beautiful beast.

Elizabeth was content to pass on the public displayed of affection for the private passions she'd come to love so much.

"Thank goodness, I thought they'd never leave," Jane said once Charles was out of the room. She slumped back onto the settee in a clumsy lump, her massive belly rolling out above her. Jane was very pregnant, and it took every ounce of effort to maintain her poise in company.

"Do you not let him see you like this at home?" Elizabeth asked. The thought of maintaining the outward poise of Jane Bennet while carting a human being her belly just sounded exhausting.

"Oh, of course I do. Still, I am a lady, Lizzie. I have to try, don't I?"

Ingrid returned with a tray of small cakes and cucumber sandwiches, both of which Jane lunged for as soon as the tray was set. Elizabeth wasn't feeling hungry.

At least, not like that.

"Pardon me, darling Jane, but would you allow me to take my leave for a moment. There's a matter I must discuss with Darcy."

Jane beamed at her, the crumbs of almond cake collected at the corners of her beautiful smile. "Of course. Do take your time!"

Elizabeth made her way out of the parlor and down the hall, trying her best not to look rushed. She wanted to catch her husband before he'd washed and changed. She couldn't quite put her finger on why, but it was urgent to her as though the kitchen was on fire.

She reached the bedroom door and gave the softest of raps. Darcy grumbled something from within, but she didn't wait to decipher the words.

She entered the room and found her husband still in his riding breeches.

"Elizabeth, darling. What are you doing?"

Elizabeth suddenly became aware that she'd been staring at him. He flashed her a wide grin, cracking his whole face apart in joy and shyness.

Elizabeth melted. She knew her husband well. He was in a rare mood.

"What?" He asked.

Elizabeth smiled and shook her head, but she didn't look away. He came across the room to her, the smell of him surrounding her all over again. He met her gaze, the smile wide on his face, his eyes fixed on hers. He paused, searching her face. Then he leaned toward her, faltered for only a second, and kissed her on the cheek. Elizabeth was surrounded for an instant by the smell of him, the warmth of him, the soft hush of his breath, the creak of the wood under his weight vibrating beneath her feet. He pulled away, searching her face, as though asking approval. His closeness sent her heart pounding, and she'd almost yelped in surprise when he leaned into her. Yet, unlike his usual forceful manner, he seemed nervous, as tender and gentle as Jane assured her Mr. Bingley was. Though Elizabeth loved her husband's forceful ways, this new side of him was almost too endearing to bear.

Still, she took a deep breath, met his gaze, and smiled. "You missed."

The smile hardened just so and his eyes darted across her face, the rarely boyish demeanor that only she could draw from him now breaking apart to show the man he showed only her. He looked down at her lips, and in one perfect movement, reached for her, curling his fingers behind the nape of her neck, and kissed her. It was soft, surface, but intent. Elizabeth smelled dust on his skin, a tiny prickle of moisture at his lips, cool as though he'd been drinking ice water. He softened and pulled away just so, then returned, another soft surface kiss. Yet, in that moment's break, in the pause between, there was expectation, a heat that invited more. Whether he intended it or not, she felt it.

He released her, letting his hand linger at her jaw when he pulled away, smiling as he searched her face. Elizabeth watched him, wordless. He turned back to the bed, patting his dusty hands on his trousers.

"I'm in dire need of a bath. I sent Ingrid to pour it, but naturally sent her to tend to Charles first. Was quite the ride today."

"Yes, I can see that."

Darcy glanced down at himself with an air of embarrassment. She smiled. If only he knew what he did to her.

"I imagine I smell like a wet saddle at the moment," Darcy said, and she smiled. It was always so wonderful to hear him jest.

Elizabeth reached to him, touching his arm, a strange compulsive urge to breach the tiny distance between them, even if for a second. "I think you smell wonderful."

He raised his eyebrows and gave her a sideways look. "What?"

"No. You smell like -" and the words escaped. Well, no. They didn't escape her – he smelled like warmth, like strength, like solid and whole, like man – like home. Yet, none of those words came out of her mouth. "You smell like a stable decorated for Christmas."

He laughed, an embarrassed but flattered huffing of breath that caught him off guard enough to make him turn from her.

"I'm not sure how long the bath water will take, but I'll freshen up as swiftly as I can and join you back in the -" He was midway through taking off his white shirt when he stopped, watching her face. "What's wrong?"

Elizabeth sat there a moment, perfectly still, despite the

racing of her thoughts. "Fitzwilliam?"

Something about her tone seemed to concern him, as he covered the distance between them in two strides. "Yes? Do you need something?"

Elizabeth nodded. "Yes."

He curled his back, lowering himself to meet her eyes. He waited patiently, the most endearing look of concern on his face. "What do you need, sweetheart?"

Elizabeth turned to face him and caught sight of his pale skin, his thick torso, the tiny pinpricks of his nipples, the divot at his hip disappearing into the waistband of his trousers.

She held her breath.

Elizabeth strode through him, forcing him gently back into the wall of the bedroom. He tensed, his shoulders lifting in surprise as Elizabeth broke the wordless barrier that exists between two people; that once broken becomes a just as wordless invitation. Elizabeth pressed her hands to his abdomen, flattening his back against the cold white wall. Elizabeth let the tip of her nose graze against his chin, then lifted her lips to his, and kissed him. His breathing changed, instantly. His hands took hold of her, fingers lost in her hair as he returned the kiss, his heavy exhales between kisses, each inviting further touch, and further destruction of whatever boundaries still lay between them.

His tongue found hers. The nerve endings in every inch of her body fired, searing from her mouth to secret places. She wanted to offer every one of them up to him. She opened to him, gasping at the sensation, and he pulled his shoulders from the wall, leaning down to consume her, filling her mouth with his exploration. Elizabeth clutched him, letting her hold on him and his on her keep her on her feet. He turned her just slightly, twisting her body to lean against his shoulder as though he were going to dip her mid-dance. Instead he held her there, pressing his mouth down into hers. His tongue's rhythm was slow, but intent, and Elizabeth finally broke from the kiss for air, finding his clear, sleepy eyes trained on hers, their pupils dilated and dark. Elizabeth rose back to her full

212

height and kissed his lips, pulling away before he could return to his languid work. Elizabeth kissed him again, teasing, flitting her tongue against his, and pulling away just enough to meet that sleepy, lustful gaze that grew darker with each passing moment. His lips were parted, glistening just so, and his breath quiet but fast. Elizabeth stared into those eyes, a dark smile playing across them despite his lips remaining still.

When he spoke, his voice was ragged and quiet, almost a whisper. "Elizabeth, darling. I really must have a bath."

The words were playful, partnered by a smile that melted her from the chest outward, yet his eyes betrayed something hopeful, something that seemed to dare her onward.

Elizabeth shook her head and smiled. "Not yet."

Elizabeth pressed her full weight against his chest, slid her hand over the smooth skin of his stomach, and without pause, cupped the hard shape Elizabeth found beneath the fabric of his trousers. His whole body tensed and his breath caught in his throat as he straightened up, startled by her touch. He could have pushed her away, he was taller, broad in the shoulder, thick across his chest – he was built like a Viking or Roman God. Yet he watched her, letting her touch him – letting her lead. The freedom of it was intoxicating.

Elizabeth pressed her nose to his cheek, her mouth open, inviting him to kiss her if he willed it. The shape beneath her fingers grew harder, like marble, and Elizabeth longed to know its nature. Elizabeth watched his face, his head tilted back, holding his breath as her hand kneaded him. Finally, the urge to feel the smoothness of his skin brought her hands purposefully to his belt buckle, whipping the straps through and unhooking him with enough purpose to pull his hips from the wall. He finally took a breath, looking down at her hands as Elizabeth unfastened his trousers.

He breathlessly said her name, "Lizzie." There was bewildered caution in his voice, but need played clear across his face. Before he could say more, Elizabeth slid her hand under the waist of his trousers and took hold of him. He gasped, watching her hand disappear under the fabric, then slumping against the wall, mouth open, eyes closed, shifting his hips to give himself over to her. Her hand moved gently, but with purpose.

"Oh dear God," he said, and Elizabeth smiled. He caught sight of it and breathlessly smiled back. "This brazen behavior could get you in trouble, darling."

Elizabeth laughed, softly, leaning in to kiss his throat. "I do hope so."

He laughed and stroked her arm, letting his fingers play at her elbow. Elizabeth couldn't take her eyes off him, off the light eyelashes that fluttered when his head tilted back, off the muscles of his arms, tensing as his hands squeezed her arm, the dark recesses that hid sight of him from her. Yet, she could feel him, long and hard, his hips moving, pressing himself into her hand to match her rhythm. Elizabeth was quickly finding this act futile. She wanted to make him weak, make him shudder. She ached to please him, wanting to offer all of herself just to hear him sigh.

Elizabeth pressed her nose to his cheek. "Touch me back."

He started at the words, despite the intimacy of what was happening to him. He met her eyes, question playing across his boyish face. Then that stern brow of his fixed as the corner of his mouth curved upward and the shy boy gave way to the man.

"Say please," he said.

She gasped, barely able to whisper the word. "Please."

He grabbed her hips and pulled her into him, pinning her hand between them as he flattened his palms against her backside, and squeezed hard enough to elicit a yelp. He laughed darkly, pressing his nose to hers as his fingers, still firmly clutching her ass, tore up the skirts of her dress, then with one hand around her waist, jammed his right hand between her legs and cleaved into the sensitive flesh there. Elizabeth cried out in surprise and he groaned, whispering into her ear how wet she was. She hadn't expected such ferocity, her hand falling useless as his fingers moved against her. He slid his fingers further, forcing her legs to part for him, then

214

claimed her mouth with his. She leaned there against him, helpless, legs barely able to support her weight, but he held her, a new, familiar side to him now claiming her wholly. Elizabeth could surrender there, happily let him have her in whatever way he pleased, wanted to, but that same foreign desire to hear his breath catch in his throat was rallying strength, ready to go to battle against an even foe. She'd never been in control like this with Darcy. He was the master – in all ways. Yet he'd relinquished power to her so freely, she felt mad with it.

She didn't want to let go so soon.

His fingers grazed over her expertly and Elizabeth cried out, only urging him onward, his kisses deeper, his fingers faster. Elizabeth steadied herself, grabbed his sex, and stroked him, determined. Elizabeth wanted to see him falter, reclaim the upper hand. He broke from the kiss long enough to meet her gaze, his eyes intent, but playful. He sensed her purpose, and with a mischievous smirk, accepted her unspoken challenge. Both their efforts doubled, she collapsed against him, and his grip tightened on her waist, his lips finding hers when they could. His breathing was ragged, labored with his effort to please her as much as with his growls of pleasure. They moved against each other, rising and falling, pressing into each other, their breathing matched in cries and sighs of need. Elizabeth lifted her knee, hooking it at his hip, and he took his opportunity with force, sliding his fingers inside her. Elizabeth cried out, unable to silence herself as his fingers moved. She opened herself to him as they ground against each other, he the pestle, and she the mortar. Elizabeth clutched his arm, feeling the muscles move beneath the skin with his effort. She pressed her forehead to his shoulder. He was intoxicating, his scent and the faint whisper of wood and horses mixing now with her need and his. Her hand stilled, unable to give him her focus anymore as her body tightened around his fingers.

He groaned so softly, whispering into her ear. "Good girl."

Elizabeth shook against him, her knees useless, and her hands useless. He held her, his hand slowing with the spasms of her body. Elizabeth turned her face to his chest, pressing her nose to his bare skin, then she bared her teeth and grazed them against him, a gentle marring. He chuckled softly, his chest shuddering.

He steadied her, before she felt his fingers under her chin, tilting her up to meet his gaze. His chin was folded into itself as he looked down at her, and he kissed her, wrapping his arms around her hips. He was still solid under the fabric of his trousers, pressed against her now throbbing sex. She let him return to his long kisses, feeling safe and small in his arms, rallying the courage to do what she was about to do.

Elizabeth pulled from his kiss, catching the sight of his face, pillowy lips parted, eyes closed, expectant and serene. Elizabeth kissed his chin, reached down to the waistband of his trousers and pulled them down. He startled, glancing down to watch as Elizabeth maneuvered the heavy fabric around his hips, careful not to hurt the hard shape beneath. They pooled at his calves, and she dropped to her knees. His cock sprung from beneath the fabric, nearly smacking her in the face as it did.

He was perfect, every inch of him was perfect. He bent to grab her, gently scooping under her arms, but Elizabeth turned from his grip and smiled up at him, pressing her hands to his thighs. His brow furrowed.

"Darling – Ah!" he said as she kissed his thigh, dodging his cock to do so. Elizabeth moved up his thigh an inch and kissed again. He took hold of her hands gently, tugging upward in entreaty.

"Angel, I can't ask you to do that."

Elizabeth smiled. "You didn't ask."

"I'm well aware!" His wide, boyish grin betrayed affection and awe at her fervor to perform this feat, but still he pulled her.

Elizabeth inched higher, kissing his thigh just beneath his balls. Elizabeth was close enough now to smell him, a subtle, musky scent.

"Lizzie, you don't have to do that."

216

"But I want to."

He looked at her agape, shocked. Then he smiled, his brow furrowed, as though touched by the notion of her wanting him in this way.

"Believe me, there's nothing I'd like more, sweetheart, but -"

He made a face, raising his eyebrows and crinkling his nose. Elizabeth laughed. "What?"

"I've been riding all day and I haven't had my bath -"

Elizabeth pressed her open mouth to his balls, rolled her tongue against them in her mouth, and sucked gently. His back slammed into the wall.

The sensation drew the softest whimper from his throat.

The hair on her body stood on end at the sound.

Oh god, she wanted to hear him make that sound again.

"Darling, please - Oh god."

He struggled with desire and propriety. Elizabeth released her hold on him, flicking her tongue against his skin. "You taste salty, that's all."

He gave a sound between a groan and a whine.

Elizabeth couldn't help but laugh at this. Elizabeth smiled up at him, taking hold of him with a gentle hand.

"Woman, I have spo -"

Elizabeth released her hold on him, wound up, and slapped his cock soundly. It swung to the side and back like a doorstop, nearly smacking her on its return. He gave a shocked gasp, then a wicked groan as he entwined his fingers in her hair. "Oh, I'm going make you pay for that."

He smiled, and she held his gaze as she took him in her mouth. Elizabeth watched his head fall back before turning her attention to her work. She lavished him with her mouth, attending to every inch, running her lips over his skin to feel each ridge. She enjoyed it, enjoyed the reaction, the way he felt in her mouth. He pinched her ear gently and Elizabeth met his eyes. He was watching her. She wanted to hear him make that soft sound again, the sound that escaped him when sensation took him by surprise, when he felt helpless to it. He held his breath, giving a shuddering exhale as Elizabeth relaxed her throat and took him wholly.

"Oh, my good Lord," he said, barely able to form the words. "What did I do to deserve this?"

Elizabeth released him, taking a deep breath. Fitzwilliam was no small man. She smiled up at him and let him hear the truth. "You needn't do anything. I love you. I want to please you."

His eyes softened. He bent down and took hold of her arms, lifting her to her feet.

"What are you doing? I'm not done with you," she said, but he'd taken hold of her and moved her as only a man of his size could. There was no fighting Fitzwilliam Darcy when he wanted something.

He laughed, kissing her jaw as he walked her backward toward the bed. "Damn right, you're not."

Elizabeth felt the bed at her back and fell backward onto it. The rumpled blanket smelled clean and of him. He fumbled at the edge of the bed, freeing himself from the rumpled mess of his clothes. Suddenly her stomach tightened and her heart began to pulse in her ears. He was naked, towering over her. He bent to grab her legs, pulling off her boots and tossing them onto the floor one by one. His fingers grazed her hip and he slipped her skirts high around her outstretched legs. Then the bed creaked beneath the weight of him as he knelt between her legs, running his hands up her thighs, pushing the skirt of her dress up over her hips. Elizabeth was bared to him, visible, and without thought, her hands shot to cover the patch of hair between her legs.

He laughed. "Shy suddenly?"

Elizabeth smiled, her cheeks burning, though she wasn't sure he could see. When she spoke, her voice was tiny, almost meek. "Yes."

"Well that just won't do," he said, slipping his hands up over her stomach, causing the muscles beneath to twist and tighten. Then he took hold of her breasts, squeezing them firmly through the fabric of her dress, pressing them together and whispering his appreciation. The dynamic had shifted, she was no longer in the lead, and couldn't take it back if she wanted to. He tugged at the collar of her dress, roughly tugging down to expose her breasts, her nipples dark against her pale skin. He clamped his mouth over one, both of them groaning in approval as it hardened to him. Elizabeth gasped, holding her breath as he pressed his teeth into her breast, the same gentle marring she'd given him moments earlier. He quickly shifted to the other breast, sucking firmly as his hands kneaded her. He knelt there, letting his cock gently graze over one thigh, then the other.

He squeezed her hips, pulling her toward him just so.

He ran his fingers over his lips before smoothing them over the head of his cock. He shifted his weight, planted one hand under her arm, and Elizabeth felt his erection against her. There was pressure for an instant, then hard fullness as her body yielded to him. Elizabeth gasped, clutching his arms, curling into herself to watch his body cleave into hers. He settled for a second, pushing into her wholly, giving her a moment to catch her breath, then retreated. Her sex ached with need, despite being sensitive from his previous efforts.

Elizabeth looked up into Fitzwilliam's face and saw the gentle way he looked at her, the way he'd looked at her when first he'd proposed and she'd said yes – a protective, endearing fondness that he showed only her. Yet, the softness of it hardened now as he moved over her. Fitzwilliam was naked, cleaving into her, the dust of his day's ride still clinging to his skin, and Elizabeth was completely open to him, in every way a woman could be.

He thrust home again, slow and deliberate, and her eyes went wide. Her body was tightening around him, her muscles contracted, the sensitive pang between her legs growing to a desperate warmth. Elizabeth reached for his ass and pulled him into her, met with a surprised chuckle and a groan of appreciation.

"Faster," she whispered.

He lowered himself onto his elbows and kissed her jaw. "They're just getting started, darling."

Her words came quickly, near desperate. "No. Faster, please."

"So demanding," he said, laughing, despite his body responding to her plea. He thrust again, then again in quick procession.

"Oh god!" Elizabeth hissed.

He shifted above her to look at her, surprised. "So soon?"

"I know!"

He thrust again, urged on by the realization of her state. His rhythm was perfect, deep and heavy. Elizabeth hummed, whined, lost the capacity for sound – and was undone. Her head fell back onto the bed and she was lost in a shuddering cry, her legs tightening around him, urging him on even as her insides spasmed against him.

He didn't slow, keeping his pace, letting her ride the sensation, prolonging it. Elizabeth sighed, and he pushed himself up onto his knees, pulling her hips up to rest on his wide thighs. He ran his hands through his hair, ruffling it, then patted her hip.

"That did wonders for my confidence."

Elizabeth laughed, breathless. "You're very skilled, it seems."

He smiled and his hips began again, her sensitive sex spasming as he moved. He went slow, watching her, letting his hands stroke over her belly, squeezing her breasts. Elizabeth hummed blissfully, her whole body relaxed and open to him. His fingers grazed over her collarbone and hesitated, then retreated all together, back to her hips. He held her there, pulling her into him in a slow rhythm. Yet, his body seemed to tense here and there, as though in preparation of something that he thought better of each time. Elizabeth felt the muscles in his arms, his hands tightening on her hips, but then the same slow thrust would follow, the energy unexpressed.

"Your turn," Elizabeth said, smiling at him.

He met her eyes, now accustomed to the light, and smiled right back. "How magnanimous of you."

She chuckled, and he leaned down to kiss her, squeezing her

breasts again as her hips slipped back down onto the bed. His hand slid over her collar again, paused, then back down, propping himself up.

"Fitzwilliam?"

He nodded, his rhythm picking up speed, but somehow, cautious. "What, sweetheart?"

Elizabeth reached down, grabbing his ass to pull him into her. He tensed, as though holding himself back.

"Ravish me."

Despite all of their nights together, his eyes blazed. He tried to hide it with a laugh.

Elizabeth pressed her hands to his hips, stopping him. He obliged, glancing down to the place where their bodies joined, where her sex began to ache with the need of him all over again. She took his hand from the mattress beside her, forcing him to lift up onto his knees, and placed his open hand on her throat. His breath caught deep in his chest, and Elizabeth felt him tense, wound tight like a guitar string, one turn away from snapping.

"Lizzie -"

She shivered. She loved it when he called her that.

"I can tell you want to and you're not doing it. I am yours. Do as you wish."

He took a moment, as though searching for words, but he did not take his hand from her collar. "I thought you wanted me to let you lead this time."

She beamed, her heart melting. He hadn't taken control like he normally would. Hadn't bent her over his knee for being forthright and difficult. He'd given her a tender side, and she'd loved it. Now he was holding back his desires for her.

Elizabeth planted her feet into the mattress and thrust her hips into him, slowly drawing him deeper. His eyes closed and he bit his lip.

"I am yours to have as you wish. Always."

Elizabeth moved there against him, his expression open-mouthed and wanting.

His eyes widened. The sight made her giggle. She'd just

221

challenged a warrior of a man, and he'd accepted. There was a whole new world of darkness in his eyes now as he shifted his weight over her, planted his knees wide on the mattress, and pressed down into her. Elizabeth braced herself, her insides clenching around him as he pushed wholly. He had been holding back, and now with all of him sheathed inside her, Elizabeth could barely breathe. He could hurt her, if he wanted.

The first thrust was just as slow as before, but when he pushed into her, he let her take all of him, to the point of near pain, then past it. Elizabeth gasped, holding her breath as he retreated, only to do it again. With each slow thrust, the pain subsided just so, but not completely.

She didn't want it to.

She searched his face, finding him watching her own, watching for reaction. Elizabeth met his gaze and silently dared him onward.

Suddenly, he grabbed her hips, pulling them upward roughly, then buried himself in her, pinning her under him, helpless. She cried out, but didn't protest. Then his hand returned to her throat, his hold gentle, but warning. The first hard thrust drew an involuntary shriek, then again as he lowered his face to hers, watching her as he took her. He was solid and hard, and each thrust pounded her insides, sending sharp pains through her, all while warming the rest of her in that exciting, familiar way. The pain subsided just enough to still her shrieks, and he retaliated to her silence by thrusting harder. Elizabeth gasped, meeting his eyes and his wicked smile, and submitted to him wholly.

"Am I hurting you?" He asked, his thrusts quickening, deeper and deeper.

Elizabeth nodded, breathless. "Yes."

He paused almost infinitesimally. "Do you like it?"

"Yes!"

All of Fitzwilliam growled. He pressed his full weight on her, moving with purpose, his breath ragged. Elizabeth reached down, digging her nails into his backside. His hand squeezed on her throat as he hummed, gratefully. "Mmm."

Then he took hold of her hands, pinning her wrists above her head, forcing her hips up higher now, giving him stronger purchase. He pressed her beneath him, each exhale harsher with his effort. He whispered something into her ear, something gentle and assuring, but Elizabeth couldn't hear it. Then his expression changed, a near sneer, like a predatory animal. He thrust into her, his body slamming into hers, and she cried out. This pain was almost too much, almost unbearable, but in that hair's breadth between, there was a sudden heat, warm and desperate, rising inside with such speed that it caught her off guard. Elizabeth cried out again as he thrust into her, pain and pleasure mingling to the point of exasperation. She gripped his hands.

"Don't stop, Fitzwilliam. Just please don't stop."

"That's it. Take it like a good girl."

Elizabeth gasped. The sound of his voice, both gentle and foreboding, intoxicated her. He thrust soundly home, bruising her both inside and out, and Elizabeth quaked beneath him. He began to rumble himself, from both sound and vibration deep in his chest. His movements quickened and her body shuddered beneath him. Then the sensation shifted. The soothing warmth of her sex close to release changed.

It was a strange searing heat deep inside, a pressure that he played perfectly.

Elizabeth was helpless to it.

"Oh my god!" Elizabeth cried, her voice tinged with an almost frantic apprehension.

He began to grunt softly in rhythm to his movement. Elizabeth clenched her legs at his hips, squeezing her thighs together against his thrusts. His grunts grew louder.

"Oh my god, Fitzwilliam! Don't stop!"

He kept his pace, but the tone of his grunts shifted with her demands, fueled at first by a growling need, and turning to a near whimpered helplessness. "I'm close."

Her body spasmed around him and she shrieked. "Please!"

The pleasure of his movements had reached its apex and

shifted. Elizabeth felt constant heat, constant tension, and suddenly with a terrified shriek, felt as though she was going to wet the bed. "Oh god!!!"

Elizabeth shuddered under him, screaming, her legs flailing out at his sides. The sensation surged in waves, down through her belly, pushing against him as strongly as he pushed into her. Elizabeth shuddered again, legs convulsing so badly, she kicked him. He seemed oblivious, his face now buried into her shoulder, his grunts constant and desperate. She clutched him to her as the last wave washed over her and his movements slowed, and then finally stopped. They lay there, entwined, their shallow breathing matched, their bodies sealed together by their sweat as much as their embrace.

He took three deep breaths before he spoke. "I'm sorry."

Her eyebrows shot up and Elizabeth pressed her cheek to his, confused. "Why?"

He groaned, rallying the strength to lift himself.

"I didn't mean to lose myself so soon," he said, hoisting himself up onto his knees. "You seemed to enjoy it rather well, yes?"

Elizabeth's face flushed and she covered her face in her hands. He pulled them away, grinning.

He grabbed her hand, pressing it to his lips and kissing it repeatedly before turning his attention to her neck. "I'll have to have my way with you before my bath more often."

He gave a quick double eyebrow raise and laughed as her hands shot to her face again, rising to his knees to tickle her sides and her feet. Elizabeth curled into herself, fighting him as he tortured her. He finally stopped, resting his hands on her knees, her legs shut tight before him. He grazed his fingertips against the bottom of her thigh, sliding down towards the warm wet place that was still throbbing from his assault. He flitted a finger against her, shooting her a mischievous glance. Then he seemed to think better of it and sighed.

Elizabeth searched his face. "What?"

He took a deep breath. "I want to taste you, but I imagine Jane is wondering where you are, and I'm still in need of a bath."

He held her legs against him, swaying her from side to side.

"They're here for several days. We're not required to entertain them at all times."

He stopped, his face split with joy and what Elizabeth couldn't deny was affection. Then he shrugged, grabbed her legs and threw them wide apart, diving his head toward her. Elizabeth twisted, shrieking as she fought to get away from his open mouth. He shot her a sideways glance once she'd settled at the end of the bed, far out of reach.

He beamed at her. "Get over here, young lady. It's your turn."

He came toward her and Elizabeth shrieked, hopping up from the bed to stand on the far end.

He gave her an appreciative whistle and moved around the foot of the bed toward her, extending a hand. "Looking at the state of your dress, I'd say you might need a bath yourself, beautiful."

Elizabeth stood her ground. He was now clearly lit from the bedroom windows, the dust gathered and smeared over his bare skin from their sweat. She glanced down at her rumpled self and blushed. All the pieces of Fitzwilliam Darcy combined to this magnificent shape, perfect in every respect, down to the perfect grin on his face. It was enough to take her breath away. Elizabeth let him take her hand, and he pulled her into him, his skin now dry and warm. He leaned down to kiss her, pinched her ear lobe then shot her a speculative, almost pleading glance.

"Perhaps you're right," she said, her shoulders rising in that same familiar shyness that had nearly stopped her from having him that afternoon. He smiled and picked her up, wrapping her legs around him as he carried her toward the bedroom door that led to the adjacent washroom.

"Wait! What if Ingrid heard us?!"

Darcy laughed. "Then she'll know damn well who the master of this house is."

# THE END

# ABOUT THE AUTHOR

**Delaney Jane** is an American author with the vocabulary of a sailor and a saucy muse. Born and bred in New England, one can't be too surprised that she was drawn to the steamier side of fiction - one has to keep warm somehow on winter nights. When she isn't writing, Delaney spends much of her time traveling to the UK, singing so loudly in the car that people think she's having a throw down argument with her windshield, and trying out some of the spicier tidbits of her imagination with her handsome husband.

Don't worry. He can keep up.

To connect with Delaney, you can find her at:
www.facebook.com/delaneyjaneauthor.
Email: delaneyjaneauthor@gmail.com

She would love to hear from you.

Watch for the sequel to The Mistress of Pemberley -

# The Fallen Lady

(Coming Spring 2018)

CPSIA information can be obtained
at www.ICGtesting.com
Printed in the USA
LVHW081254130122
708513LV00017B/201

9 781981 225996